A Brother's Oath

CHRIS THORNDYCROFT

A Brother's Oath
By Chris Thorndycroft

2015 by Copyright © Chris Thorndycroft

www.christhorndycroft.wordpress.com

For Maia for her constant encouragement and my parents for their unwavering support

Sweons

Geats

Eastern Sea

The Islands

Danes

Jutes

Angles

Saxons

Northmen

Western Sea

Frisians

Britta

The Northern World C.A. 435 A.D.

Anglo Saxon Society

Ealdorman – 'Elder man'. A chieftain.

Aetheling – An informal title for any noble-born man.

Thegn – A noble warrior in service to an ealdorman or king.

Ceorl – A freeborn commoner such as a farmer or a craftsman. Often called upon to fight in times of war.

Theow – A slave. Often captured from another tribe during war but some are born into a life of slavery.

Scop (pronounced 'shop') – A singer and a composer of tales and poetry.

Gealdricge – 'Yell Woman'. A woman who sings the funeral dirge to carry the slain to the afterlife.

Wicce/Haeg – A witch, a seer, a prophetess and a healer. Skilled in rune and herb lore.

"In the meantime, three vessels, exiled from Germany, arrived in Britain. They were commanded by Horsa and Hengist, brothers, and sons of Wihtgils. Wihtgils was the son of Witta; Witta of Wecta; Wecta of Woden…"

- The History of the Britons, Nennius

PART I

*(Eh) "Eh byþ for eorlum æþelinga wyn,
hors hofum wlanc, ðær him hæleþ ymbe,
welege on wicgum, wrixlaþ spræce,
and biþ unstyllum æfre frofur."*

(Horse) "The horse is a joy to princes in the presence
of warriors. A steed in the pride of its hoofs,
when rich men on horseback bandy words about it;
and it is ever a source of comfort to the restless."

Jute-land, 432 A.D.

Horsa

The door to the stable burst open under a heavy kick. Two large men shouldered their way inside, their faces red with rage. The horses in their stalls nickered in alarm at the sudden intrusion.

The boy and girl, who lay upon the straw, looked up in sudden fright. They had seen no more than thirteen winters apiece. Keen for each other, they had succumbed to their burning desires in a secret hideaway they had thought was safe.

One of the men held a heavy length of timber that had been fashioned into a crude cudgel and the other held a vicious looking saex; one of the long-bladed knives that were common in that part of the world. Its silvery edge glinted in the afternoon light that streamed in from outside.

The girl cowered as they advanced, frozen in fear, one small breast bulging above the top of her dress.

"Cover yourself, slut!" said the nearest of the men, as he dealt her a resounding crack with the flat of his hand that snapped her head backwards.

The boy scrambled to his feet and made a futile dash for the door. The two men caught him between them, and he was knocked backwards by a powerful fist to his jaw, that sent him tumbling into the hay.

"So," said the larger of the two men, "you thought you could treat our sister as if she were a common whore eh, rich boy?"

"No!" cried the girl, looking to her brothers. "Don't hurt him, please! We love each other!"

But her pleas fell upon deaf ears as the two men hauled the young boy roughly to his feet. His head hung loose and swayed from side to side as he was dragged out of the stable and into the yard. He tried to say something. It may have been an insult to the two men who held him in a vice-like grip, but the words came out through his bloodied teeth as incomprehensible mumbling.

He was thrown to the dirt in the yard outside where a crowd had begun to gather, drawn from the simple huts and pens that made up the settlement, distracted from their daily tasks by the promise of entertainment in the form of a public brawl.

The larger of the two brothers raised his cudgel and brought it down hard upon the boy's back, flattening him under the force of the blow. The youth tried to crawl away on his hands and knees. He cried out in pain as another stroke of the club fell upon him, crushing the wind from his chest.

The second of the two brothers stood nearby, testing the sharpness of his saex with his thumb, grinning at the beating that was being inflicted upon the youth. The screams of the girl could be heard from the doorway to the stable as she pleaded with her brothers to stop.

An elderly man called out from the crowd, "Take care, lad. That boy is the ealdorman's son."

"Mind your own business, old man!" replied the brother with the club. "This little runt dishonoured our sister. He must be made to pay!" He raised his club again but was thrown off balance as somebody crashed into him from behind, sending him flailing to the ground.

He looked up into a long face and a pair of blue eyes that crackled with a cruel intelligence. The one who had knocked him down was not much younger than he was - perhaps sixteen - with long, fair hair that hung in tidy braids. He was tall and slender with the beginnings of a beard growing on his chin that was fairly impressive for his age.

"The old man is right," said the youth with the braided hair. "He is the son of Ealdorman Wictgils. As am I."

"Look here, Hengest," said the fallen man, scrambling to his feet and picking up his club. "Son of the ealdorman or no, your brother does not have the right to lay his hands upon whatever girl takes his fancy."

Hengest walked over to his battered and bruised brother, extending a hand to him. Blood streamed from Horsa's nose and between his teeth, but he grinned, glad to see his older brother. It was not the first time Hengest had helped him out of a sticky spot.

"No, he does not," replied Hengest. "But if you feel that your sister has been wronged by my brother, then he at least deserves a fair hearing at the Folcmot before you take your club to him."

There were murmurs of agreement from the crowd. The ealdorman's sons were well liked and Hengest was always one to stick to the formalities of honour. Besides, the simple folk put much faith in the authority of the Folcmot.

"Folcmot?" exclaimed the man with the club in astonishment. "Fair hearing? We just caught the little bastard with his hand up our sister's skirt! There is nothing further to discuss!"

"Nevertheless," replied Hengest. "I will not allow you to beat my brother half to death in vengeance."

The crowd watched, enthralled as the two pairs of brothers faced off. This was going to be good.

"Now, if it is a case of repayment for your sister's virtue, then I am sure that we can come to some sort of agreement. Name the price."

Horsa snorted at his brother's suggestion. "Virtue? There was precious little of that left by the time I got to her."

Ripples of laugher made their way through the crowd and the faces of the two young men glowed red with indignation. Their sister, who had been watching the altercation from the stable door, ducked back inside, her own face red.

"I've heard enough," said the larger brother, his rage erupting. "Gold is not the issue here, but my family's honour is, and by the gods I'm going to reclaim it!"

He launched himself at Horsa, his club raised high. The blow was intercepted by Hengest, who twisted the attacker's arm around, hurling the big man to the mud for the second time that morning.

The younger man with the saex followed up the attack but was met by Horsa who gripped both of his wrists. The two of them rolled and thrashed in the mud, fighting for possession of the long knife. Horsa soon prised it from his opponent's grasp and tried to move back, but a savage kick in the belly made him drop it. The knife fell to the mud with a wet splat. His opponent scrambled forward to retrieve it, knocking Horsa backwards.

Hengest had subdued the older of the two brothers who now lay in the mud, dazed; his face pounded and bloody. Hengest turned and saw the younger brother advance on Horsa, six inches of cold, glittering steel in his hand. He moved quickly, for the knife was already making its way towards Horsa's chest. Quick as lightening, he flung himself upon the younger man and began to press his face down into the mud.

Still gripping the knife, the man slashed at Hengest with it. It drew blood from his shoulder but did not cut deep. Hengest grabbed the arm by the wrist and twisted the blade away from him until he heard the bone snap. The man screamed and dropped the knife. Hengest stood up, leaving his opponent writhing in the mud, grasping his broken arm.

The crowd cheered wildly at the victory of the ealdorman's sons. The elder of the defeated brothers, bruised and humiliated, helped his sibling to his feet and together they staggered away through the crowd, ignoring the jeers.

Their sister scurried from the stable and, pausing to shoot a venomous glance at Horsa, fled after her brothers, her face still burning crimson.

The entertainment over, the crowd dissipated and returned to their chores. Horsa did his best to wipe the mud from his clothes. He breathed a sigh of relief and then hooted with laughter. Hengest strode over to him and cuffed him soundly on the ear.

"What the hell were you thinking?" he demanded. "Those men are the sons of Wulfgar, one of father's thegns. They were ready to kill you, and quite rightly so if you ask me."

"I'm sorry, brother," replied Horsa. "I didn't know the bitch was Wulfgar's daughter. And I didn't know she had two brothers the size of oxen either."

"Even so, you are the son of Ealdorman Wictgils. It does not become you to whore and brawl as if you were a common ceorl."

"Oh, give the lectures a rest, Hengest!" snapped Horsa in irritation. "We both know that you are the only son our father gives a damn about. I might as well have been sired on a local fishwife for all the care he pays me!"

Several heads turned and stared at the two brothers, wondering if a new fight was about to break out. Conscious of this, Hengest seized his younger brother by the scruff of the neck and marched him away towards their father's hall.

Hengest

The lands of the north were dark, brooding places ruled by feuding, tribal communities under the disinterested gaze of indifferent gods. Hammered by the broiling waves of the Eastern and Western Seas and blending into the thick, dark forests of the south, this part of the world had been ignored by the more civilised lands that lay beyond the Rhine; the lands that had fallen long ago to the iron legions of Rome.

But the time of the great Caesars was over. Their empire had split in two and was now ruled by corrupt officials and half-mad boy emperors. Rome's armies, which contained more barbarians than Romans, struggled to hold its borders in check while the denizens of its once great cities cowered in their churches and fearfully called on their Christ-messiah for salvation.

But, beyond the black forests of Germania, the pagan gods of sea and sky still ruled and the altars to their names were splashed red with the blood of sacrifice. The fires in the halls of kings and ealdormen burned bright, and within were recited the sagas of great heroes who battled fire-drakes and sea-wyrms. In the countryside beyond, the people still lived in fear of the trolls and the Aelf-folk who were said to dwell in the dark forests and hills.

The domain of Ealdorman Wictgils was nestled between two sweeping curves of a great river that wound its way through the land of the Jutes and out into the Western Sea. His hall was an impressive construction of timbers, with a turf roof and a single smoke hole that emitted gentle wisps into grey skies. Down on the banks of the river, clinker-built vessels were moored, bringing trade from the coast in the form of fish, timber, skins and amber. Drying racks stood nearby from which herring gently swayed in the soft breeze.

The various dwellings and workshops that lay strewn between the wharves and the great hall hummed all day long with their activity; the blacksmith clinked away on his anvil and the smell of honey drifted from the huts where bees were kept and mead was brewed. Around to the side of the ealdorman's hall were his stables where Hengest and Horsa had spent many hours of their childhood playing among the bales of hay.

The horse was a sacred animal to the Jutes. The wild creatures that galloped freely across the vast flatlands and rolling moors were a brother race to the sons of Woden who, over time, had tamed them and brought them into their fold to be treated not as slaves, but as equals. Ealdorman Wictgils was a passionate rider and owned the finest horses in all of Jute-land. His fondness for the beasts was demonstrated by his naming of his firstborn, 'Hengest', which meant 'stallion' in the Jutish tongue. His second son was given the less illustrious name of 'Horsa' which meant simply, 'horse'.

The golden glow of the spring afternoon gently receded across the thatched rooftops of the ealdorman's hall and stables. A few theows wandered about the yard attending to the last duties of their day before they could go home to their families. Other than that, the place was deserted. Hengest, who had been dragging his younger brother with him from the village, finally released the struggling boy and shoved him roughly.

"Who do you think you are, pushing me around?" said Horsa angrily. "Just because you're father's favourite!"

"Do you wonder why I am his favourite?" demanded Hengest. "Do you wonder why I lecture you?"

"Because you think you're better than me," replied Horsa sulkily. "Because you're older than me."

"No. It is because of your irresponsible antics like today. Because of your careless disregard for the honour of our family."

Horsa was silent, his eyes cold. Hengest sighed. He hated to lay into his younger brother like this. They had always got along well and had rarely fought, even as children. Horsa had always looked up to his older brother but, as the years of adolescence had gripped him, he had changed. He had become bitter and argumentative and Hengest began to worry that he would turn against him just as he had turned against their father.

Father did favour Hengest, it was true. He always had warm praise and hearty encouragement for his eldest son but when it came to Horsa, he was only scathing and overly critical. As the ealdorman's heir, Hengest had always been kept by the side of his father who instructed him in the ways of ruling a people. But Horsa was often left to his own activities, and it was no wonder that the younger brother got into as much trouble as he did.

"Look, Horsa," Hengest said, as they entered the stables. "I'm on your side. The more you fight and rebel against Father, the tougher it will be for you. Do yourself a favour and try and keep on his good side. Try and do what I do …"

"Oh yes, that would suit everyone perfectly, wouldn't it?" snapped Horsa. "If only I could be more like Hengest! I've heard it all my life. Perfect Hengest! Apple of Father's eye!"

"It's not like that …" began Hengest.

"Yes it is! It's always been like that! Father would have been happier had I never been born!"

He stormed away, kicking a pail across the yard as he went. Hengest watched him leave with a heavy heart. Perhaps he was wrong to act like the voice of authority. They were, after all, brothers.

He thought back to their childhood years. Playing together and getting into trouble together; sharing everything. Life had been so simple, so black and white. But somewhere along the line, somehow, things had changed. *Horsa* had changed.

Ealdorman Wictgils was in a furious mood that night. News had reached him of the fight in the village between his sons and the sons of his thegn, Wulfgar. He sat on his great carved chair at the head of the hall and seethed. Theows brought him mead which he drank in large quantities, fuelling his boiling rage.

He was a big man, grey-haired but strong. His beard was long and fell down to his broad belt. His right leg was missing, taken by an axe-blow in a territorial dispute years ago. The stump still gave him pain on cold mornings and only added to his ferocious temper. He was held in that odd mixture of fear and awe by the people he ruled. His judgements were accepted as just and yet, when one of his moods took him and he could be heard roaring and bellowing like a branded ox, theows and thegns alike did their best to avoid him.

His wife, Aedre, was a kind and loving woman who put up with a great deal in life. She was of that noble stock of women who had been trained from childhood to know when to acquiesce to their husbands' whims, and when to lay down their own brand of quiet authority in the form of honey poured into their ears. Aedre's ever graceful light touch could often mean the difference between life and death for some poor soul who had incurred the ealdorman's wrath.

Her sons held her in the very highest regard for she was the only person they knew who had the courage to stand up to their father. Wictgils also treated her with a grudging respect, listening to her advice on occasion and letting her have her say when it came to the raising of their boys.

Aedre sat next to her husband, speaking softly into his ear in an effort to cool his temper. She held his mighty forearm as if restraining it from striking out at Horsa. Hengest stood nearby, his words of support for his brother largely ignored by the ealdorman.

"Are you aware of the situation between myself and Wulfgar?" Wictgils demanded of his youngest son. "His land dispute with his neighbour, Osfrid, has already put me in a difficult situation. By favouring Osfrid I have alienated Wulfgar; a slight that he has not taken easily. My efforts to placate him have come to naught. And then you take advantage of his daughter and brawl with his sons in the street! Would you have me lose Wulfgar's loyalty altogether?"

"Father," began Horsa, his face burning crimson at being chastised before the whole of his father's hall, "I apologise. Had I known that the girl was the daughter of Wulfgar, I would never have laid a hand on her."

"So you thought she was just some common wench you could use and cast aside, eh? Her fine clothes and good graces clearly held no meaning for you. Now the issue is to be brought before the Folcmot next month. *Eala*! Our family is to be shamed in public because of your actions! Why do you never think, boy? Why must you always cast a shadow over my name?"

Horsa's red face transformed from humiliation to anger. "I might ask why I must have a father that takes the side of his own thegn instead of his son's?" he snapped. He would have liked to have said a good deal more, but the warning look on Hengest's face made him bite down on his rage. Their father was quick to violence.

"Get out of my sight!" Wictgils roared. "Insolent wretch of a boy! Oh, would that the gods had gifted me with two sons of the same quality!"

Horsa spun on his heel and marched out of the hall. Only Hengest saw the tears that had begun to well up in his eyes spill down his cheeks.

Aedre got up and hurried after him, leaving her husband with his head in his hand. Hengest sat down in his mother's chair and summoned a theow to bring them both more mead.

"Please don't be too hard on him, Father," he said, handing him his horn. "He tries hard to please you."

"He doesn't try at all!" snapped Wictgils, accepting the horn and drinking deeply from it. "He thinks only of his own pleasures. Why is he so insistent on shaming me? What have I done to deserve it?"

"He does not do it on purpose," said Hengest. "He just ... doesn't think at times. Acts without prudence. He means no harm."

"What good is someone who means no harm but causes it anyway? What am I supposed to say at the Folcmot next month? Am I to defend my son, this defiler of nobleman's daughters? Or am I to punish him as Wulfgar will undoubtedly demand?" He grasped Hengest's arm tightly and leaned close so that his son could smell the sickly sweet mead on the old man's breath. "You are my true son; my heir," he said. "Do not let him drag you down with him. I have great faith in you, Hengest. You will be ealdorman after I am gone. Forget your brother. Do not waste your time protecting him from his own weaknesses and folly."

"He is my brother, Father," said Hengest. "If I do not protect him, then who will?"

"Oh, this is tiresome," said Wictgils in a resigned tone. "We have more important things to discuss. I want to send you on an errand, Hengest."

"Of course, Father," Hengest replied. His father often sent him on missions of diplomacy within his territory, not only because the old, one-legged ealdorman found it difficult to get about, but because he wanted his eldest son and heir to get a feel for the responsibilities of being an ealdorman. An ealdorman, his father had explained, must use his own intuition to settle disputes for the good of everyone. And by the gods, that was a fine art.

"A married couple came to me the other day," Wictgils explained. "The woman was called Ebba and the man, oh I can't remember. Anyway, they were upset by the actions of some relative. He's been mistreating his niece apparently. She's only a girl, about fourteen. Her parents were taken by a fever last winter and she inherited their farm; some broken down old place over West Hastham way. Naturally, the girl cannot take care of the place on her own, being young as she is and without the wealth to purchase theows, so her uncle has taken it upon himself to be her guardian.

"He's living with her now and this couple claim that he keeps her locked up and treats her like a common theow, forcing her to work and beating her if it's not up to scratch. This Ebba woman is her cousin and she's desperate to get the girl to come and live with her and her husband, but the uncle will have none of it. Says she's his charge and he won't budge."

Wictgils cursed as he spilt mead down his tunic and irritably brushed it off.

"I can't say that I'm much interested in the family affairs of ceorls, and I told this couple as much the other day. But they damn near got on their knees, begging me to help. They are convinced that this fellow is up to no good; trying to get his hands on the farm."

"But the only way he could manage that, legally speaking, would be if he married the girl," said Hengest.

"I daresay that's what they're afraid of."

"And you want me to go over there and see what's to be done?"

Wictgils smiled at him. "For the sake of appearances at least. I can't have the people speaking ill of me, saying that I refuse to intervene just because it's a ceorl who asks. Personally I don't give a damn how this fellow treats his niece. But, as I say, appearances …"

"What's the girl's name?" asked Hengest.

"Oh Gods, I can't remember," said Wictgils, staring into space for a while whilst the drunken parts of his brain tried to shuffle themselves into some sort of order. "Halfritha I think it was. Be a good lad and nip over there in a day or two. See what's up. I can send several thegns with you just in case the uncle dares to give you any nonsense. And you'll take Ebba and her husband with you, of course. No point in making a show of things if there's nobody around to see it."

Horsa

At the entrance to the hall Horsa looked up at the star-filled night through frustrated tears. How he hated this place! If only he could get away from it all. There had to be more to life than playing second fiddle to Hengest. But where? Who did he know? He may be the son of an ealdorman, but he felt as trapped as the lowliest theow.

He felt a hand on his arm.

"Don't go," his mother said. "Please. Your father is an ill-tempered man and he says things that he does not mean."

"He means them," replied Horsa, wiping the tears away with the back of his hand.

"He loves you, I know it. But you both have the same hot blood in your veins. You are too similar and that is why you do not see eye to eye. Hengest has more of my blood in him. Cooler, more thoughtful. Your father fights you because he sees himself in you and that frightens him. But he loves you nonetheless, Horsa, trust me on this."

"I need to go, Mother."

"Where?"

"I just need to clear my head. I can't stay in this hall a moment longer. The heat stifles me."

She let go of his arm and he stepped out into the cold night air.

He did not return that night.

Hengest

Hengest's horse snorted and scraped at the earth as he stared down at the small farm. It was in a shambles. A broken fence that had not been maintained surrounded a cluster of dirty huts. A few stray chickens seemed to have the run of the place and clucked about, scratching in the dirt for worms. A pig had died in a nearby pen and its owner had not been bothered to remove the carcass, leaving it to fester with flies buzzing about its jellified eyes.

"A damned disgrace," said Cynebeald behind him. "This used to be a respectable homestead. A good family home."

"Is there anybody else living here with him apart from the girl?" Hengest asked.

"No, just him and my poor cousin, Halfritha," replied Ebba. "Her parents were too poor to afford any theows."

Ebba and Cynebeald had accompanied Hengest along with six thegns. Cynebeald was a woodcutter and Ebba was a kind wife with a good heart. They were not young, although not yet in the winter of their years.

Hengest led the way down to the farm; Ebba, Cynebeald and the six thegns following close behind, harnesses jingling. Nobody was in sight as they entered the yard but the ferocious barking of several dogs could be heard from inside the main house. Hengest dismounted, strode up to the door and rapped smartly on it. The owner of the farm took his time opening it and when he did so he only opened it just wide enough to peep out at Hengest.

21

"Clear off!" he said. "I set the dogs on the last lot of beggars who came round here and don't think I won't set them on you!"

The door slammed shut.

Hengest turned to the six thegns and nodded. They came forward and with three heavy stamps, broke the door down and dragged the wretched creature out into his own yard. From somewhere inside the dogs were going berserk, and Hengest assumed that they must be tied up for none came running out to defend their master.

The man had clearly realised his mistake and grovelled at Hengest's feet. "My apologies, aetheling!" he whimpered, cowering under the drawn swords of the warriors who surrounded him. "I thought that you were no more than common ruffians."

"Never mind that," said Hengest. "We are here about the girl."

"Girl?"

"Your niece. The one these people say you keep locked up."

The man seemed to notice Cynebeald and Ebba for the first time and his face turned to one of loathing. "My lord," he protested. "That girl was entrusted to my care by her parents. It was her father's dying wish. You cannot expect me to hand her over to these two who are little more than strangers to her."

"You're a liar!" shouted Ebba, stepping forward. "Your brother would never have asked you to come and live in his home and care for his daughter, for he learned many years ago what a vile creature you are!"

"Show me the girl," said Hengest.

"Ah, she's er, sick," said the man. "She can't possibly be brought before company I'm afraid."

Hengest noticed that the man's eyes kept darting over to a tiny sunken hut on the opposite side of the yard; a sad, dilapidated building of the kind that was used for storing meat. He turned from the man and made his way towards it.

The farmer scrambled to his feet and ran to keep up with Hengest, putting himself between him and the hut, spouting some remarks about the girl being a troublemaker possessed of a violent temper and that she had to be restrained from time to time. Hengest's men seized the farmer and hauled him away from their lord.

The door to the hut was shut fast with a dirty length of rope tied around the handle and nailed into the doorframe. Hengest drew his saex and sliced through the rope, heaving the door open.

The hut stank of rotting meat and flies buzzed around erratically. Within the darkness, something moved. Hengest saw the dirty hem of a dress, half hidden in the shadows.

"Come into the light, you there," he said. "I'll not harm you."

A small figure moved quietly from the shadows into the rectangle of light thrown in from the doorway. Hengest's eyes widened as he saw her.

She was filthy. Her dress was little more than rags and her feet were bare. Hair, the colour of straw fell down to slender shoulders. She was not unattractive, despite her filthy appearance. Her pale, frightened face was marked by several purplish bruises. She looked up at Hengest, squinting as if she was unaccustomed to daylight. He held out his hand to her and she took it, cautiously at first, never taking her eyes from him, but then her trust deepened and, gingerly, she let him lead her out into the yard.

Ebba cried out and ran to her, wrapping her arms around the frightened girl and weeping tears of joy.

"She is to go back with you," Hengest told the kindly woman. "Look after her." Then he turned to the uncle who stood in sheepish silence between two thegns.

Rage boiled inside Hengest. He wanted to kill this revolting man, or bolt him up inside the hut as he had done to his niece and leave him to rot. But he was on his father's business, and the ealdorman would not be best pleased if he began dispensing self-made justice with too heavy a hand. He tried to calm himself and spoke coolly.

"You are lucky that your niece was still alive when we found her," he told the man. "For if she had not been, then it would have gone very badly for you. As it stands, you are relieved of your guardianship of this girl."

"The girl is simple," protested the uncle. "Touched in the head. She often has violent outbursts and I am forced to lock her up. She lies too. You can't believe a word she says ..."

"Silence!" bellowed Hengest. "This home is no longer your own. You are to leave it immediately."

"But ..."

"I am returning the ownership of the farm to Halfritha, to be held until she comes of age by Cynebeald and Ebba. And if, in the interim, any destruction or damage should befall it, then I will come looking for you. Mark me on that!"

The man looked at the ground and kept his mouth shut. Hengest was aware of the girl's eyes watching him.

24

She still had not uttered a word, but she stared at her uncle with hatred in her blue eyes. There was also a fierceness there. 'Simple', the man had said. 'Touched in the head'. But there did not seem to be anything wrong with her as far as Hengest could see.

"See that this worm leaves this land," Hengest said to two thegns. He mounted his horse and the remaining four warriors followed suit.

Ebba carried Halfritha upon her saddle and they made their way up the rise and away from the farm. As they crested the hill, Hengest caught the girl looking back down at the nest of ramshackle buildings that was her birthright.

She did not look sad to see the back of it.

Horsa

The month leading up to the Folcmot passed slowly for Horsa. He avoided the hall and had not spoken to his father since their altercation. He would not have admitted it to anyone, but he was frightened. His father would surely take the side of Wulfgar in order to keep his thegn's favour.

Punishments handed out by the Folcmot could range from the payment of a weregild – an amount of compensation to be paid to the injured party by the offender – all the way up to exile or even execution. He did not think that his crime warranted such an extreme measure but, for the first time in his life, he felt like he was the centre of the town's attention and he did not like it one bit.

His name was discussed throughout the settlement by fisherman and baker's wife alike and he did his best to avoid everyone in the days coming up to the meeting. But still, he was aware of people eying him in the streets, muttering to each other once his back was turned. Thegns, ceorls, theows; it did not matter what their station. All were watching him, titillated by the whiff of scandal.

There was some distraction in the form of a Jutish trading vessel that had returned from the land of the Northmen bearing a cargo of seal skins and timber. Timber was scarce in Jute-land but the northern lands across the sea were said to be covered in tall pine forests that lined their jagged and glittering fjords.

The vessel put in at one of the wharves and many flocked to it to barter for goods. Aedre sent Horsa to purchase some furs that she wanted, and it was during the bartering that Horsa met Ketil, a native Northman who travelled with the Jutes on their trading runs.

Ketil was an astonishing looking man; tall and muscular with a great cascade of tawny hair that he usually kept loosely bound at the back of his head. His left ear was missing, lost to some enemy's blade during one of his many adventures, leaving a ragged rim of scarred flesh around a gaping hole in the side of his head. Most striking about his appearance, however, was a bearskin cloak complete with its grinning head that hung down from his shoulders.

It had been taken from no ordinary bear, for although it was filthy with soot and mud, it had once been a creamy white, the colour of goat's milk. These white bears, Ketil told Horsa, were to be found on the islands far to the north where they fished under the ice for seals, dragging them out with their powerful claws and razor-sharp teeth.

Horsa was fascinated by the tales Ketil told about the places he had visited and the adventures he had endured. He had been a slave as well as a raider in his time and it had been the sword of a rival raiding ship that had taken his ear. He had journeyed far, from Dane-land right up to the northern reaches of the world where the ice bears roamed.

It was here that Ketil had stared across the vast frozen wastes that were the home of the frost-eotuns; the kindred of mighty Ymir whose bones the gods had used to form the land of men, his skull the sky and his blood the oceans. Here the sun hardly ever shone during the winter months; and yet in summer, night never descended.

Most fascinating of all to Horsa, was Ketil's telling of the colourful bands of light that swirled about in the sky: reds, blues, greens and purples, more vibrant and eclectic than any dull vegetable dye that was used to colour the clothes of mortals. It was said that this bizarre phenomenon was the bridge to Esegeard, the land of the gods, where the golden halls of Waelheall stood; a glorious kingdom only attainable to men who died honourably in battle.

Thunor, or 'Tor' as he was known in the dialect of the Northmen, was the god Ketil followed; the lord of thunder who could summon mighty storms and could strike down those who displeased him with bolts of lightning from his hammer.

"Tor is the god of all seamen," Ketil explained in his heavy accent. He spoke the Jutish dialect well, but none would be fooled into thinking that he was one of them. "He must be kept happy. When you are out on the great whale-road, with the waves hurling your small craft about and the wind tearing at your arse, you will understand why."

Horsa had never been out on the open sea before. His father had often taken his two sons on diplomatic visits to other ealdormen along the network of rivers, but they had always been short affairs and river boating was nothing like venturing out across the turbulent whale-road.

Ketil's tales ignited a passion for adventure in Horsa and he found himself longing to travel far from Jute-land. There were lands across the sea for him to discover, adventures to be had and glory to be gained. Out there on the gannet's bath life was harsh but men made their own way with their own hands. He could be anybody he chose out there; not Horsa, son of Wictgils, the second son of a minor ealdorman, but a man of his own making.

He yearned for a life like Ketil's but he knew nothing of the sea and it would be many years before his father would let him venture out on his own.

As the days passed, Horsa hung around the boats more and more, listening to Ketil and the sailors of other vessels talk. They would drink and play dice on the wharves amidst the racks of drying fish and piles of wares. Sometimes they let him help out, unloading goods from the boats and sorting out the ropes and equipment.

He was unused to hard work and his hands were soon raw with blisters, but the good-natured attitudes of the men and their hearty slaps on his shoulder as they passed gave him a wonderful feeling of acceptance.

They apparently didn't know that he was the ealdorman's son; or if they did they didn't care. His birthright didn't matter here amongst men who cared only for a man's own merits; not the achievements or sins of his father. For the first time in his life, Horsa felt as if he almost belonged.

Halfritha

The door slammed as Cynebeald entered the house carrying an armful of firewood. The sudden noise startled Halfritha who sat sewing by the fire.

"Ouch!" she yelped, pricking her finger. A bead of blood welled there and she set down her needle and sucked at it, silently cursing herself for being so skittish.

"Oh, you poor dear," fussed Ebba. "Here, let's put the sewing away for today. The light has gone anyway." She took the garment Halfritha had been working on and put it away in the deep chest in the corner of the room.

It had been a week since Halfritha had come to live with her cousin and, for the most part, she was doing well. The big portions of food that Ebba heaped upon her had helped to gain some weight back and it felt good to sleep in a bed again.

Cynebeald regularly checked on her birthright when he was out looking for good trees to cut down. He had even made some repairs in preparation for her return once she had reached womanhood. That was something Halfritha dreaded. Womanhood and her return to the home of her parents. It was a black shadow on her horizon. How would she cope in that lonely old farm all on her own? She feared the long shadows of night with only the ghosts of her parents and the memories of her uncle for company.

But for the time being, Halfritha was in good, warm company. Ebba would often take her to visit her friends or they would visit them - a great gaggle of mothers and daughters - and they would sit about the hearth mending the clothes of their menfolk and sharing gossip.

Gossip was something the women thrived upon out on the moors, where it was several miles between homesteads, and the close-knit community of the riverside villages was absent. Marriage was often the subject; who was courting who, when they were expected to get married and who was struggling to find a sweetheart and why. Halfritha listened to these women silently for she was unused to female company. She was unused to any company at all.

Her childhood felt as if it had happened a century ago, even though less than a year had passed since her parents had been claimed by the fever. The dark days following the arrival of her uncle in her life had almost erased the happy memories of childhood from her mind. But now, sitting with Ebba and her friends, warmed by hearth and companionship, she felt like she had returned to an innocence she had thought forever lost.

Content to simply sew and listen, Halfritha rarely talked, which alarmed the other ladies. They prompted and probed her with questions so that she was forced to speak up on occasion, blushing furiously as she did so. But the women showed nothing but kindness and understanding for which Halfritha loved them.

But when darkness came and the old house was quiet, the nightmares clouded her mind like stormy skies. She wanted to talk, to open up to Ebba who was so kind to her, but she just couldn't. Some days she would cry for no reason at all and would run off to hide so that Ebba would not see her and become distressed. Halfritha knew that she should be happy and grateful in her new home and she was terrified of offending her hosts.

No matter how her life had changed for the better, it was as if a dark shadow was clutching at her, keeping part of her in darkness whilst the rest of her yearned and struggled for the light. It was the shadow of her uncle. Her fear of him was still strong and the thought that he was somewhere out in the wilderness cursing her name terrified her.

"Why don't you eat something dear?" Ebba asked. There was a pot of hare stew bubbling over the fire which she occasionally stirred with a long wooden spoon.

"No thank you," replied Halfritha.

"Have you given any more thought to the ealdorman's feast yet?"

When Halfritha had heard that there was to be a feast at the ealdorman's hall in a week's time in honour of the spring festival of Eostre, her feelings had been a mixture of joy and panic. She knew very well that the ealdorman's eldest son, Hengest – the one who had rescued her from her uncle's farm – would be there and she longed to see him again.

The memory of that tall, well-built youth with the sandy hair and beard, who had stood bathed in sunlight spilling into her world of misery, was a strong one for her. She had asked herself many times over the past days if she would have felt so strongly for him had he not been the one who had rescued her from the darkness. It was an impossible question to answer. All she knew was that she desperately wanted to see him again and, if possible, to thank him.

But on the other hand, the thought of walking into the ealdorman's hall and standing face to face with him again terrified her. What if she made a fool of herself? What if he was not interested in talking to her? There must be a hundred local girls who fought for his attention, and what was she to him? And he had seen her at her most destitute: filthy and flea ridden. She must have repulsed him that day and she felt ashamed.

But then, there had been that look on his face when he had opened the door. She had been dazzled by the sunlight at the time and his face had nearly been a dark silhouette, but she had seen something in his eyes. A look of pity, yes, but there was something else too, a feeling of outrage and anger at what had been done to her. That meant that he cared, surely?

"I think I'll go," she told Ebba.

"Oh, that's wonderful," Ebba replied, beaming at her. "There'll be dancing and singing and good food. It will do you the world of good to get out and meet people. And of course you will be able to thank the ealdorman's son for what he did for you. We all will."

"Will many people be there?"

"I expect so," replied Ebba, not noticing the fear in her cousin's words. Halfritha dreaded crowds and staring faces.

A thought struck Halfritha and she began to panic. "But I have nothing to wear!" she protested, her mind recoiling at the thought of turning up in front of all those noble families wearing the garments of a common farmhand.

Ebba chuckled. "Not yet. But I have some very fine cloth that would make a lovely dress for you. Here," she reached into the chest and showed Halfritha a bolt of material so blue that it looked like it had been cut out of the sky itself. "We can work on it together. With some nice jewellery you will be the gem of the feast."

33

Halfritha highly doubted that but Ebba's kindness had done something to allay her fears and for that she was grateful. So grateful that tears began to spill from her eyes once more and her body was racked with sobs. Startled, Ebba hurried over to her and wrapped her arms around her, cradling her small body. She whispered soothing words as she rocked her back and forth and, not for the first time, cursed their uncle's name for what he had done to her.

The following week they rode to the feast with Cynebeald between them, his head held high and proud as if he were some gallant thegn chaperoning two ladies.

Halfritha felt extraordinarily uncomfortable in the dress she and Ebba had spent the past week perfecting. It was a beautiful dress, but she had never worn such a fine garment before and she was terrified of falling off her horse and getting it muddy.

Cynebeald broke out into a song about the goddess Eostre, and although it was a nice, respectful song, Cynebeald had no voice with which to do it or its subject justice so after a while Ebba hushed him.

"Just greeting the good Lady of Spring in my own way," said Cynebeald, beaming at his wife.

"Well you don't have to hurt the ears of all Jute-land in doing so," said Ebba.

Cynebeald grinned and continued humming the song under his breath. He was in high spirits. "I'm getting drunk tonight," he said, as if commenting on the nature of the weather.

"You are not," replied Ebba firmly. "I don't want you showing me up like you did last year. And you're to stay away from those servant girls too. I don't want my husband rolling around between the benches like some mead-addled letch."

Cynebeald snorted. "As if I could possibly outdo old Wictgils. Our ealdorman is famous for drinking himself under the mead bench at the first opportunity."

Ebba hushed him urgently, looking around to see if anybody was nearby. "Don't speak of the ealdorman so!"

Halfritha smiled as she listened to the couple argue. She had to admit that she was in high spirits too; despite her nerves which were stretched close to breaking point. She thanked Eostre, for the Lady of the Spring and the Dawn surely had something to do with her euphoria. The life of the new year thrummed about their ears. Crickets and frogs chirped in the undergrowth and birds newly arrived from wherever they had spent the winter sang shrilly in the trees above them. Streams that had been frozen for months now ran freely and sang to them in their chuckling rhythms.

As they rounded the bend in the river, Halfritha saw for the first time the settlement of Ealdorman Wictgils and the Great Hall on a rise in the middle of it. Many other families had also arrived and were milling around in the yard; some drifting in through the wide doors of the hall from which came the musical beat of skin drums and piping.

They dismounted and handed their reins to a theow. Lifting up the hem of her dress so that it would not trail in the mud, Halfritha followed Ebba and Cynebeald into the hall.

The warmth inside enveloped her like a comforting blanket. The hall buzzed with activity. Tables groaned under the weight of the food provided by the ealdorman's kitchens. Salmon, boar, hare and lamb were in abundance; the steam rising from them and mingling with the wood smoke in the rafters to create a tantalising aroma. Freshly baked bread was piled high in baskets and cooked onions, leeks, peas and cabbages steamed in their bowls whilst cheeses oozed on wooden boards in the heat. Mead and ale was in high quantity and the guests dipped horns and cups into barrels, fuelling their rosy-faced merriment. The ealdorman's scop plucked out a tune on his lyre and there was singing and dancing. Later on there would be wrestling as the drunken men showed off their athletic abilities.

Halfritha immediately spotted Hengest on the other side of the hall talking to a nobleman and his family. An older woman, whom she guessed must be his mother, stood by his side. The woman turned and, upon seeing them, wove her way through the crowd, bringing Hengest with her. Halfritha's heart hammered in her chest as he approached, knowing that the time had come and she would have to speak to him.

"Hengest, you remember Ebba and Cynebeald," said Aedre, one hand on his shoulder and the other on Cynebeald's. "The couple who took in that poor girl. In fact, here she is, my goodness, Halfritha, you are looking pretty tonight!"

Halfritha was astonished by the woman's ability to recall her name even though they had never met.

Hengest gazed upon Halfritha, as if drinking in her appearance.

"We want to thank you for what you did, my lord," said Ebba, "from the bottom of our hearts."

"Don't mention it," Hengest replied, barely taking his eyes away from Halfritha's.

"If you and your father had not stepped in," continued Ebba, "well, I don't like to think what might have happened to my dear cousin. Halfritha, wouldn't you like to say something to Hengest?"

Halfritha opened her mouth as if to say something, but her voice seemed to catch in her throat. With a sudden movement, she stood up on her tiptoes and kissed Hengest on his bearded cheek. It was an action so out of place and unexpected, that several heads in the hall turned to stare.

"I'm terribly sorry," said Ebba, her face flushed. "She's not quite adjusted to society yet. Her time with her uncle has been a strain on her mind."

"Not at all," said Hengest, waving the woman's apologies aside, a flicker of a smile crossing his face.

Aedre's attention was suddenly caught by another couple who had walked into the hall and she tugged gently on her son's arm. "Oh, Hengest, you must come and say hello to Raedgar and his wife. Come along."

Halfritha watched Hengest being led away from her and she caught a glance of an apologetic shrug in his shoulders.

Her face burned with embarrassment at having kissed him. And in front of the whole hall too! But her wits had deserted her upon coming face to face with him and something else had taken control. She cursed herself for a fool at having blown her chance to properly thank him.

Sensing her turmoil, Ebba took her gently by the arm and led her over to a table where mead was being poured. "Don't fret, my dear," she said soothingly.

"I made a complete fool of myself!" whispered Halfritha, on the verge of tears.

"Oh, I wouldn't worry too much about it. Hengest is a decent and kind man. I'm sure he understood. Did you see how he looked at you in any case? I'd say the lad was a tad smitten with you, my girl!"

Such a thought had not occurred to Halfritha. She had been too wrapped up in her social faux pas. *Smitten?* Could that possibly be true? Or was Ebba merely trying to allay her fears with kind falsities?

The evening wore on and Halfritha watched Hengest and his mother doing the rounds of the hall. She watched as he greeted various noblemen and their families, but no matter how courteous his manners, he always remained aloof with them and somehow distant.

She saw how all the other young girls acted around him; the daughters of thegns and noblemen. She saw their simpering smiles and how they laughed at his jests. They clustered around him as if he was handing out gold rings, pouring compliments on him. And she had not spoken a word to him.

Jealousy raged within her. She didn't know why, but she felt a hatred for those other girls in their fancy clothes and gold ornamentation. She knew it was foolish but she felt utterly plain next to them. But why should they bask in his presence and not her? What did they know of him? It had been her that he had rescued, not them. She felt a connection to Hengest, a link that these other girls did not share and it made her feel possessive of him.

A hand touched her shoulder. It was a heavy, male hand and she instinctively shrank from it. She turned to meet the eyes of a young man standing beside her who looked no older than she was. He had dark brown hair and a beardless chin and was dressed in fine garments of green and red befitting a noble rank. But there was something familiar about his eyes. Did she know this boy?

"I'm sorry, I didn't mean to startle you," he said.

"You didn't," she replied, a little defensively.

38

"I couldn't help but notice you standing here alone. Very unwise, if I may say so, being as beautiful as you are. Any scoundrel here could come and carry you off."

Halfritha felt confused and uncomfortable. There was a glimmer of a smile on the young man's face that suggested a jest. Was he making fun of her?

"Who are you?" she asked.

"My name is Horsa," he replied. "And you?"

"Her name is Halfritha, and she is no concern of yours," said a deep voice beside her. She spun around to see Hengest at her side.

"Ah, the girl my brother is so fond of," said Horsa with a wicked grin.

Halfritha looked to Hengest and was alarmed to see the handsome young man blushing furiously.

"Why don't you go and work your charms on one of the serving girls, Horsa?" he said.

"Can't," replied the ealdorman's youngest son. "Father would have my skin if he saw me causing trouble among his servants."

"Where is he?"

Horsa nodded in the direction of their father. Ealdorman Wictgils was surrounded by a group of his thegns, roaring with laughter, a mead horn in his hand. "He's already as drunk as a dead warrior at Waelheall. I'm staying away in case he starts bawling at me as he usually does when he's falling out of his chair."

"Very wise. How about running outside and seeing if there's any wrestling matches to bet on? Here." He tossed his brother a couple of silver bits. "I know that your usual lucky streak has been neglecting you of late. Let's hope Eostre favours you this night."

Horsa beamed at his older brother. "You know, I think she might." As he turned to leave, he flashed a smile at Halfritha and said; "Heed my advice, sweetheart. Beware of scoundrels trying to carry you off!" He chuckled and dodged a kick Hengest aimed at his hindquarters before vanishing into the crowded hall.

"My brother," Hengest explained to Halfritha sheepishly.

"Siblings …" said Halfritha. "I have none, and perhaps I should be thankful for it."

He laughed and it was a pleasant thing to see. "Are you settling in well?"

"Oh yes, my cousin is very kind. And I wanted to thank you for coming to my aid. If you hadn't, I would still be my uncle's captive."

Hengest smiled. "I'm only glad that I could help," he said. "You needn't worry about your uncle anymore. If he steps within a hundred yards of you, his body will be dangling from the nearest oak tree."

She looked down at the ground, not doubting his sincerity, only his ability to make good on his promise.

"He was going to force me to marry him," she said. "I thank the gods every day that you saved me from that fate."

There was an awkward silence until Aedre's voice called out to her son to come and meet another nobleman and his spawn.

"My duties are never finished," Hengest said with a sigh.

"There you are!" Aedre said, approaching them. "I've been looking for you, Hengest. Hello, Halfritha. Are you enjoying yourself?"

"Yes, my lady," replied Halfritha. "It's a wonderful feast."

"Well, I'm glad. Make sure you try the lamb. Our head cook has his own way of doing it."

Halfritha promised that she would, and did not have time to say goodbye to Hengest before he was dragged away from her once again.

As the evening drew to a close, the guests drifted away beneath a clear moon. The ride back home was a slow trot and a constant battle for Ebba to stop her husband from singing at the top of his voice and falling off his horse at regular intervals. But her chiding lacked any severity for they had both drunk much that night and their spirits were high.

Halfritha stifled a yawn as she led her horse into the stables. The stillness was broken only by the nickering of the horses in their stalls and the playful squealing of Ebba in the adjoining building as Cynebeald chased her around. Halfritha unsaddled her horse and began to brush its glossy coat. It was a dun filly with a pale mane. As she ran her fingers through those golden locks, she was reminded of Hengest's hair and considered how like a horse's mane it was, only the mane of a stallion of course, as befitting his name. She thought that she would very much like to run her fingers through his hair.

A scream sounded from the house so sudden and terrifying in its intensity that Halfritha instantly knew that it was not one of Ebba's playful cries of protest at her husband's games. There came the sound of Cynebeald's raised shouting and the crash of some heavy piece of furniture breaking.

Halfritha dropped the brush in a panic and made to leave the stable. As she rounded the timber support of the stall a pair of rough arms grabbed her around the waist. She let out a cry of terror as her attacker dragged her across the straw. He stank of sweat and shit. What little light the moon provided was suddenly blotted out as a sack was pulled over her head.

Terror flooded her veins as she felt herself being dragged outside and hoisted up over the saddle of a horse that danced and swayed beneath her. Its rider placed a firm grip on her wrists, pinning them behind her back. Of Ebba and Cynebeald, there was no sound.

She cried out in fury at her abductors but they did not answer. The horse jerked forward and soon she felt the cool darkness of the night rushing past her as she was carried away from the place she had so briefly called home.

Hengest

A young ceorl had been on his way home across the moors when he passed by the home of Cynebeald to witness the kidnapping. He had galloped all the way to the ealdorman's hall and now stood on the steps panting for air and slick with sweat. He had tried to get into the hall to see the ealdorman or one of his sons, but the guards had halted him.

"The feast is over, lad!" said one of them. "Be off with you, unless you've come to help scrub the tables and clear out the straw."

"But I must see the ealdorman!" he protested. "There has been a kidnapping and murder in my lord's lands!"

"What's the problem here?" asked Hengest from the doorway, a horn in his hand. He had drunk little during the feast, wishing to keep a clear head, and now that the evening was at its end he was allowing himself to relax. His father, on the other hand, was dead drunk and snoring loudly in his chair while the theows cleaned up around him.

"Aetheling!" panted the ceorl.

"Let him approach," Hengest told the guards. The men stood back and the youth fell to his knees at Hengest's feet. "Now, what's this all about?"

"There has been a kidnapping," said the boy. "Over at Cynebeald's stead. They were waiting for them to get back from the feast. They took that young girl with them."

Hengest wasted no further time asking for details. "Come with me," he told the ceorl and set off at a stride towards the stables.

Several guards were sitting about drinking nearby. "You lot," Hengest snapped to them. "Get your weapons and saddle your horses. We ride out tonight! How many men did you see up at Cynebeald's farm, boy?"

"Not many," the youth replied. "Two at least."

Hengest cursed. If any harm had come to Halfritha he would carve up those who had laid a hand on her and leave them screaming.

It took a matter of moments for the five men to prepare their horses, and soon they were galloping out across the shrouded fields, the moonlight reflecting off their helms and the night wind in their long hair. On they thundered, across the moors, the water of the streams splashing up silver beneath their hooves.

Hengest pushed his steed hard, the men at his back struggling to keep up. He swore under his breath, his words muffled by the panting of his horse as he urged it on, calling upon every god he could name to give him more speed.

Cynebeald's stead rose up in the distance like the shadow of a ghost, silent and deserted. No firelight showed from its openings and the thinnest of smoke was barely visible from its roof. The horses slithered to a halt in the yard and their riders dismounted. Hengest drew his sword and entered the house.

The hearth fire had died low. Furniture lay smashed about the place. Two dark objects lay in the corner of the room and Hengest knelt down to inspect them. It was Cynebeald and Ebba, their bodies run through by blades. Hengest screwed his eyes shut and ground his teeth.

"Search the outhouses," he told his men.

It did not take them long for the stead was small and its buildings were few. Hengest sat by the glowing remains of the hearth, his hand touching the still warm body of Ebba who he had seen alive and laughing but a few hours ago.

"Nobody about, Aetheling," said one of the guards, returning.

"No more bodies?"

"None. The horses haven't been taken though. It doesn't make any sense."

"Yes it does," replied Hengest through clenched teeth, as he covered the glassy-eyed stare of Ebba with her own cloak. At least Halfritha was still alive. And that gave him a very good idea of who was responsible.

Halfritha

Halfritha stared at the scratched and marked surface of the tabletop. She knew every nick and cut that the dim light picked out on that rough wood. How many times had she scrubbed it clean? Scrubbed it cleaner than clean to please her tyrant of an uncle who could never be pleased. She remembered eating her meals at that table with her parents when they had been alive and the memories brought the slightest shimmer of tears to her eyes. She fought down the urge to cry. She would not give him that satisfaction.

On the other side of the hearth sat the two men her uncle had employed to capture her. They had the hard, emotionless faces of mercenaries. Her upper arms still throbbed with the finger-marks of the one who had grabbed her.

She was racked with worry – not for herself – but for Ebba and Cynebeald. Did they live? Or had they been slain defending her? All of it had been useless, worse than useless in fact. She was right back where she had started and nothing had been gained except death for those who had shown her kindness.

"Well, niece," said her uncle, entering the room. "What have you got to say for yourself?"

Halfritha resisted the urge to rise out of respect; an urge he had engrained in her during her time with him.

"You left me, girl," he said, staring down at her. "Your own blood. Have you no shame?"

She remained silent.

"Well, I'm not waiting any longer. I have asked the holy man to come first thing in the morning to marry us. Once we are man and wife, not even the ealdorman himself can remove me from this farm. There'll be no more of your tricks now, my bride to be." He smiled at her and the sight of his yellowed teeth nearly made her sick.

"I'd rather die than marry you!" she spat.

"Don't push me, girl," replied her uncle. "I'll remember every insult, every betrayal, and save your punishment for when you are my wife."

Horses could be heard in the yard outside. The two mercenaries leaped up and Halfritha's uncle spun around, his eyes wide. "Go and see who it is," he told them.

Halfritha watched her uncle keenly, allowing herself to enjoy his moment of panic.

"Did you really think that nobody would come looking?" she asked him, surprised by her own audacity. But her anger at him outweighed her fear now. He had taken her away from her only chance at happiness and had harmed those she loved most dearly.

He glared at her and seized her by the arm. "With me," he said. He hauled her through the doorway that led into what had once been her parents' bedchamber. There, in the darkness, he pushed her down into a corner, concealing her from the light of the doorway. He left the door slightly ajar, letting only a sliver of light penetrate the gloom.

There came the noise of fighting from the yard outside, blows of swords and the slither of steel. A cry of pain called out in the darkness and then all was silent once more. The door to the house crashed open and several pairs of footsteps strode across the hard-packed earth floor.

Halfritha watched her uncle. Sweat stood out on his brow as the footsteps approached. Silently, he drew a saex from his belt and Halfritha saw it winking in the gloom. She desperately wanted to cry out to whoever was in the next room, to alert them to the presence of the poised knife that waited behind the door, but it was as if her voice had been stolen by a runespell.

The door creaked open slowly and the large frame of a man with long, braided hair filled the doorway. Halfritha knew that it was Hengest and her heart nearly broke at the thought of the man she loved about to be slain by her uncle.

Anger gripped her. She had always been terrified of her uncle. She had suffered all kinds of cruelties at his hands and she had borne them because of her fear. But now he threatened the people who had tried to save her from him and she felt an anger she had never felt before; a resolute strength within her that fed her body, giving it vitality and purpose. It was as if a voice within her mind shouted 'No! I will not let you take this man from me!' and for the first time in her life she felt she had the courage to do what needed to be done.

A tool chest sat in the corner of the room, left by Cynebeald from when he had recently repaired the roof. Within it was a long iron spike used in the joinery of the building. Halfritha snatched it up and turned to see Hengest step into the chamber. Her uncle lunged forward, saex held high, directed at his throat. Halfritha hurled herself at her uncle and drove the point of the spike into his back.

The metal sunk through, finding a path through the man's ribs and puncturing his vitals. She saw the look of shocked horror on Hengest's face as he stumbled backwards out of reach of the stricken man, his eyes flitting from the face of her uncle to hers.

Halfritha gritted her teeth and wrenched the spike free with a loud sucking sound. Her uncle gasped and collapsed face down on the floor. She let the spike fall to the ground. The fear and exhaustion drained from her body to be replaced by shocked relief and she began to weep.

Hengest rushed forward to clutch her in his arms. Halfritha felt the warm, crushing embrace of his powerful body holding her close. She also felt a tight, hard feeling of dread within her. She had killed a man; her own uncle. She knew then that this was something she would carry with her for the rest of her life.

"It's alright," Hengest said, holding her tightly.

He lifted her chin so that he could look her in the eyes. "Thank you," he said. "You saved my life."

"My cousin, Ebba …" she managed. "Is she … are they?"

Hengest shook his head. "I'm sorry. They're both dead."

Halfritha buried her face in his chest and finally allowed the tears to fall freely.

Hengest

"Marriage?" exclaimed Ealdorman Wictgils around a mouthful of meat. "I send you to settle a simple dispute and you go and develop a fixation on the girl!"

Hengest chewed on his meal. He had chosen this time to broach the subject with his father. The hall was empty but for him and his parents. A few theows were clearing up and Horsa was eating down at the wharves with his newfound friends as he did most nights.

"I love her, Father," he said, knowing that such softness would do little to impress the ealdorman.

"Love?" scoffed Wictgils. "What use is love? A child's fancy that is soon lost once a man comes to deal with the hard reality of life. I didn't love your mother when our parents decided that we should be married. But we learned to love each other over our years together. It takes time to learn to love. And it is the duty of an ealdorman to ensure that his sons marry well into families that will benefit his people."

Hengest had been afraid of this. The son of an ealdorman was often married to the daughter of one of his father's friends or rivals in order to secure an alliance or to end a feud. Wictgils had never mentioned such a union for Hengest as the tribes of Jute-land were in a state of relative peace in recent years. But there was trouble brewing over in Dane-land and he feared that if war broke out, his father would begin to consider his options.

"Am I to be traded for favours like some lowly theow?" he asked.

His father raised his eyebrows in surprise at his tone. "You're beginning to sound like your brother," he said. "And that is a trait you can most certainly do without."

"She is a good girl from an honest family," interjected Aedre hurriedly.

"They're ceorls!" protested Wictgils. "She's no fit bride for an aetheling!"

"There's no law against it!" said Hengest.

"I think that it is time you put aside thoughts for personal gain," said Aedre, "and put the heart of your eldest son first. He clearly loves the girl deeply."

Wictgils threw up his hands in exasperation. "I might have known a woman would take this horseshit seriously! There is not time for this at present. I have one useless son whose fate is to shame me at the Folcmot in a matter of days and another coming to me, starry-eyed and spouting nonsense about love. Wait until this blasted Folcmot is over, Hengest, and then we will discuss your future at length."

Hengest nodded. That was as good an answer as he had hoped for from his father and, for the time being, it would have to do.

Horsa

The Folcmot was held several times a year. In a violent world, where minor disputes could so often lead to blood feuds that transcended generations, it was the only acknowledged system of law. Any free man could attend the Folcmot and for everybody else it was something of a spectacle. People flocked in droves from miles around to see cases put to the assembly and often placed wagers as to their outcomes.

It was held in a sacred grove on the edge of the settlement where the sparse trees of Jute-land had clustered together, almost as if summoned by the gods. It was dedicated to Woden, the one-eyed god of wisdom and chief of all the gods. Woden was a wanderer and a master of disguise who ruled Esegeard from his mighty hall, Waelheall. It was said that all men were descended from him.

A gigantic carven effigy of the Allfather's head stood at one end of the grove beneath the gently swaying canopy of trees. At its feet lay a stone altar with a wooden bowl atop it which always contained blood as a permanent offering to the god. A circle of wooden logs was laid out all year round for the noblemen to sit upon. For generations, meetings had been carried out here in this sacred place beneath the single all-seeing eye of the high god.

More people than usual had come to see the case of Wulfgar verses Horsa. The brawl had been the talk of the village for a whole month and thegns had come with their sons from miles around to play their part in the deliberations. Horsa watched them with a heavy heart as they made their way into the grove, taking their seats, greeting old acquaintances and laughing jovially.

He was unbearably nervous. Hengest stood by his side and offered words of encouragement to him, but nothing could allay the gut-wrenching feeling of helplessness as he watched the cheerful faces of the men who would be deciding his fate. Their father was not there yet. It was customary for the ealdorman to be the last to arrive so that the proceedings could begin immediately without him having to wait.

There was some excitement at the other end of the grove and many heads turned to watch three men stride into the clearing. It was Wulfgar and his two sons. The thegn was a well-dressed man in a blue cloak with red trimming. His face wore the stern expression of a man determined to get what he wanted for his troubles. His two sons limped sheepishly behind him, one with his arm in a sling and the other with a face that was still yellowish from its bruises. They ignored the sniggers of the crowd and fixed their glaring gazes upon Horsa as they sat down next to their father in the front row.

A silence fell over the grove and all rose respectfully as the ealdorman arrived, hobbling on his crutch, refusing the aid of his theows. Next to him walked Oeric, the elected law speaker who would preside over the assembly.

Oeric, stooped and ancient, turned to the effigy of Woden and picked up the birch twigs from the bowl on the altar. As he splashed the blood on the face of the god he spoke,

"Allfather Woden, Chief of the Ese and Lord of Waelheall, may you bless this meeting and ensure that an honourable and just end be brought to all disputes."

The hand flicked and droplets of blood ran down the cracked and warped wood. "Grant us a part of the wisdom that you gave your eye for, when you hung from the world tree for nine days, so that we are right in our judgements. Hail Woden!"

There were many other murmurs of 'Hail Woden!' and Oeric replaced the birch twigs and turned to face the assembly.

"The first item of this Folcmot is the dispute between Wulfgar, son of Octa, and Horsa, son of Wictgils. As is the custom, the injured party may speak first."

Wulfgar rose and took the time to arrange his cloak before speaking. "Members of the Folcmot," he began, his voice carrying over the soft breeze that stirred the leaves above them. "I am, as you know, a man of honour and principle. Never has there been a time when I have allowed the honour of my family to be sullied without standing up and fighting for it. Last summer I was stuck a blow which was not easy for me to take. I need not remind you of the Folcmot's decision to support the claim of Osfrid against me. I lost land because of that decision but I accepted it for it was the will of the Folcmot. But now an insult has been made towards me that I cannot accept. My daughter, my beautiful Eadyth, who was a pure and virtuous girl, has had her virtue taken, her purity robbed. Robbed by Horsa, son of Ealdorman Wictgils!"

He paused for effect before carrying on. The assembled crowd shuffled their feet impatiently.

"Is this the kind of behaviour we are to expect from the son of our ealdorman? My daughter has nearly reached the age to be wed. I had hoped to marry her to one of you good, noble thegns who sit here today. But after she has been defiled by Horsa, who now would marry her? She is doomed to be a spinster for the remainder of her life for I cannot allow her to marry a lowly ceorl in place of a thegn. For this I demand justice be done! I demand a weregild be paid!"

There were many cries from the assembled thegns, some in support of Wulfgar's demand and some against it. One rose and addressed them.

"A weregild is paid when the life of one is taken. Your daughter is still alive, Wulfgar, so the demand for such a payment cannot be taken seriously."

The cries of agreement at this shouted down the cries against it. Oeric pleaded with them to come to order.

"Very well," said Wulfgar. "Not a wergild then, but surely I am due some sort of compensation for the loss of my daughter's honour. If not, then I suggest that the matter be settled by single combat. A fight to the death between the ealdorman's son and one of my own!"

Horsa felt sick to his stomach. He hadn't considered that it would come to this. It was not uncommon for disputes to be settled by single combat before the council. Like all noble-born members of society, he had been trained well in the use of sword and spear but he had not wielded either outside of the training yard. The thought of fighting for his life against one of the sour-faced sons of Wulfgar made him queasy. And this time Hengest would be powerless to intervene.

But there was nothing he could do but accept the man's offer. To do otherwise would earn him the mark of a coward and a man without honour. His heart hammering, he stood up and raised his voice above the babble of the excited gathering.

"My lord Wulfgar, I ..."

"Be silent!" shouted his father, and the sacred grove instantly quietened at the sound of the ealdorman's hoarse bark.

Wictgils heaved himself out of his chair and leaned on his crutch. "My youngest son has disgraced not just your family but mine too, Wulfgar. Had this been any other man then I would agree with your proposal for single combat. I understand your anger, and you are right to call for the blood of the one who defiled your daughter. But, I beg you, do not let this ugly matter claim the life of my son. Take payment from me instead. I am willing to be generous in reaching a settlement that is agreeable to you."

The grove was silent as Wulfgar considered this offer.

"What manner of payment do you have in mind, my lord?"

But Wictgils was already motioning to a group of his theows who stood at the edge of the trees. A magnificent horse was brought forward from where it had been hidden; a white stallion with a sleek, plaited mane and a speckling of grey upon its hind quarters. The theows led the creature around the circle of benches as if they were parading a war trophy.

Horsa recognised the beast at once for it was the pride of his father's stables, the only horse he and Hengest were forbidden to ride.

"This is the finest horse in my possession," said the ealdorman. "He has carried me on many hunts and has never failed me. I had planned to give him to Woden at the winter festival of Geola, but instead I give him to you, Wulfgar, in payment for your daughter's stolen virtue."

Wulfgar's eyes goggled as he watched the stallion canter around obediently, showing no resentment of the bridle. Horsa seethed inside. His father had planned this all along. The horse had been hidden in the woods before the Folcmot had even assembled.

"Well, Wulfgar," said Oeric. "Do you accept this in payment?"

The thegn hesitated before answering, weighing up the thought of seeing Horsa's blood spilt against owning the finest horse in the entire territory. It was apparently a hard decision to make.

"I accept," he said at last.

Then somebody began to thump the handle of his saex upon his bench. This was taken up by one more and then another, until the whole Folcmot was hammering their acceptance; a rousing, rhythmic roll of thunder that echoed throughout the glade.

"He knew that Wulfgar would accept the horse!" Horsa said to Hengest, as they made their way down the hill after the Folcmot had come to a close. The council members and spectators were making their way home, some milling about in small groups, talking. "Why did he not just tell me what he was planning?"

Hengest shrugged. "There was no guarantee that Wulfgar would have accepted," he said. "Perhaps father didn't want to risk getting your hopes up only to see them dashed."

"Huh," said Horsa with a snort. "He knew. That was just his way of punishing me by making me suffer."

"Perhaps. But he did trade his best horse so that you would not have to fight. That has to count for something, doesn't it?"

"And what exactly does it count for?"

"It's proof that he loves you enough not to want to see you perish in battle with one of Wulfgar's sons."

"Are you so sure that I would lose if it had come to that?" asked Horsa. He looked over to where Wulfgar was leading his newly acquired horse by its bridle. His two sons followed close behind. "You don't think I could beat one of them?"

"The younger one, perhaps," said Hengest. "But his arm is broken. It would have been the older one you would have fought."

"I saved your life today, boy," said Wictgils, hobbling over to them. "But you cost me my best horse. It is a debt I want repaid one day."

Hengest and Horsa were silent as their father hobbled off. They watched as Eadyth, the daughter of Wulfgar and subject of the whole messy affair, came to greet her father and brothers at the foot of the hill. She looked over to Horsa and he saw that one of her eyes was blackened and swollen. He felt pity for her but knew that he could never speak to her again after what had happened.

"You said you loved me, Horsa!" she cried out to him. "Why did you not claim me for your own? You said you loved me!"

"Aye, I'll say anything for a quick fumble in the hay," he called back.

It was a bitter comment and he regretted it as soon as he had said it. But it had to be made clear that their affair was over. There would be no more secret meetings in stables from now on.

The sons of Wulfgar turned sharply to him and looked ready to renew hostilities at the insult, but their sister's face spoke more than their blows could ever do.

"I hate you Horsa!" she shouted. "I hate you and curse your whole wretched family!"

Her elder brother grabbed her roughly and she was dragged away, weeping.

"Nicely done," said Hengest, his voice dripping with reproach.

"Oh, lay off," replied Horsa. "It's hard enough giving her the elbow. She was a sweet treat."

"Well, try to plan ahead a bit before you strike up another blossoming romance, eh?" Hengest said not unkindly, grabbing his little brother around the neck playfully.

Horsa was not in the mood and he squirmed free from his brother's grasp.

"What's up?" Hengest asked.

"I'm sick of this place," Horsa replied. "I'm sick of its gossiping old nags and its snooty bastards."

"People gossip everywhere."

"In little shitholes like this, yes, but the world out there is big; so big that you can wander for days and not see the same person twice."

"The world out there?" queried Hengest, raising his eyebrow at him. "You've been listening to the Northman again, haven't you? What's his name? Ketil?"

"So what if I have? He's an interesting man. He's been all over and even he hasn't seen everything the world has to offer."

"Well, when you reach manhood, perhaps Father will agree to let you go on a voyage with someone he knows. That ought to satisfy you."

"And would you come?"

Hengest shrugged. "Father needs me here. Besides, I get seasick."

That brought a smile to Horsa's face as he remembered the trip downriver to the coast they had taken with their father a year previously. Hengest had turned green as clover as soon as they were out on the water, and spent the rest of the voyage hurling the contents of his stomach over the bulwarks. It had become a regular joke around the hall that the ealdorman's eldest son would get seasick standing in a puddle.

"What's so funny?" Hengest asked.

"Oh, nothing. Just the thought of you as a sailor."

Hengest took a swipe at his brother, and the two of them chased each other about all the way home.

Hengest

Later that night Horsa was nowhere to be found. The ealdorman was getting drunk in his hall and doing his best to forget the day's proceedings. Hengest searched for his brother in the surrounding stables, storage huts and craftsmen's dwellings, worried that he too might be drinking away his sorrows in the arms of some other woman or gambling away all his wealth on a dice game. He couldn't find him anywhere and, with the moon high above the gables, he was prepared to give it up and leave Horsa to his own troubles.

Outside the hall he was approached by one of his father's theows, a youngish lad with an untidy mop of flaxen hair. He had a message for Hengest that he was to meet his brother in the sacred grove.

"When did my brother give you this message?" Hengest asked.

"A few minutes ago, master," said the theow sheepishly. "I was detained by one of your father's attendants and I had to fetch more mead …"

"Very well. Be about your business then." Hengest left the lad to his chores and made his way up the hill to where the Folcmot had been held a few hours previously.

The grove was silent and eerily unreal in the silver moonlight. The chisel marks in the great carven face of Woden were all the deeper, making him even more sombre and grim. Alone in the grove stood Horsa. Beyond him, faintly visible in the shadows of the trees, awaited a small pack pony.

"What is it, little brother?" asked Hengest, as he stepped into the grove. "Why all this secrecy? And what's the pony for?"

Horsa turned, startled by the soft approach of his brother. His face was almost as grim as Woden's.

"I'm leaving," he said.

"What?"

"I'm going away. Far away."

"Be sensible, Horsa. It has been a tough few weeks for everyone. Don't let it force you into hasty actions you might regret. Besides, where would you go?"

"I'll head to the coast and get work onboard one of the trading vessels, or maybe a raider. It'll be a better life than sticking around here. Don't try to persuade me otherwise. I've made up my mind. It's better for everyone if I go."

"It'll kill mother."

Horsa looked down at his feet. "I know. But she'll understand. One day I'll return. I'll be rich and I'll repay Father for the horse. You'll all be proud of me, you'll see."

"What do you know of the sea?" asked Hengest.

"I'll learn. How hard can it be? Besides, I'm a good fighter and a hard worker. It will come to me."

"I can't stop you, can I?" said Hengest in a resigned tone.

Horsa smiled. "No."

They were silent for a time, both sharing the moment in the presence of the Allfather. They both knew that a turning point had come in their lives. They were no longer children. Their old life was slipping away from them like leaves on the autumn wind, and there was nothing either of them could do about it.

"There is something I wanted to do before I left," said Horsa. "Something I wanted to show you. I haven't always been the brother I should be and you have helped me out of more scrapes than I can count.

62

You saved my life when Eadyth's brothers attacked me and … well, here I am saying thank you. I hope you will think well of me when I am gone, for I know that when we see each other again, I will be the brother you deserve."

"Horsa, there is no need for this …" began Hengest.

"Let my actions speak now instead of words, Brother," interrupted Horsa. He stepped up to the altar, stained with the blood of a hundred sacrifices, and spoke to the high-one himself. "I come to your sacred grove, Woden, Allfather of men, to perform an act in your presence. I wish you to witness my pledge to my brother, Hengest. He saved my life and I vow before you that I shall return the favour one day. I swear this by all that is precious to me."

Hengest watched in stunned silence as his younger brother rolled up the sleeve of his left arm then drew his saex. With a long, fluid motion, he opened up a vein in his arm and allowed the blood to run freely into the wooden bowl, mingling with the congealed blood that was already there.

"I offer you my blood, Woden, keeper of knowledge," continued Horsa, "as you offered your left eye. In exchange, I ask you to help me make true my oath to my brother. Let not water, earth, or fire stand between me and its fulfilment. Help me shiver the shields and break the swords of those who would prevent it. Let not the waves of the great sea stand as a barrier, nor the marshes, nor the forests of Middangeard."

He picked up the birch branch and dipped it in his own blood. With several flicks of his wrist, he splashed the blood upon the face of the god. He stepped back and tore of a strip of his tunic to bind his wound.

"I hope that you realise what you have done," Hengest said. "An oath made in the presence of the Allfather is not one to break."

"I know," replied Horsa. "I'm serious about this, brother. I will return to you one day and fulfil my vow. But until that day, I have my fortune to make and my name to prove. Goodbye, Hengest."

The two brothers embraced and Hengest watched Horsa walk away through the trees to where his pony was waiting. He heaved himself up into the saddle, and with one final look towards his older brother, he set off through the trees.

Hengest remained until the darkness had swallowed Horsa whole. He could hardly believe it.

His little brother was gone.

PART II

(Lagu) "Lagu byþ leodum langsum geþuht,
gif hi sculun neþan on nacan tealtum,
and hi sæyþa swyþe bregaþ,
and se brimhengest bridles ne gymeð."

(Ocean) "The ocean seems interminable to men,
if they venture on the rolling bark
and the waves of the sea terrify them
and the courser of the deep heed not its bridle."

Frisia, winter, 444 A.D. (twelve years later)

Hnaef

Many leagues off the western coast of Jute-land, several boats cut a southerly direction, their oars rising and falling in tight, disciplined strokes. Nearly sixty men were carried between them, dressed in mail and boiled leather. Saexes and swords hung from their belts. Their shields, painted in an array of different colours and devices, hung from the bulwarks.

In the stern of the foremost of the ships, Hnaef, son of Hoc, King of the West Danes, sat wrapped in furs. His hair was golden and his face possessed the kind of noble handsomeness that charms and commands men. His family was old and his tribe ancient. The Hocings were a small, proud people, rarely considered a threat by their more powerful neighbours.

But Hnaef had been born with an ambition that could never be contained by the borders of his father's territory. He was a man the gods had marked for greatness, so his people said. Ambitious and ruthless in equal measure, Hnaef had led his tribe to victory over their neighbours in battle after battle, and had forged a confederation of Danish clans that he ruled as the first King of the West Danes. But his ambitions did not stop there.

Hnaef had set his sights on uniting the whole of the northern world under a single king – Jutes, Saxons, Danes, Angles, Frisians, even the Geats and the Sweons – all paying homage to the Hocing dynasty that would rule for a thousand years or more. A futile dream perhaps, but it was his dream and he would stop at nothing to see it come to fruition.

"Is there any other feeling in the world like it, Sigeferth?" Hnaef asked the man at his side. "Cutting through the waves at the head of a warband; the smell of salt on the air, the slapping of the water against the strakes of good, strong, Danish longboats! I have spent too long on land, Sigeferth. The sea lanes are my real home."

"My own people are born seafarers," replied Sigeferth. "I too have missed the smell and motion of the whale-road."

Sigeferth was a slender, fair youth and an aetheling of a tribe called the Scegan; one of the many peoples that had fallen under the banner of the West Danes. As part of the peace treaty between Hnaef and Sigeferth's father, it was agreed that the young aetheling would accompany Hnaef on one of his expeditions, so that the two families might be bonded by camaraderie.

"But as for the warband," continued Sigeferth, "is it wise to bring such a large force to the home of your brother-in-law?"

Hnaef shook his head. "I specifically brought few enough men so as not to insult our host by making him think that we are heading an invasion, but enough to ensure that he knows who, out of the two of us, holds the upper hand."

They stared over the helmeted heads of the rowers at the thin grey line on the horizon that marked the coastline of Frisia. The purpose of Hnaef's voyage was to spend the winter festival of Geola with King Finn of the Frisians.

Cunning in trade and fine seafarers, the Frisians rivalled the West Danes and Finn was a ruler of wealth and power almost great enough to rival Hnaef. Hnaef knew that one day, when the lands of the Angles, Jutes and Saxons that lay between Dane-land and Frisia eventually fell under the Hocing banner, West Dane and Frisian must face each other with no buffer between them.

Always thinking ahead, Hnaef had married his sister, Hildeburh, to Finn, thus forging a blood-tie between the two kings that could not be broken without great shame. The loyalty of the Frisians had been bought without a single drop of blood being shed.

Hengest

On one of the boats behind Hnaef's, Hengest gripped the bulwark and focused on breathing deeply. The deck lurched beneath his feet and his stomach lurched with it. The white caps of the waves rose and fell with sickening regularity, and the swell beneath the shallow keel tossed the small craft about as if it were driftwood.

Hengest hated the sea; the nausea, the constant wind and wet spray and the thought of the vast, black chasms yawning beneath them and the nightmarish creatures that dwelt in those dark depths. The distant coastline of Frisia was a dull grey bulge on the horizon beneath a leaden sky. Another winter was coming.

Twelve years had passed since Horsa had left. It had all but destroyed their mother when she had learned that her youngest son had run away. Hengest had remained with her the night he told her, comforting her as she wept until the dawn came. Their father had ranted and raged as could be expected; but on the whole, as much as Hengest was loathe to admit, life went on just fine without his little brother.

Hengest had married Halfritha and the two of them had moved into the farm she had inherited. He had purchased theows to work the land and their home had been a happy one. Halfritha had borne him two children; a daughter they named Hronwena and a son they named Aesc. Both were nearing adolescence now and he missed them terribly.

Year by year, news of Horsa trickled back to Jute-land like the melt of spring. There had been rumours of him taking up with a crew of Angle raiders and enjoying great success plundering the merchant vessels and coastal towns throughout the northern world. One year a messenger arrived with a large sum of silver to be paid to Ealdorman Wictgils. It had been sent by Horsa to repay his father for the horse that had been given to Wulfgar. Wictgils accepted the money but said nothing. As far as he was concerned, Horsa was dead to him.

But the happy and safe home Hengest had built for his family had been thrown into turmoil by the recent rise to power of Hnaef. There had long been enmity between the Jutes and the Dane-tribes; blood feuds and territorial disputes that reached back further than anyone could remember. With this new upstart uniting the West Danes, the Jutish ealdormen began to worry that they would be next to fall to this Dane's boundless ambition.

Their concern was well-founded. Ealdorman Guthulf, a good friend of Wictgils, was the first victim and was slain along with his wife and two sons. A third son, Garulf, had escaped the slaughter with a few of his father's retainers and had fled Jute-land. Another ealdorman, Herebeorht, was next to fall under Hnaef's shadow and there was talk of a treaty between the two.

Wictgils was outraged at the idea and sent Hengest to Herebeorht's hall to persuade the chieftain not to join with Hnaef on a point of honour and for the pride of all Jutes. Upon arrival, Hengest was shocked to find the negotiations already underway and King Hnaef a guest of Herebeorht.

Far from being a bloodthirsty tyrant as Hengest had been led to believe, he found Hnaef to be a fair and sensible man with strong political opinions and a heart that was big enough to feel for the misfortunes of the common people. As the mead flowed and the three men got to speaking freely, Hengest had begun to like Hnaef.

73

The Danish king was the exact opposite of his father. Wictgils was content for his earldom to live in total independence and isolation. That was the way it had always been; an ealdorman looked after his people and left others to look to the protection of their own leaders. But Hnaef proposed a new era of unity throughout the northern world and an end to the petty blood feuds and territorial arguments.

Hengest saw in Hnaef a visionary and he wanted a stock in this new world that was to rise from the ashes of the old. That night, with the gods watching from Esegeard, he had pledged his allegiance to the king of the West Danes.

As could be expected, his father was furious. Instead of preventing an alliance between Herebeorht and Hnaef, his son had sealed the union and had joined the Danish tyrant himself, dishonouring his people and shaming his family.

The waves that rushed past the strakes of the boat could never wash away the bitter memories of that argument. Hengest remembered his mother weeping whilst his father had raged at him and, for the first time in his life, he had felt as if he had taken the place of his younger brother.

He had stood his ground, refusing to let the old ealdorman's wrathful words deter him. He was a grown man and he had the right to follow whatever banner he chose. Wictgils made his choice plain; break his oath to Hnaef or be disinherited and exiled from his lands.

Hengest had chosen exile. His father had cursed him for a wretched ingrate and proclaimed at the top of his voice for all the hall to hear, that he no longer had any sons. But it was his mother's weeping that remained with Hengest. He doubted he would ever see her again and it broke his heart to see her suffer the loss of two sons.

Forced to leave the farm that was within his father's lands, Hengest had sold his theows and moved Halfritha and his children further south where Brand – one of his father's thegns in the old days, before he too had been exiled for some petty thing – now lived, far away from Wictgils's reach.

Brand was closer in age to Hengest and the two had always been good companions. Now Brand showed compassion for his old friend and offered shelter for Hengest's family.

Spring had come and Hengest had joined the warband of Hnaef, as he had promised to do so for the period of one year. Ironically, his father's title and lands would now pass to Horsa, who had always been the unlikelier of the two sons to succeed the ealdorman.

If Horsa ever returned to claim his title.

Hengest often thought of his brother. He was glad that Horsa seemed to be doing well in his life as a raider but wondered if their paths would ever cross again. The lands of the north were brutal and harsh. Once two companions parted ways, there was no certainty that they would ever meet again.

Silently, Hengest offered up a prayer to the Wyrd Sisters, those three women who sat at the foot of the world tree and wove the fates of men into their great tapestry. He hoped that they wove a bright future for him and his family.

"The king's boat is changing course," shouted Guthlaf, an elderly Danish thegn and one of Hnaef's highest captains.

Hengest looked out across the choppy water to the other boat. He could just make out the figure of Hnaef standing in the stern with his fur cloak billowing about him.

"He knows this coastline," replied Hengest. "He'll know the best place to come ashore. Hard to steorbord, Ordlaf!"

Ordlaf the steersman gave out the order and the twenty oarsmen raised their oars, and the boat turned gradually to match the speed and angle of the king's vessel.

They were a good crew though Hengest barely knew them. Even most of their names eluded him apart from Ordlaf and Guthlaf who were chief among them. As Hengest knew next to nothing about seamanship, it fell upon the two Danish thegns to make most of the decisions. He knew that his presence on the trip was little more than a chance for Hnaef to flex his political muscle and flaunt his ability to surround himself with the sons of powerful rulers. *Well, let him flex.* Once winter was over, he would be returning to his family to plan their future.

After beaching the ships on the dark sand of Frisia, a company of King Finn's thegns rode down to greet them upon the powerful black stallions that were native to Frisia. They were beautiful beasts with glossy coats that seemed to twinkle even in the dim afternoon light. Behind them, sandy dunes prickling with clumps of long grass swept away from the sea leading to flat, green pastures. Cattle farming formed the backbone of Frisian agriculture and they passed many herds of the black and white type that Frisia was famous for on their way to Finnesburg.

King Finn's chief settlement was divided down the centre by a river that wound its way across the flatlands like a glistening worm. The water had been diverted, either by nature or by man's hand, around a small island that formed the central point of the settlement. It could be reached from either side by timber bridges, and it was upon this island that King Finn had built his hall. Two other halls had been built on opposite sides of the river, and around them the various dwellings and workshops were clustered, lain out along streets of wooden planks that rested on the mud.

Most of the town's populace turned out to watch the procession of the Danish king, making its way through the muddy streets, following their Frisian hosts. It was an impressive sight; sixty Danish thegns in war-gear forming a large column of toughened leather, chain mail and polished helms. Shields were carried upon their backs as a sign of peace but spear tips prickled the air.

Hengest looked up at the carven gables and thatched roofs of the settlement, and at the mass of people that crowded in the streets. From the many workshops and storage huts the sound of industry hummed and the tantalizing smell of freshly cooked food and brewing ale competed for dominance with the stink of unwashed bodies and human and animal excrement.

The sheer size of the place put any settlement in Jute-land to shame. The village his father ruled was a mere cattle pen compared to this. But then, his father was an ealdorman and Finn was a king, and therein laid the difference.

And a king's hall, Hengest discovered as they crossed the bridge to the island, was far more impressive than an ealdorman's. A great pillared entrance supported a massive thatched roof with gables carven into the grinning visages of drakes. Stone steps led up to gargantuan oak doors also carven with swirling motifs.

"Have you ever been here before?" he asked Ordlaf, not taking his eyes from the entrance to the massive building.

The young Dane shook his head. "Not I. Guthlaf has though. He's been in Hnaef's service longer than anyone and came here when Hildeburh was married to Finn."

"I've never seen a hall so impressive."

"You should see King Hnaef's," replied the Dane with a smile. "Finn's whole hall could probably fit inside his."

Hengest did not reply. He had never even been to Dane-land. He came to the conclusion that such extravagance must be a king's prerogative to show his might and wealth in one symbolic gesture.

A royal welcome awaited them at the steps to the hall. King Finn was there with his wife, Hildeburh, and a select few of his most trusted thegns. Finn was not a tall man but he was stocky and handsome. His dark hair was tied back under a simple gold circlet that served as a modest crown.

"*Hwæt*, Brother!" said the Friesian king, as the Danes approached. "Welcome to Finnesburg!"

"*Hwæt*, Finn!" said Hnaef and the two kings embraced. Hnaef then looked to Hildeburh with great fondness in his eyes. "Hello, Sister. It has been too long."

"That it has, Brother," replied Finn's queen, letting Hnaef kiss her on both cheeks as they embraced.

She possessed a cold kind of beauty. She had flaxen hair like her brother and was blessed with the high cheekbones and intelligent air that marked the house of the Hocings. But there was an icy sadness to her, a melancholy that did its best to hide behind her queenly façade. Hengest wondered what ailed a woman who lived in the seat of luxury and wore the finest of furs and gold rings with a handsome king for a husband.

"And where is my fine nephew?" asked Hnaef, looking about for Frithuwulf, Finn's son. "He must be at least fifteen by now. Not come to greet his uncle?"

"He is with a friend of mine," replied Finn. "I fostered him to a local family. A good family."

It was common for noble families to foster their sons during their years of adolescence. It helped establish alliances as well as providing the young boys with experience and education they might not have otherwise got from their own fathers.

"They are coming to celebrate Geola with us so you may see him then. But come now!" Finn placed a hand on Hnaef's shoulder and addressed the sixty-odd Danes who stood at his door. "Inside, and warm yourselves by my hearth!"

The interior of Finn's hall did not betray its exterior and was truly vast, a testament to the wealth of the Frisian kings. The floor was paved with stone flags and in the centre of it was a huge fire pit over which two spitted boars were already crackling. The wooden pillars that supported the roof were carved with exquisite shapes and designs and were banded at top and bottom with gold. Brightly coloured tapestries depicting many heroic tales of Finn's ancestors hung down from the rafters and on the walls. In one, a Frisian king led his men to victory over their Saxon neighbours whilst another showed the hunting of a mighty boar. The tapestry above the royal dais showed the hero, Sigemund, slaying the dragon, Fafnir; a legend well-told around hearth fires throughout the northern world. Upon the dais stood three great chairs for the king and his family.

The guests were asked to sit and theows brought them empty drinking horns. Queen Hildeburh walked between the benches with a large jug of mead and filled up the horns of the guests until they were brimming; a symbolic gesture of the host's humbleness that he would send his own wife to serve mead. King Finn arose from his carven chair and raised a horn in salute to his guests.

"King Hnaef of the Hocings, ruler of the West Danes," he said. "We welcome you and your thegns who journeyed with you across the sea from Dane-land and hope that you will enjoy the winter here with us. Frisians and Danes – brothers!"

"Brothers!" echoed the rest of the hall, and a hundred mead horns were raised to the rafters in a toast before being emptied down thirsty gullets in one movement. There was cheering and clapping and more mead was brought forth.

"Fetch the gold!" Finn commanded, and a large chest was heaved in and set down before the king's chair.

Finn flipped the lid open with his boot and dug deep into it, pulling out handfuls of golden rings, torques and coins which he tossed onto the feasting tables. The gold glittered in the eyes of the Danes who marvelled at the generosity of their host as they plucked up chosen treasures. Jewels and worked metals from far-off lands such as Britta, Frankia, Burgund and the Eastern Roman Empire twinkled in the light of the torches. Roman coins depicting the heads of various

Caesars long dead were spread out across the dark oak. There was cheering and toasting to the Frisian king's generosity and all about the hall was a buzz of excitement.

And then Hnaef ordered his own gifts to the host be brought forward. It had taken six men to bring them from the boats to Finnesburg. Three chests were carried up to the king's throne and Hnaef opened each himself. All in the hall were silent as Finn was presented with a magnificent gold-rimmed shield decorated with animal symbols, a sword forged by the finest blacksmith in all Dane-land, and last of all a large bronze bowl, the sides of which depicted hunting scenes and the images of the forest deities of the Celts.

The gifts were accepted with much gratitude on the part of Finn, for even though a king may be the wealthiest man in the world, he always hungers for strange and exotic items that might stir his interest. Another toast was made and then the feasting began.

They ate and drank heartily. Boar meat, sizzling and dripping, warmed hungry palates. Steaming fish was carried around by theows on large platters and flat loaves of freshly baked bread were heaped up at the ends of the tables. There was cheese and honeycomb and autumn berries. Mead flowed freely and there was ale too for those who wished it. The hall rang with song and laughter and, as faces turned rosy with drink, there was dancing and wrestling. People got up and moved about freely, conversing and tale-telling. The men eyed the women hungrily and some were rewarded with shy smiles and the occasional wink. Hnaef, who sat at the king's table, called Hengest over and introduced him to the Frisian king.

"This is Hengest of Jute-land," said Hnaef, pouring them both some more mead. "As you can see, there are at least some Jutes who would have an alliance with me!"

The Frisian king fixed a gaze on him and spoke, "Am I right in thinking that you are the same Hengest who is Ealdorman Wictgils's son?"

Hengest groaned inwardly. He knew that the matter of his father would come up sooner or later. "Your knowledge of petty chieftains stretches far, my lord," he replied. "I am that Hengest. But you have no doubt heard, also, that I have little to do with my father these days."

Finn half smiled. "I had heard something of the sort."

"Hengest shows more sense than his father," said Hnaef. "His pledge to me is a gesture that I hope all Jutes will eventually follow. The world would be much simpler if the West Danes held Jute-land instead of it being mired in pointless rivalry; do you not think so, Finn?"

Finn smiled but there was little humour in it. "A world of Danes and Friesians? Then there would be nobody left for you to conquer, Hnaef."

"Ha! There are always the Saxons, or the Angles. Or even the Geats. There is no shortage of tribes to fight, old friend. But at least the Scegans have shown me their loyalty. Have you met Sigeferth, by the way?" He called over the young aethleing and grabbed him roughly about the shoulders in playful affection. "We two are not the only royal-born in this hall tonight. His father sent him with me as a token of his allegiance, and I am very glad that he did. Sigeferth here is a fine seaman and a good fighter by all accounts."

The young Scegan aetheling blushed and Hengest smiled. Hnaef had no sons as of yet and it was not hard to see the Danish king taking on the role of a proud father to the sons of others.

"We are old men, Hnaef," said Finn. "The young of today are twice the boys we were and it is in them that the future lies."

Hildeburh approached and filled up Finn's horn with mead. He grasped her around the waist and kissed her hard on the neck. She smiled and wriggled playfully, but it seemed forced to Hengest; a worn-out pretence.

"I am twice blessed by Woden," said Finn. "Once with this beautiful queen of mine and again with my wonderful son. Few kings are as lucky, I think. Hengest's horn is empty, my dear. Be a good hostess to him."

He released Hildeburh and she moved over to Hengest, her long dress sweeping the stone floor and the beads and ornaments that decorated her bosom twinkling in the firelight. Finn and Hnaef continued talking behind them. Hengest held out his horn for her to fill and she searched his face as she poured.

"You're a quiet one," she said, mustering a warm smile. "Does the entertainment of my husband's hall bore you?"

"Far from it," he replied. "But the talk and power play of kings is a game I cannot join. I am but a humble son of an ealdorman, and an exiled one at that."

"Exiled?" asked Hildeburh, her eyes showing some mild interest. "For what crime?"

"For the crime of being stubborn and disagreeing with one's father," he said.

"I see," she said. "It is a crime many men are guilty of. And women too."

"Are you such a woman?"

She smiled weakly. "No. I did as my father asked, or brother I should say, for Hnaef took his place as head of our family at a young age. Do not be hard on yourself for your choices, Hengest. For between exile and a prison, the comparison favours the former."

He wanted to ask her what she meant by that, but she was gone before he had a chance, and he watched her make her way to the other side of the hall where other drinking horns were waiting to be filled. He heard Finn calling his name.

"My lord," he said, rejoining the two kings.

"Tell me, Hengest, as a Jute," began Finn. "Do you find any difficulty in following Hnaef here, the man whose family has long pushed the borders of their territory further and further into your homeland?"

"Well," replied Hengest with a grim smile, "I don't exactly have a homeland anymore. But if you mean to ask if I resent the West Danes for their incursions into Jute-land, then I would say no. Jute-land is not a united territory such as Frisia or West Dane-land. It is made up of many clans who would just as gladly fight each other as the Danes. King Hnaef's movements represent a push for a better world, a united world where peace is much more achievable. That is why I would rather follow him than the chieftains my father favours."

"I see," said Finn. "You are an idealist like Hnaef. And you, Hnaef. Are you content to have Jutes in your warband, even the sons of ealdormen who despise you with a passion?"

"I judge men on their own merits, not on the stubbornness of their fathers," said Hnaef.

"I am glad to hear you say that," replied Finn. "Because the nobleman I have charged with the fostering of my son is coming to Finnesburg in three days, and he is a Jute."

"Oh?" replied Hnaef with interest. "Anybody I know?"

"In a manner of speaking. You see, Hnaef, I am something of an idealist myself. I want this winter to be a milestone in friendship between the tribes. I want old feuds to die and be buried under the frost, to shrivel up never to rise again."

"Who is it?" asked Hnaef, his face devoid of any of the humour and good cheer it had possessed a few minutes ago.

"Garulf, son of Guthulf," replied Finn.

Hnaef's face turned ashen. "That whelp? I drove him into exile many seasons ago. Killed his father. He won't be pleased to see me!"

"I am aware of the history between you both," said Finn patiently. But Garulf is a good man. Since his exile, he and his followers have been living in Frisia as refugees. They are under my protection and have been good allies these past few years. That is why I have invited them here to winter with us."

"You play a dangerous game in sheltering enemies of my family, Finn," warned Hnaef. A noticeable tension was growing in the air and much of the hall had fallen silent. All eyes were on the two kings.

"You yourself said that you wished peace amongst the coastal tribes," said Finn. "I am merely asking that two guests of mine get along for one winter. If you can manage that then perhaps peace can be reached between Jute and Dane."

"There is peace between Jute and Dane," snapped Hnaef. "The right sort of Jute anyway. Jutes like

Hengest here. Not vicious little urchins like Garulf and his kin."

"Would you like some more mead, Hnaef?" asked Finn.

"No thank you," replied Hnaef. "My belly is full and my head is thick with drinking. I am no longer in the spirit of merrymaking."

"Then I shall have someone show you to your sleeping quarters," said Finn.

Several Danes departed with Hnaef but the feasting continued, albeit a little muted. Hengest walked over to where Ordlaf and Guthlaf were betting on the outcome of a wrestling match between a fellow Dane and a bulky Frisian.

"What do you make of all this then, eh?" Guthlaf asked him. "Finn's got some balls inviting a bunch of Jutes here. I was with Hnaef's warband when we killed old Guthulf and took his lands." He started suddenly as he remembered that Hengest was a Jute and said; "Sorry, did you know him?"

"No," replied Hengest. "But my father did. It was their friendship that caused the rift between us."

Guthlaf whistled. "What a hornet's nest! I'd be greatly surprised if no blood is spilled this winter."

"That's something I've never understood," said Ordlaf, turning to Hengest. "Why did you join Hnaef? The word is that you forfeited your birthright in doing so."

"Hnaef represents the greatest military force these lands have seen," said Hengest. "Maybe I just wanted to be a part of something bigger."

"Well, if I were the son of an ealdorman with my future secured, there's no way I'd let myself be dragged off into some war," said Ordlaf. "I'm the son of a blacksmith and proud of it, but a life at the forge was no life for me. That's why I headed out on my own and found service with the king."

Guthlaf scratched his greying beard. "You chose a different path to your father, just as Hengest did," he said. "For myself, I was born a warrior and I'll die one. I'm just glad that it'll be alongside my chieftain and not some foreign warlord who pays my wages. But that's just me."

The feasting did not carry on much longer. One by one, the Danes slipped off to bed. They had been given a hall to themselves that was on the other side of the river, although many simply slumbered where they dropped in the king's hall, shoulder to shoulder with the Frisians.

Hengest paused at the bridge and watched the black water that rushed beneath him, flecked with the reflections of the stars in the night sky. He gazed up at the constellations. Frigg's Distaff hung from a carpet of black velvet and The Eyes of Thjazi blazed with potent anger at having been cast up into the blackness by Woden back in the Dawntime. He wondered if Horsa was watching these same constellations, wherever he was. Out on the ocean or drunk in a tavern, the same gods looked down on all men and their signs were visible on clear nights such as these.

The peaceful serenity was broken by the loud slopping sound of Ordlaf vomiting over the side of the bridge a few meters away. Hengest made his way to the hall where the snoring of the Danes could be heard as they slept around their king.

Horsa

The grim, grey sky of late autumn hung over the crashing surf that hammered upon the shores of Dane-land. Leaden clouds boiled overhead and the waves boomed rhythmically as the *Bloodkeel* surged through the white caps, its oars digging at the water and thrusting the vessel ever closer to the coastline.

Horsa stood at the prow of the ship and stared past the carven drake's head at the coil of acrid black smoke that rose up from the distant strip of land. Waves broke in a frothy haze upon the wet pebble shore beneath the walled settlement of Grimburg, but no guard stood watch by torchlight.

"Something's wrong," Horsa called over his shoulder to his captain.

Ingvar Wolofson, captain of the *Bloodkeel*, strode down the deck between the rows of oarsmen who strained against the waves to where his first mate stood. Ingvar was an Angle; nearly six feet of solid muscle crowned by a thick head of flaxen hair into which he had woven several ornaments of bone and bronze. He looked along Horsa's pointed arm to the bare stretch of beach ahead.

"Too much smoke for any hearth fire," he agreed. "No one to meet us either. I just hope we haven't been beaten to it."

And that was the crux of the matter. It was far too late in the season for a raid this far from safe ports. But it had been a complicated summer. Mutiny had divided the once large warband of Ingvar Wolofson and after a savage sea battle the Angle had been left with just one of his three ships and a meagre crew of thirteen to man it. This attack on a remote Danish settlement was a last-ditch attempt to salvage something from an otherwise disastrous season. Soon winter would set in and the sea lanes would become too rough to travel, forcing the raiders back to their homelands. But all knew that their captain's pride had been dented and by the gods he would not return home empty-handed.

The twelve years Horsa had spent at sea had toughened him. When he left Jute-land he had been a boy – a thin stripling of a lad – but now his body was hard and lean. His beard was full but kept carefully trimmed. His hands were calloused from pulling on oars and salty ropes and his face was burned brown by the glare of the sun. He had joined Ingvar's crew five years ago, after he was forced to flee the first group of raiders he had taken up with due to a dispute with the captain's brother.

The rest of the crew was an assorted gallery of rogues, mostly Angles with a sprinkling of Jutes and the occasional Saxon and Geat. Most of them were outlaws and outcasts with prices on their heads leaving sea-roving the only career open to them.

The shallow keel crunched against the stones as the boat was beached. Its crew shipped their oars and jumped out into the foaming surf to haul the vessel up out of the water. The beach was silent save for the cawing of gulls and the booming surf. Horsa doubted that there was anything of value here. If there was then the men of Grimburg would be amassed on the beach to defend it amidst a blowing of horns and clashing of shields.

Ingvar led the way up the grassy knoll towards the wooden palisade of the village. The crew followed close, gripping their axes and shields tightly in case any ambush awaited them. As they crested the hill they stopped and stared at the carnage before them with sinking stomachs. Their fears had been well grounded. Someone had got there first.

Charred stumps were all that remained of the halls and buildings of Grimburg. The wooden palisade had been completely burned away in places and the sod huts within had been torn up, their contents looted or destroyed. Black smoke still rose up in great plumes, choking and offensive to the nostrils. The corpses of the townsfolk: men, women and children, lay along the trackways, hacked open and blackened by the fire and smoke. Ravens had descended in their hundreds to gorge themselves upon the grisly feast. Whoever had done this had shown no mercy.

"Bastards!" howled Ingvar at the grey, overcast sky.

It was a sentiment shared by all the crew of the *Bloodkeel*. The stinking corpses and glowing embers of the town symbolized the failure of their raid and a miserable end to a terrible season. They descended the slope and made their way through the ruined town. Horsa prodded a nearby corpse with his spear, cracking open the charred skin and he watched the liquids ooze freely.

"These bodies are nearly fresh," he said. "This raid was recent."

"We didn't pass any ships on our way here," said Beorn the Bald, leaning on his axe.

Beorn was the crewmember that Horsa liked best. He was a towering mountain of an Angle who wielded a two-handed battleaxe as his choice weapon. His head was completely shaven but for a long, blond braid that hung down on the right side.

"Perhaps they came from inland," said Ingvar. "A tribal feud maybe?"

"This one's still alive!" shouted Aelfhere; a Jute and another man Horsa considered a friend. He was crouched over the limp form of a young warrior, little more than a boy, but he had clearly fought hard against the attackers, for the battered and chipped sword he clenched in his hand was coated in dried blood and matted hair.

"He has been pierced through the stomach," said Beorn grimly, inspecting the boy. "Nasty way to die."

"Give him water," said Ingvar.

"It'll kill him," warned Horsa.

"Nothing we do can save him now, but we can at least make it a little easier for him to talk," replied Ingvar.

Horsa was not fooled by his captain's apparent concern for the boy. He had once seen Ingvar cut the thumbs off a ten-year-old lad who would not disclose where his father had buried a hoard of silver ingots.

The nozzle of a water skin was pressed to the dying boy's lips and he drank a little, glad of it, but wincing at the same time.

"What's your name, boy?" asked Ingvar, as the youth opened his eyes and stared at the men who were standing over him.

"Ulf, son of Brecca," replied the dying boy in a wheezing voice.

"Now then, Ulf, tell us who did this."

"Men from the south. Evil men. *Wane-worshippers.*"

He had whispered the last words in a frightened voice but the crew of the *Bloodkeel* heard it well enough and exchanged glances, scarcely able to believe what the boy had just told them.

"Woden's eye!" said Ingvar. "I thought they were wiped out long ago."

91

"So did we all," replied Horsa grimly.

The Wanes were an ancient race of gods, older even than Woden himself. They belonged to a darker time. Malicious water and earth spirits mostly, who knew the dark secrets of the void before creation. Their evil cult had once been widespread in those lands but had since been driven away by the sons of the one-eyed god of wisdom. Now they were considered little more than folklore by many.

"We were in league with them, may the gods forgive us," continued Ulf, tears beginning to stream down his grimy cheeks. "We were led astray by promises of wealth and fertility. In our blindness we burned our sacred grove to Woden and reared in its place a shrine to the mother goddess, Gefion. But it was all a lie. The following year our crops failed and our stream dried to a trickle. As we began to starve, we realised the error in our judgement and so rebuilt the temple to the Ese. But it was too late. Not two days hence, men from the south came to punish us, bringing fire and sword to Grimburg. They slaughtered us and took our gold. May the true gods forgive us for our heresy!"

He began to weep violently even though every movement was clearly agonising for him. Ingvar stood up suddenly.

"Find horses!" he bellowed. "We leave before nightfall."

"We are going after them?" asked Horsa in disbelief.

Ingvar nodded. "They have the gold that otherwise would have been ours. Two days' start on us is not much. We can catch up with them and …"

"Madness," interrupted Horsa. "It's too late in the season as it is. We should be making preparations to return home, not chasing robbers across the Danelands."

"You would rather go home to a cold hearth, empty-handed and with nothing to show for a whole season?" replied Ingvar, rounding on him.

"We don't know how far away these people are, or how strong they are in numbers," insisted Horsa. "And even if we do take a large haul of gold, we may not leave ourselves enough time to get back home."

"Perhaps you forget how long winter is," snapped Ingvar. "Too long, let me tell you, to sit in a damp hall with no stories to tell around the fire. Or will you be returning to your father's hearth this winter, Horsa, to bask in the warmth of your high-born family?"

Horsa's face seethed and the crew were silent at their captain's words. Very rarely was the matter of Horsa's noble birthright brought up and when it was it was usually met with ferocity by the young warrior. Yes, he was the son of a Jutish ealdorman, but he had chosen his path a long time ago. He had forsaken his family and become a rogue and brigand, and a damned good one at that. He clenched his teeth and restrained himself from striking out at the captain. The other crew members stirred uneasily in the background. This whole confrontation smacked too much of the mutinous quarrels that had dominated the early part of the season.

"I do not agree with your decision in this matter," said Horsa coldly. "If I were captain, I would not risk the lives of my crew on the word of a dying farm boy."

"Then perhaps it is a good thing that you are not captain!" replied Ingvar. "I however, am. And as captain I have decided that we shall track these bandits for three days. If we do not catch up with them, then we shall return to the ship and make for home. What say the rest of you?"

There were various non-committal murmurs from the crew. Nobody wanted to stay here longer than necessary and all had thoughts of hearth fires burning. On the other hand, returning home empty-handed and shamefaced was not a pleasant prospect.

"I'm with the captain," spoke up Beorn, with an apologetic glance at Horsa. "We track them for three days only, though. Then I want to go home."

"Me too," said Aelfhere the Jute.

"And I," added Heathlaf the Geat.

One by one the crew of the *Bloodkeel* agreed to their captain's plan, although with varying degrees of reluctance.

Horsa could see that they all had a glimmer of hope in their eyes and the faint scent of gold in their nostrils. They were desperate and their captain had provided them with a final opportunity for success. He, on the other hand, had a sick feeling in his stomach. He had never been one to balk in the face of danger, nor care much for the future, but something about this whole business felt wrong. They were far from home in strange lands. And the talk of Wane-worshippers made his spine ripple with repulsion.

He touched the amulet at his neck. It was an arrowhead made from flint, the workmanship of some craftsman in an age gone by, lost in the dirt for centuries. He had discovered it one winter at Beorn's farm and had bound it with twine, making a necklace of it. Now it dangled below his breastbone beneath the folds of his shirt as a mild defence against bad fortune.

94

"All right," said Horsa at last. "We go south."

"What about him?" asked Beorn, indicating the dying boy.

The youth looked up with pleading eyes. Ingvar drew his sword and in a single, downwards chop, severed the boy's head from his body.

Hengest

The next few days were occupied with the preparations for the festival of Geola. The weather was getting noticeably worse. The Western Sea was choppy and as grey as the sky. Frost had begun to form each morning on the thatched roofs of the settlement and puddles froze in the streets.

All were busy in preparation. Cattle had been slaughtered and their meat preserved for the coming months. A great boar was being fattened in a barn, awaiting the axe that would make it the centre piece of the king's table during the feast. Storage huts were loaded with dried fish, cabbages, peas, onions, wild apples and hazelnuts, and the children went out every day to collect bird eggs and set traps for rabbits.

Finn regularly led large groups of Frisians and Danes out on hunts and they speared hart and boar to add to the growing stores. Hnaef usually accompanied Finn on these trips but it was clear to everybody that the friendship between the two kings had soured somewhat since it had been learned that the son of Hnaef's enemy would be joining them for the winter.

Hnaef was grumpy most days, and during the evenings he sat and brooded over his mead, refusing to take part in the singing, dancing and wrestling that had so pleased him that first night in Finnesburg. His temper was volatile and even his own men did their best to keep out of his way.

Hengest occasionally joined the hunts but they reminded him too much of home, for his father had been a passionate hunter and had often taken his sons out with him. Instead he spent much time alone, exploring the settlement and admiring the king's horses in their stables. One day, when the settlement was more or less empty of royalty and thegns during one of the hunts, he decided to borrow a horse and ride out to the coast to check on the boats.

The wind was chilly and the overcast sky drifted past rapidly. The long grass wavered and the distant islands that formed something of a barrier between Frisia and the open sea were grey smudges on the flat horizon. The boats were safe enough from the crashing surf, beached high up on the sands. Frost clung to the ropes and strakes like fur.

Another rider appeared on the crest of the dunes, wrapped in a long cloak. It was Hildeburh. He cantered up to her.

"I come here sometimes to be alone," she told him. "Whenever my husband is out hunting and I have no urgent tasks to attend to. It is peaceful even when the sea is rough and the sky is dark. A quiet kind of violence, don't you agree?"

"I know exactly what you mean," replied Hengest.

They looked out over the choppy surface of the water at the ring of islands for a while, savouring the silence.

"Have you travelled much, Hengest?" she asked him.

"No. Only around my father's lands. I haven't even been to Dane-land, though I follow a Danish king. My brother, Horsa is the one who travels."

"I long to venture out across that sea," she said.

"Is it really so terrible for you here?"

She looked at him, startled for a moment. "I'm sorry. I am wrong to complain to you. I am happy here. I love my sons very much. And my husband."

"Sons?"

"Yes. Frithuwulf and Frealaf. Did you not know I had two?"

"No. Only the one was mentioned. The one who is fostered by Garulf."

"Frealaf is only four years old. But he is sickly and is mostly confined to our chambers."

"I have a son also. And a daughter. They are nine and eleven."

"You must miss them. Children truly are gifts from the gods. They give us light and hope in the darkest days of our lives."

Hengest nodded. "It is hard to spend so much time from them. You must miss Frithuwulf very much, as I miss my own son."

"Yes. It has been a hard few years, but my heart gladdens with the knowledge that he will be back by my side in a few days."

They watched the surf for a while.

"What did your words to me mean the other night?" asked Hengest. "When you told me that exile is better than a prison."

"Oh, I apologise. I was not feeling myself. I merely meant to warn you against becoming trapped."

"Trapped?"

"There are many types of prisons, not all of them visible. We all talk of being bound by things; honour-bound, loyalty-bound, bound to our families and lands. I believe that the human spirit is a free thing and the bonds of our society are hard to break."

"But why say these things to me?"

"I don't know. Maybe because you are a Jute who follows a Dane. And there seems to be no reason behind it."

Hengest laughed. "Nobody seems to understand it. My father especially."

"You are young, Hengest. Do not let yourself fall into the trap of loyalty and blood-oaths as so many young men do."

"But without oaths of loyalty there is no trust in the world and there can be no peace between men. I follow your brother because I believe in him. I believe that he can change the world and I want to be a part of that change."

"Then make sure that it truly is what you want. My brother has a habit of drawing men to him with many fine promises. An oath can easily become a prison; a cage for the soul if your heart yearns for other things."

"My heart yearns for nothing but a safe world for my family. And you, do you feel trapped?"

"I have my duty to my husband and to my children. And to my brother."

"It was Hnaef who forced you into marrying Finn?"

She nodded. "My father died when we were in our adolescence. Hnaef was always mature for his age and he wore the mantle of leadership well. I was but one of his many game pieces to be played."

"Do you love him?"

"My brother? Dearly. It was out of love for him that I accepted his decision to marry me to Finn. I knew deep down that it was for the best, even if it took me many years to learn to love Finn."

The clouds had darkened and daylight was spread thin. The wind skimmed the tops of the waves sending their spray inland.

"I must return now," Hildeburh said.

"May I accompany you?" asked Hengest.

"No. It would not be proper for us to be seen riding together. Besides, I am fast and would outrun you."

"You think so? Then you have not heard that we Jutes are the greatest riders in the northern world."

Hildeburh laughed and it was the first time Hengest had seen her smile. It was a fine sight.

"I do not mean to insult your horsemanship, Jute," she replied. "But nevertheless, I ride on alone."

She set off at a gallop, leaving Hengest alone watching the drumming of her mount's hooves on the sand. He had to admit, she was fast.

Horsa

The last golden rays of sunlight receded over the bleak and rugged land. Onwards the horsemen galloped, hooves churning up the marshy soil.

It had taken some considerable time to round up thirteen horses from the ruined settlement and its surrounding fields and those they did find were frightened and half wild. By the time they had got going, the day was almost gone, but Ingvar was determined to set out before nightfall.

The land was comprised of rolling heaths and moors, dotted with clumps of dry bracken and the occasional cluster of gnarled trees, stripped of their leaves by the oncoming winter. No mountains or even hills could be seen for miles around, only the endless flat plains vanishing into a hazy horizon.

Eventually the warriors stopped for the night. Clustering around a meagre fire by the shelter of a large boulder, the crew of the *Bloodkeel* ate some of the dried meat and fish they had brought with them from the ship. It was bitterly cold and the atmosphere was little warmer. The confrontation between Horsa and Ingvar still hung heavy over them. Few talked. Horsa watched the faces of his comrades by the flickering light of the fire. The words he had spoken to Ingvar echoed in his head.

If I were captain.

What if he *were* captain? What then? He could lead this crew and probably do a better job of it than Ingvar. What could stop him? He would have to fight Ingvar for the position of course, but that was not an uncommon occurrence in such groups of lawless men. If he could guarantee the support of the crew it might not be a problem. Beorn would be with him, he could count on that. Probably Aelfhere too, just out of Jutish loyalty, and the rest would surely follow. But when to make his move?

Not yet. Let this whole business play out a little first. If they survived the next few days and made it back to the boat, then he would strike.

One by one, the companions dropped off to sleep and Horsa savoured dreams of commanding his own crew. He dreamed of the rolling deck of his own ship beneath his feet and of his name held in honour and high regard across the northern world.

The following day was long and tiring. The rolling moors gave way to soft marsh into which the hooves of the horses kept sinking, forcing the riders to dismount and continue on foot. Soon everyone was plastered in the black mud and in foul temper. They could smell salt on the air and knew that the coast must curve around them for these were not freshwater marshes. They had not seen a single person for nearly two days now, and their spirits were low as their leader plunged ever onwards into unknown lands.

As night began to fall once more, a thick fog descended and cloaked the fens in an eerie gloom. The companions began to talk of finding a place to spend the night and some of turning around and heading back towards the coast. But out of the blackness, a faint pinprick of light could be discerned; a beacon on some dry bit of land.

"A settlement of some kind," said Beorn.

"We'll make for it and seek shelter with them," said Ingvar. "They may know something about these Wane-worshipers."

"They may *be* the Wane-worshipers," warned Horsa, but nobody said anything.

They continued onwards through the mist. Flat areas of water prickling with long reeds lay on either side of them. They could smell fish and wood smoke on the air. In the darkness they could make out a sturdy looking gate illuminated by a single torch.

Movement.

A horn, warning the village of the approaching strangers.

In the dim light, several figures in iron helms could be seen approaching. They formed a protective shield wall in front of the gate and their leader stepped forth.

"State your name and business, outlanders!" he called.

"I am Ingvar Wolofson of Angle-land! We are lost and seek shelter for the night."

The guard approached, his troop following close, shield wall tight. His face was thin and pale in the moonlight. "How many of you are there?"

"Thirteen. We are all that is left of a punitive force sent against the sea raiders by Ealdorman Aescgar. We were defeated in battle and flee from those who would butcher us in revenge. Our boat is hidden in a small inlet on the coast."

A good enough tale, thought Horsa. Raiders were hated everywhere, and Ealdorman Aescgar had made enough of a name for himself fighting them, to be known even as far out as this backwater place.

"Why did you not seek shelter at Grimburg?" asked the guard. "Surely you could see it as you approached the coast."

"Grimburg has been razed," Ingvar replied. "Burned to its foundations and all slain."

103

There was murmuring amongst the soldiers and their captain said something inaudible to one of his comrades. The man scurried off into the settlement; apparently to speak with someone in authority. He returned presently bearing news for his captain.

"You can enter our village," the captain spoke, "but you must leave your arms outside before entering my lord Herogar's hall. There you will find food and shelter for the night."

"I would thank your lord Herogar for his kindness," said Ingvar. "But you show an awful lot of distrust towards a band of good-natured travellers. Surely you can see that we are not bandits or murderers."

"It is a bad time for these lands," the captain replied. "You said yourself that Grimburg has been destroyed. We cannot be too careful whom we let within our walls."

The shield wall parted to let the companions pass and they were shown to a small outhouse where they were told to disarm and leave their weapons. Theows came to take their horses to the stables. Feeling naked with only their saexes at their sides, the crew of the *Bloodkeel* were escorted to the hall where a golden glow spilled out onto the glistening mud outside.

It was a modest hall, not excessive in its carvings or tapestries. A large hearth illuminated the walls and smoke-stained rafters and several warriors sat about drinking and playing dice. They eyed the strangers closely. Mead was brought and Horsa felt glad of the warming liquid as it settled in his belly.

A side door opened and an elderly couple entered, clothed in the colourful garments of nobility, but sparing in their use of gold ornamentation. All in the hall rose out of respect and waited for the couple to sit down at the head of the largest table.

"We have new friends tonight," said the elderly man, smiling in their direction. "I am Ealdorman Herogar of the Hrolfingas. I welcome you to my home."

Ingvar stood up and raised his mead horn in polite salute. "Hail, Ealdorman Herogar! My name is Ingvar, son of Wolof. I am the captain of the humble men who sit before you. We thank you for your kindness and hospitality."

"You are most welcome," replied the Ealdorman, raising his horn in appreciation. "But tell me, what is an Angle sea-captain and his crew doing in this remote part of Dane-land?"

"We have been separated from our lord by defeat," replied Ingvar. "Ealdorman Aescgar, perhaps you have heard of him?"

"Indeed, I know the name, for his wars against the raiders are well told of throughout the Dane-lands. You sail with good company then."

"We put in to Grimburg for supplies," lied Ingvar, "but found the settlement raided and destroyed. We heard of another settlement nearby and it took us nearly two days to find you."

"You heard of our little settlement?" inquired the Ealdorman. "That is curious for we rarely have dealings with the Ealdorman of Grimburg. *Eala!* Though it saddens me to hear of his downfall. He was a good man."

An eel stew was brought, along with loaves of coarse bread and the warriors feasted well. Opposite Horsa sat a young woman with her child as she tried to get him to eat spoonfuls of stew. The child's attention was wholly transfixed on the rough-looking warrior before him. Horsa smiled at the boy.

"Don't stare, Eadgar," chided his mother. "It's rude. Now come on, eat some stew."

The boy took the spoon from his mother and, without taking his eyes from Horsa, began to eat.

"I apologise," said the woman to Horsa.

"Don't," he replied. "He is a fine lad. How old is he?"

"Six."

"Nearly seven!" Eadgar chimed in.

"Do you have children of your own?" the woman asked Horsa.

"No. But I think my brother has. I haven't seen him in many years."

"You keep a good table my lord," said Ingvar, addressing the ealdorman around a mouth full of eel. "Do you see much trade in the summer months?"

"Oh, we have little use for traders," replied the ealdorman, sipping mead from a gold-rimmed horn. The land meets all of our needs."

"Has it been a good harvest?" asked Beorn, for he was always keen for some indication of how his own crops may have fared back in Angle-land.

Herogar shrugged. "Not as good as it could have been. The sea levels are rising. This used to be good land, but the meadows are fast turning to salt marsh."

"It's the same everywhere," said Beorn. "Even in western Angle-land where I have my stead. People are leaving in droves seeking better lands elsewhere."

"Successful crops depend on so much more than good tending and favourable weather," said Herogar. "This wasteland that is visited upon us is a punishment of some kind, mark my words. The gods have not been shown the proper honour."

"You mean sacrifice?"

"Yes. Our ancestors thought that the very land herself must be appeased before her fruits can be harvested and so they spilt blood or milk upon the soil to ensure its fertility."

There were some smiles and chuckling around the hall at this. The superstitions of their forefathers were laughable.

"That reminds me," said Ingvar. "In the ruins of Grimburg, we encountered a young lad who told us that these lands were troubled by Wane-worshipers; heathens who kneel before demons of antiquity."

"Indeed?" inquired Herogar. "I have not heard these rumours. Perhaps this is true in the lands further south. I can assure you that we have no trouble with heathens here. Although we are familiar with the tales of those people who dwelt in these lands before us and worshipped the gods of barley and sun." He motioned to a thin, quiet man in the corner of the hall who sat sipping his mead, watching them with beady eyes. "Scop! A song if you will, about the Wane-goddess and her followers."

The man coughed gently and put down his mead horn. From a bundle of rags at his side he removed a beautifully carved lyre and set about tuning it with his long, delicate fingers. He began to play. The tune was a mournful one and his voice, beautiful and melancholy, drifted around the hall, seeping into the very wood as it told its story.

These lands hold a lake, lost to time,
Formed in the beginning, when the world was barely born.

Around its still depths the settlers dwelled,
Wane-worshippers they were, wiccan and wise,
And from whence they came none now know.

The mere-dweller was their matron; a goddess of guile,
A queen of the land from long distant legend,
In shadow-haunted woods was she worshipped,
And in moonlit circles, her slaves were sacrificed,
And blood ran red on the runestones to her name.

Her name was Gefion; a goddess of giving,
And in her image an idol, iridescent was made,
Of glittering gold, gleaming and smooth,
With eyes of jade and studded with gems,
No finer fashioned idol was ever forged.

Rome rose and fell and the rumours remained,
Of the Wane-goddess and her worshippers,
By the shores of the lake, in luxurious wealth,
Denying the new gods, no glory to them,
Of Woden and Frige, frightened were they not,
Nor of Thunor and Tiw, truth they already knew.

The Sons of Woden, heard whispers of the Wanes,
And set out with shields, and spears sharpened
bright,
Of greed they thought, to gain glory for their gods,
And pillage and plunder, to fill their purses.

Red ran the lake, as the looters found victory,
Over the children of Gefion who were butchered and slain.
The golden statue was stolen away,

A goddess defeated and her devout left dead.

Around the idol, the ill-meant victors revelled,
Until mead and merriment, muddled their minds,
And they slept, strewn in the statue's shadow.
But dawn broke over barbarous ruin,
The warriors' corpses were cloven and clawed.
None had awoken during the slaughter, and the stolen statue,
Was stolen once more.

The women wept for Woden's brave sons,
And the missing idol spoke of mischief and malice.
None knew who had slaughtered their stout sons,
And the hills hide their hideous secrets.
No names give the nighted fens,
And the forests feed no answers to the fearful.

Gefion and the Wanes are forgotten but by the few,
But some say they have seen strange sights on the moors,
Of troll-shapes in the mist, murderous and monstrous,
And strange lights beneath lakes at night,
In league with the lake-dweller they liken these things,
And the Wane-queen's vengeance will never wilt,
Nor will the shape that haunts these lands.

The scop finished his song and his audience pounded the tables with their knife hilts in respectful applause. Horsa and his companions followed this example half-heartedly. It was a chilling tale, a world away from the heroic, rabble-rousing sagas they were used to hearing in the halls of their homelands.

"I drink to your tale," said Ingvar, raising his horn in the direction of the scop. "And I am glad that the

Sons of Woden did indeed rid the land of the foul heathens so many years ago."

Ealdorman Herogar smiled and took a sip of his mead. "Then perhaps you would be interested in joining us for a short ceremony a day from now in the Allfather's name."

"Indeed we would," replied Ingvar. "But I am afraid I am a little ignorant of customs in these parts. What ceremony is this?"

"Oh, just a local tradition that welcomes the onset of winter and gives thanks for the harvest. I conduct the ritual myself with my priests standing by."

"Very good. We would be honoured to join you."

"To friendship then," said the ealdorman, raising his horn.

They ate and drank some more and soon tiredness crept over them. The fire died down to a glow and the ealdorman and his wife retired to their chamber. The women and children departed and the companions were shown areas to sleep around the hall. Soon the rafters were filled with the sound of snoring.

Horsa did not sleep. He lay awake for several hours, stroking the arrow amulet around his neck thoughtfully. For all the generosity and friendliness of their hosts, he looked forward to leaving this settlement and heading back to the boat. Ingvar's three days were nearly up and they had seen no sign of the raiders they sought. It would soon be time to head for home.

If Ingvar kept his word.

And if he didn't? What then? The crew were already unhappy with their captain's decision for the most part. He had failed them this season and that was why they were pursuing brigands into foreign lands with winter snapping at their heels. They would be happy to turn home and if Ingvar insisted on leading them further on this wild goose chase, then perhaps they would be happy for a change in leadership.

He could not sleep. He got up and left the hall to breathe in the cool night air and look at the stars. The fog was still as thick as a shroud and the village was as silent as a grave.

But somewhere, somebody was weeping.

Curious, Horsa followed the sound, treading softly across the mud so as not to startle anybody. As he rounded a corner he saw the huddled form of a woman leaning beneath the thatched awning of a house, her face buried in her hands. She started at Horsa's approach.

"I don't wish to intrude, lady," Horsa began, "I just heard weeping …"

It was the woman who had sat opposite him at the table that night, the one with the boy, Eadgar. Her face bore a look of terror and her cheeks were glistening with tears in the starlight.

"It is a cold night to be out of doors," said Horsa. "And that boy of yours must be missing his mother."

At this the woman burst into a fresh batch of tears and fled, vanishing from sight into the shadows of the buildings. Horsa shrugged and turned back. The coldness of the night was pressing in on him and he now yearned for the warmth of his fur by the hearth.

As he neared the hall, a glimmer in the darkness caught his eye. Beyond the palisade, way up upon some rise out on the moors, several faint pinpricks of light could be seen. They were too close together and too distant for Horsa to count, but they were a cluster, suggesting some encampment or procession of people out in the blackness. But who would be out on the moors at this time of night, and in this bitter cold?

Then, one by one, as if aware of their detection, the lights winked out until only the darkness of the moors remained, leaving Horsa with doubt in his mind as to whether he had seen them at all.

He continued back to the hall, muttering to himself. The sooner they left this settlement the better. It had too many strange goings on by half.

PART III

(Feoh) "Feoh byþ frofur fira gehwylcum;
sceal ðeah manna gehwylc miclun hyt dælan
gif he wile for drihtne domes hleotan."

(Wealth) "Wealth is a comfort to all;
yet must everyone bestow it freely,
if they wish to gain honour in the sight of the Lord."

Horsa

Morning broke over the Dane-lands, its golden light reflected off the still waters of the fens forming a perfect mirror of the sky, broken only by the occasional flapping wings of some marsh bird taking off with a fish in its mouth.

Now that it was daylight, Horsa and his companions could better make out the nature of the settlement and its surroundings. It was nestled on the edge of a large body of water, broken in parts by little islands of mud and reeds. Parts of the settlement seemed to hover above the water, supported by long posts that sank down into the mud. This had all been farmable land when the ealdorman's hall had been built. Now it was a doomed settlement existing on borrowed time. Slowly, the sea was creeping in to claim the land.

After a breakfast of oatcakes and creamy goat's milk, the crew of the *Bloodkeel* were left to their own devices and spent the morning milling around the village and exploring their surroundings. Horsa walked down to the wharves where several boats were being taken out to check the eel traps. There, staring out over the flat water he found the woman he had seen the night before, hugging herself, her face vacant of any emotion.

"Hello, again," he said, as he approached.

She turned to look at him, but her face showed neither surprise nor embarrassment.

"I'm sorry if I startled you last night. I just thought you looked like you needed company."

"No, I'm the one to apologise," she replied. "I did not know that anyone could hear me. I thought I was alone."

"No Eadgar today?"

"Who?" asked the woman.

"Eadgar. Your son," repeated Horsa. "Is he not well today?"

The woman frowned. "I'm not sure who you mean."

Horsa blinked. "The boy I saw you with last night. Eadgar. Your son …"

"I have no son," she replied, her face rigid. "You must be mistaken."

She turned and left Horsa with his mouth open in astonishment. She was either mad or lying. Either way it was just one more bizarre thing to chalk up against this place. And there was that blasted ceremony they were expected to attend later that day. He wished that Ingvar would just make the decision to turn back to the boat.

Late afternoon approached and with it the preparations for the ceremony. The procession led away from the village and up on to the high moors. Here lay many crumbling stone tombs of a people long forgotten. Great slabs formed barrows that were known as 'giant's beds'. Horsa looked about him as they ascended, searching for signs of the campfires he had seen the previous night but there were none. The wind billowed up on the high ground and a small stream wound its way below them, feeding the marshes from some hidden valley.

Some fifty people from the village formed the procession: warriors, farmers and fishermen, along with their women and children. Ealdorman Herogar led the way, dressed in his white priest's robes that the wind whipped and billowed about him. Four other priests followed him holding staves of yew which were carven with many runes. There was singing as they went, drumming on tambourines and shaking bells, although the songs were not familiar to the ears of the raiders.

The procession stopped at an ancient slab of stone that stood alone on the rise and obviously held some spiritual significance.

"We of the Hrolfingas," began the ealdorman, "have gathered here to pay thanks to Woden, the God of wisdom, who gave his eye in exchange for supreme knowledge at the well of the giant …"

He continued on with the usual cornerstones of any religious speech devoted to the Allfather, bestowing thanks upon the high one and proclaiming their humility in his presence. Horsa had heard it all before and every time the Allfather's name was mentioned he was reminded of his oath to his older brother.

He wondered where Hengest was now. At home with mother and father? Or was he the ealdorman now and their father dead in his barrow? Twelve years was a long time. Too long. How could he fulfil his oath if he was not by his brother's side? All the more reason to put his plans into action sooner rather than later. Once he had command of the *Bloodkeel* and a good, honest crew beneath him, he would return to Jute-land; the man he had promised to become.

The four priests scratched various runes upon the stone slab with charcoal and eventually the rites came to their end. A barrel of barley beer was brought forth and broken into with an axe. Herogar dipped in a horn and brought it out, splashing the golden liquid upon the stone, washing away the charcoal runes. He continued until the stone was dark with moisture and the runes had been completely removed, as if they had never been written.

"Now, my friends," he said, turning to the crew of the *Bloodkeel*. "Will you honour us by drinking first upon this happy morning, to Woden, lord of the Ese and ruler of Waelheall?"

"Very well," said Ingvar, accepting the horn brimming with beer. "Gladly."

Full horns were passed around and each held them up in salute of Woden before knocking back the barley drink, enjoying the strong, sour taste on the chill morning.

The next few hours were muddled in Horsa's memory. He remembered much music and capering about. Drums and bells and chants ran through his mind like a rippling serpent. The barrel of beer was finished but Horsa did not remember drinking much from it. The women of the village made him and his comrades feel very welcome and Aelfhere made a spectacle of himself, rolling about on the ground with two of them like a drunken letch. At one point, Horsa saw Ingvar stumbling about with a daft crown made from the sheaves of barley corn on his head, roaring with laughter. The only one of them who did not seem to be enjoying himself was Beorn.

"This is not the correct way to honour the gods," he grumbled.

Horsa's head began to feel heavy upon his shoulders and he was hit by an uncommon feeling of drowsiness. Through blurred vision he saw Ingvar stumble beside him and pitch headlong upon the earth. Cruel laughter filled his ears, echoing as if the distance between him and the villagers was rapidly increasing. His own knees gave way and he fell, consumed by darkness.

He awoke with a burning pain in his limbs. He tried to move but was unable to. Rope bound his hands and feet securely to an upright piece of wood. His head swam and throbbed and slowly the events of the past few hours slid into focus.

The procession, the rites, the beer. He hadn't drunk all that much. It had to have been drugged. His vision was blurry but he could see that the sun had moved far across the sky and the leaden clouds formed towering and foreboding shapes above him. The scenery had changed too. No longer was he atop the moor. He was in the shaded valley below it. One side was steep and rock-strewn, the other rose up under the shade of twisted and withered old trees. The stream trickled past, emerging from a yawning, black crack in the rock ahead of him.

He craned his neck and saw his fellow shipmates, all in identical situations to him – bound tightly by the wrists and ankles to thick wooden poles thrust upright into the dark earth, as if they were scarecrows. Several of them had also regained consciousness and began to twist and turn in their bonds.

Voices from high above carried to them on the wind and Horsa looked up to see the villagers lined along the valley ridge. The four priests were there along with a grotesque form, a man in a headdress fashioned from the skin and skull of a gigantic wolf. The beast-like creature waved its arms about and shouted to them in a fury. The voice was that of Ealdorman Herogar.

"Sons of Woden!" he bellowed. "Your arrogance shall be paid for with your lives!"

"Ealdorman Herogar!" howled Ingvar, straining at his ropes. "Release us immediately!"

"Silence heretics!" the masked man yelled back. "The blood of the followers of Gefion shall be paid for in kind! Your beating hearts shall be collected by Her children; the shadows in the night, the prowlers of the heaths. Their dripping talons shall make you scream for Her forgiveness!"

"Woden curse you, Herogar!" cried Ingvar, his voice hoarse with fear and rage. "I'm going to carve your screaming lungs from your back and feed them to your own dogs!"

"Your one-eyed trickster has no power here!" was the reply. And then the ealdorman and his minions were gone, vanished beyond the ridge of the valley like phantoms in the fog.

An unsurpassed feeling of rage and frustration overwhelmed each of the crew members as they struggled fruitlessly at their bonds. They had been deceived, a fate made all the worse for having wandered blindly into it. The ceremony in Woden's name had been a sham, a deceit. Herogar and his followers *were* the Wane-worshippers. It had been they who had destroyed Grimburg.

The sun sank behind the ridge; cloaking the valley in a premature night. A thick mist had begun to roll in off the moors and spill down the slope towards the thirteen wooden posts. Soon the gaping black cave ahead was hidden by a curtain of grey.

One by one, the posts ahead of Horsa with their struggling captives became dark silhouettes in the mist, eerie ghosts of themselves as the fog crept ever closer. Horsa struggled until blood began to run from where the bonds cut into his wrists. If only he had something sharp to cut with, but all their weapons had been left in the village and his saex was gone from his belt.

But then he remembered his amulet. *Of course!* A piece of flint, fashioned hundreds of years ago was still sharp, undulled by the effects of time. He tucked his chin in and nosed around in his shirt for the familiar object. Catching hold of it with his teeth, he slowly reached up to the rope that held his hands.

He had to pull his hands down as far as the rope would allow, wincing as it chafed his wrists, but he could just touch it with the arrowhead. The rope smelt old and musty. He began to move his head back and forth rhythmically, sawing at it with the sharp piece of flint.

He could feel each fibre snap as he cut through it with the ancient tool, and sweat beaded upon his forehead with the effort. Finally the last strand of the old rope twanged as it broke and he felt himself tumbling forward, his arms swinging numb and useless at his side as he landed face down on the muddy ground.

Taking the arrowhead in his hands, he twisted around and began to work on the ropes that bound his legs. Soon he was loose and he scrambled to his feet, rubbing some life back into his limbs. Only a few of his comrades were still in sight. Aescwine – an Angle and the youngest member of the crew – was the nearest and the young warrior squirmed in startled surprise to see Horsa heading towards him.

"Woden's eye, Horsa! How did you get loose?"

"A little help from our ancestors. Hold still, damn you! I'm cutting you loose!"

Horsa worked his way from post to post, sawing at the bonds that held his comrades, spilling each one loose into the wet mud. As he was cutting Ingvar free, he looked over to the last post, the one furthest from him and nearest the cave. The dim form of Heathlaf could be seen.

"By all the gods, Horsa, I'm glad to have you with us!" Ingvar said. He was still wearing the ludicrous crown of barley grass.

Horsa's attention was transfixed upon Heathlaf. It may have been a trick of the light or the ghostly fog playing on his mind, but for a brief moment, he thought he could see a shape looming near the post. Hunched over, ape-like, the form seemed to extend a long, thin arm towards the lone warrior like a thing out of the dark depths of some nightmare.

The rope snapped and Ingvar struggled free, tearing the crown from his head. When Horsa looked back up, the shape was gone.

And so had Heathlaf.

They splashed through the mud towards the lone post. It had been stripped of its occupant. There was no sign of Heathlaf save for the frayed remains of the rope that had bound him and a few confused tracks that led away into the fog.

"What happened to him?" said Ingvar.

"Something took him," replied Beorn. "As if it were the mist itself …"

"Let's get moving," said Horsa, unwilling to mention what he had seen to his already frightened comrades. "We should head over to the trees and wait there until daylight."

The comrades silently headed up the slope of the valley. Just as they met the tree line, a terrible cry sounded out in the darkness. Neither human, nor animal, the sound froze every one of the companions in their tracks.

"Gods, what was that?" said Beorn in a hoarse whisper.

"Keep moving," said Horsa, but half of the crew were already dashing up the slope and vanishing into the darkness of the trees. The cry was answered by another from a different part of the valley and Horsa ducked into the trees, his heart pounding in his chest. He slid behind the cover of an elm and crouched down.

He listened. He could hear his comrades rustling about, seeking similar hiding places, but he could hear something else too. The light footsteps of several other beings pattered through the forest.

A bush next to him burst aside and a figure slid down in the mud next to him. It was Beorn.

"What are they?" Beorn whispered, his face pale with terror.

"Keep quiet!" replied Horsa.

They sat and waited as the rustlings and scampering of several creatures hustled by. They listened some more. Somebody somewhere screamed. Other than that, silence prevailed.

After a while, Horsa stood up slowly and beckoned Beorn to follow him. They found Ingvar and several of the others in a small clearing, huddled together with cold and fright, their faces pale in the shimmering moonlight.

"Where are the others?" asked Horsa.

"Aescwine was right behind me," said Aelfhere in a shaky voice. "Those … *things* were following close, I could hear one of them grunting! I ran and ran and when I looked back, Aescwine was gone."

A tree rustled close by and everyone leapt up in terror.

Three more crewmembers stumbled into the clearing.

"Captain," said one. "You'd best come and look at this."

All followed the three men back the way they had come. A few feet away, in a broken thicket lay the mangled remains of a man. Blood, black and sticky coated every branch surrounding the corpse. Protruding ribs glistened white in the moonlight.

"Gods! That's Aescwine!" exclaimed Beorn.

"Not anymore," added Ingvar grimly.

"What could have done this?" asked one man.

"A troll perhaps," said another.

"My father saw a troll once," said Beorn. "On the headland. Horrible, disgusting thing it was."

"Is that what they sacrificed us to?" said Ingvar. "That's their goddess? A troll and her spawn? Those demented heathen bastards!"

"We have no weapons," said Aelfhere, panic gripping him. "We can't fight trolls! We'll be slaughtered! Just like Aescwine and Heathlaf! We …"

"Calm yourself, Aelfhere," cut in Horsa. "I can't hear anything at the moment, can you? The trolls – or whatever they are – have moved on, probably looking for food elsewhere."

"That cave!" said Beorn. "The one down where the stream runs. I'll bet that's their lair!"

"We could sharpen some sticks. Go in and drive them out …" Aelfhere forwarded.

"We'd be fighting them on their own ground," said Ingvar.

"Why are we even considering fighting it?" asked another. "Why don't we just head back to the boat?"

"Because that bastard Herogar and his people sit between us and the coast," said Horsa. "That troll-cave may be our only hope. We might get hold of some useful weapons in there. Trolls are hoarders and thieves according to the tales."

"But we can't just wander in there and take them head on," snapped Ingvar. "It would be suicide."

"They're out hunting at the moment, that much is sure," said Horsa. "If we're quick we could rob their cave and be on our way before they return."

"Alright then," said Ingvar. "But quickly and quietly, though."

The rest of the crew were not at all happy with the prospect of poking around in a troll's cave, but they could see the truth in Horsa's words. There was no other way they would stand a chance of getting back to the *Bloodkeel* otherwise.

They set about covering Aescwine's body with rocks – a small cairn to keep the wolves away – and said a prayer for his soul. It was the best they could do under the circumstances. With the moon shining high overhead, they walked silently back down the hill, leaving the woods behind them.

It was eerily quiet in the valley. The thirteen posts stood vacant before the black mouth of the cave, casting long, thin shadows across the wet mud. Only the gushing of the stream could be heard, a pulsing melody that wound through the earth. It was as if the whole area was cursed, a sacred place for the heathen worshippers of old, forever scarred by the terrible rites that had occurred there.

Sounds could be heard behind them, and as the men looked back they could see the foliage shaking, wavering back and forth in the pale moonlight as things moved about within.

"They're still looking for us in the woods," said Horsa. "That's good."

They splashed through the stream and hurried into the narrow cave entrance, slipping single file into the blackness. At once they were overpowered by an awful stench of faeces and rotting meat. The passageway continued in complete blackness as it curved around to the left with the stream rushing along the right-hand wall until at last opening up into a wide cavern.

The ground was pitched at an angle and thick clumps of moss grew near the water. A fire smouldered, sending smoke and embers up to the damp ceiling where lichen hung in slimy tendrils. All around lay evidence of the cave's inhabitants. Bones, both animal and human, were piled up around the walls and several crudely cured hides and stinking furs served as beds. War gear belonging to various unfortunate individuals who had met their fate in this cave was piled up in one corner. Rusted helmets, shields, coats of mail, shoes, belts and other indigestible objects were heaped up along with ancient swords, axes and spears.

The companions delved into the pile, salvaging anything that might be of use. Horsa gripped the hilt of a rusted sword and Beorn tested the weight of a heavy battleaxe. The others chose spears that still had some strength left in their ash shafts and many took saexes and hand axes as secondary weapons.

A heavy footstep fell outside the cave's entrance and all froze. There was a splashing as something moved through the water, entering the cave. Beorn plucked up a burning log from the fire and used it as a torch as he moved back towards the entrance, his newly acquired axe gripped steadily in his other hand. The others followed him, tense for a fight.

A bellow of anger sounded throughout the cavern and the shadows of several beings fell on them as their hidden enemy rushed in. The flaming brand was knocked from Beorn's fist as something slammed into him. The light sputtered and flared as it hit the floor and all was confusion.

Swinging blades and stabbing with spears, the companions howled and cursed oaths as they drove on at the creatures, ready to die, desiring vengeance for their lost comrades. Iron punctured flesh and blood ran warm, encouraging the warriors that they faced beings that were not mere wraiths summoned by dark sorcery.

And then it was over. A light flared somewhere and Horsa turned to see Ingvar holding a new torch he had plucked from the fire. The crew of the *Bloodkeel* were bruised and bleeding from scratches and claw marks, but they were all still alive. They looked down upon the motionless forms that lay strewn about the cave, horribly mutilated by sword cuts and spear wounds.

Far from being the ghastly trolls they had imagined, their enemies looked surprisingly human. They were dressed in simple garments befitting farmers and huntsmen. Beorn rolled one of them over onto its back with the toe of his boot. The dead, pale face of a man in his middle years looked up at them with glazed eyes. Around his mouth blood was smeared as if he had been eating raw meat.

"Is this what we were fighting?" asked Ingvar. "Are these our trolls? Menfolk?"

"Maybe they turn human after they are killed," suggested Beorn.

"I doubt it," said Horsa. "I think we've been letting our fears get the better of us. These creatures are as human as we are."

"They must be deranged," said Beorn. "To live out here in a cave, eating human flesh. It's disgusting!"

"I wonder who they were," said Ingvar. "Exiles from the village perhaps?"

"Or offerings," said Horsa. "Men sent by Herogar and his priests, condemned to live like beasts in the wilderness."

"But why?"

"To serve Gefion," said Horsa. "The Wane Queen. They became her children. And we, like many before us, were to be their food."

A shiver went through the crew as the horrible reality of the cult of Gefion dawned on them. They retreated further into the cave and lit more torches to better search it for items that might be useful.

"Captain!" called Aelfhere. "Look at this."

Behind a clump of matted furs, two wide, terror-stricken eyes peered out at them. Horsa instantly recognised the boy.

"It's Eadgar, isn't it?" he said, addressing the boy in what he hoped was a friendly voice.

"He must have been hiding here the whole time," said Ingvar.

"Come on out," continued Horsa. "We'll not harm you."

The boy edged himself out from beneath the furs but kept his distance from the warriors.

Rage boiled inside Horsa. This poor child had been taken from his mother and given to these creatures. For what purpose? To be raised as their own? The old tales said that trolls were once menfolk, enchanted by evil magic, cursed to a life outside the warmth and friendship of society. In a way, that was exactly what had been going on here. That was the purpose of the cult of Gefion. To create trolls: the children of the goddess. And the child's own mother had barely put up a fight. There was a sickness eating away at the heart of the Hrolfingas; a sickness that revolted him.

Eadgar's eyes glanced quickly to the cave's exit and before the warriors could stop him, he made a break for it, his spindly legs splashing through the stream. The darkness without the cave swallowed him.

"Let him go," said Ingvar. "We have plans to make and weapons to sharpen."

They rummaged about in the piles of discarded junk for any food that might satisfy their rumbling bellies, but aside from an old skin of sour mead, they found nothing. Though, there was one aspect about the cave that had escaped their notice, until Beorn pointed it out to them.

"Look here," he said. "There's an entrance to another cave back here."

He was right. The river that flowed through the cave emerged from a large crack in the rock at the rear of the chamber that was so hidden in shadow it could easily have gone unnoticed. The cold water bubbled freely and there was a gap between it and the rock hinting at a second chamber beyond. One by one, they waded into the river and ducked beneath the rock, pulling themselves into the space beyond.

They emerged into an enormous cavern. Moonlight shone down from a small aperture in the roof and illuminated the space below. It was as ancient as time itself. Gigantic stalactites hung from the ceiling like teeth, dripping down onto their counterparts below that had reared up over the ages like the spires of some lost city. A large pool in the centre of the cavern fed the stream, its still depths concealing its source. The light of their torches fell on a reflective substance that seemed to coat the rock surrounding the lake, and as the companions inspected closer, their eyes widened in awe.

"Gold," said Ingvar. "It's gold!"

Gold it was, and in huge quantities. A thousand glimmering surfaces winked and twinkled back at them like a scene from legend. Coins and rings glittered like stars, along with torques and bangles and circlets studded with jet and amber. Treasures from the furthest reaches of the world were piled up in huge heaps. Jewels plundered from the Franks and Burgundians, Roman currency long since disused and even gems from the eastern lands once conquered by Alexander of Macedon. Armour forged for kings and princes lay scattered about: finely worked mail, golden helms, ceremonial shields, spears and drinking horns studded with vivid stones. And most magnificent of all was a golden statue mounted upon a pedestal high above the silent pool, watching over all with cold, jade eyes.

It was the size of a fully-grown woman. Long hair fell down over beautifully worked shoulders and curled around full, plump breasts, framing high cheek bones and sensuous lips. Slender arms hung relaxed, palms angled outwards over wide hips as if in offering.

"That's her," said Horsa, his whispering voice echoing around the cavern. He did not need to explain further, for each of the warriors knew that they gazed upon the image of Gefion, the lost statue of legend, hidden for so many years in this dark and dank cave of wonders beneath the moors of Dane-land.

Gefion, the mother goddess of their ancestors, held them all with her mesmerising beauty. But beyond the beauty, beyond the wondrous facade of gold, they all saw an evil, wicked thing. In those eyes they saw the horrors that had been committed in her name over the ages. They saw the blood that had been spilled on the altars at her feet.

"I knew this was to be true," said Ingvar, as if in a dream. "A statue of solid gold! There is enough of it in her to make us all kings forever!"

They began to laugh; their fear of the goddess fading in the face of their greed. At first it was a childish giggle that rippled through the cavern but soon it bubbled up out of their mouths as roaring bellows of joy. *As rich as kings!* They danced and capered and delved deep into the piles of treasure, hauling up items of wonder in a shower of twinkling gold.

Ingvar, a boar-crested helm upon his head, drew a gold-hilted sword from its scabbard and held it aloft. It was a magnificent thing, a treasure that surely had been wielded by kings of old. Its shimmering blade was wavy with the patterns of the folded metal that had been made during its forging and it was inscribed with ancient symbols. As he could not read runes, he passed it to Horsa to translate.

Horsa ran his fingers along the chiselled marks, recalling the lessons of his childhood. His eyes suddenly lit up.

"This is the blade *Hildeleoma*!" he exclaimed. "The legendary sword of the Jutish kings, lost for an age! It is said that it was forged by Weland, himself, the lord of the Dark Aelfs, who forged Thunor's hammer deep in the bowels of the world where the furnaces burn brightest. Truly, I thought it had vanished from the world of men forever."

"It has returned!" said Ingvar, snatching the blade away from Horsa. "It shall be held by the hand of an Angle now, to cut a bloody swathe across the land as it once did an age before!"

"Why should an Angle wield it?" asked Horsa. "It was made for the Jutes. Would it not better fit a Jute's hand? There are plenty of other swords here that would serve you just as well."

"This is the pride of the heap, Horsa," said Ingvar. "As captain, I claim it."

"You claim it?" demanded Horsa, his face flushed. "What have you done to earn such a reward? I rescued our crew from bloody sacrifice and led them into the woods. It was also my idea to raid the troll's cave. If anyone here has the right to that sword, then it is I."

"So, it is now that you choose to enforce your noble birth upon us, is it?" said Ingvar. "You may have once been the son of a Jutish chieftain, Horsa, but now you are nothing. Nothing but an embarrassment to your family and little more than an exile in your own land!"

Horsa might have killed him for this, as he had indeed taken the life of a man once before for a far lesser insult.

"I am the captain," said Ingvar, "and as such I claim the hoard, this sword and that statue in the name of the *Bloodkeel*. You shall have your share, Horsa, once we are far away from Dane-land."

"That statue cannot go with us," said Horsa, the sword momentarily forgotten.

"We're not leaving without it," Ingvar replied.

"We can't carry it for a start. And there is something about it that does not sit well with me. Something ancient. Something evil."

There were murmurs of agreement from the crew and it seemed at that moment that Ingvar was the only man among them who did not feel acutely uneasy in the presence of the golden statue.

"The crew and I have made up our minds," said Horsa. We take what we can carry and we leave. Now!"

"The crew and you is it?" replied Ingvar, his voice dripping with condescension. "Fancy yourself a captain as well as an aetheling now, do you?"

Horsa stared into Ingvar's eyes and Ingvar stared right back. "What if I do?" he said coldly.

"I have tolerated your insolence for too long, Horsa. No more! You fight me now or you hold your tongue!"

"We don't have time for this!" shouted Beorn. "Let's just go!"

"No," said Horsa quietly. "This ends now."

In perfect synchronism, the two men drew their blades. The rest of the crew stood back. With a yell of rage, Ingvar slashed out at his first mate with *Hildeleoma*; a glittering sliver of steel in the dim light of the cavern. Horsa deflected the blow with his own rusted blade and sidestepped, cutting in at his captain.

Back and forth the Jute and the Angle raged, steel clanging and slithering, echoing around the cave. The other crew members yelled out at the two warriors to stop, but the matter had gone too far past the point of reconciliation. This would end in death for one of them.

Horsa dodged a lunge from *Hildeleoma* and bashed it aside with his own blade, throwing Ingvar off balance. Seeing the chance to finish him, he lunged forward, thrusting his sword up to the hilt in the Angle's chest.

Cold steel slid noiselessly through warm flesh. Blood spilled outwards and rained down on the wet stone. Ingvar stared at Horsa, his eyes wide in momentary disbelief. Then they glazed over and he sank to his knees as the blade was ripped out in a gush of crimson. Horsa whipped the blade through the air and severed the Angle's head from his torso, sending it bouncing across the floor of the cavern. He turned with wild eyes to his silent comrades.

"I, Horsa, son of Wictgils, have slain Ingvar, son of Wolof and hereby take his place as captain of the *Bloodkeel*. If any man here disputes my claim, let him step forward now."

None did.

Horsa bent down and plucked *Hildeleoma* from the stiffening hand of the dead man at his feet. "This sword shall return to the hand of a Jute, where it belongs." He looked up at the statue of Gefion. "And as for that damned thing, it has witnessed the last bloodshed it shall ever see."

In several leaps he was up upon the rock that hung above the pool as a pedestal. Setting his shoulder to the golden figure, he heaved with all his might. The statue began to move, grating against the moss-encrusted rock where it had rested for generations. He pushed harder and the idol started to tip, slowly at first, then gathering momentum as gravity reached up to claim it.

There was a brief silence as the statue fell through space, and then the pool erupted as several tons of gold plunged into it with a tremendous splash that showered water across the whole cavern. Horsa was not the only one who imagined that he could hear a shriek; a terrible sound of dismay and rage that tore through them and was then sucked away, dragged down into the blackness along with the statue, to be consumed by the choppy surface of the pool.

None spoke as they began the task of selecting which of the treasures they would carry back to the ship. They worked fast and followed Horsa's orders to the letter. He smiled. They had accepted him as their new leader before Ingvar's ugly head had hit the floor.

He was the last to leave the cavern. As the other crewmembers waded through the stream into the cave beyond, he took one last look around. It was then that he saw something in the dark depths of the pool that sent an icy shiver through him.

It may have been nothing more than a reflection or the dim light playing tricks on his tired mind, but he was sure that he could make out a face staring back at him from the black depths of the water; a female face with wavering tendrils of hair and piercing eyes full of hate. He blinked and it was gone but the image remained with him until his dying day.

Outside the cave, the slow light of dawn was creeping across the moors. It was bitterly cold. They had a long, hard fight ahead of them before they could drop oars aboard the *Bloodkeel*. The odds were against them, but a thirst for cold, bloody vengeance made for a powerful battle-companion.

They found a comfortable spot with a cluster of trees at their back and got a fire going with some embers they brought from the cave. Several of the men went chasing after wild pigs with spears and soon all were enjoying the succulent taste of roasted pork as they watched the sky turn pale over the marshes to the west.

"I say we attack as soon as possible," said Beorn, around a mouthful of juicy meat. "They're probably still sleeping off the effects of last night's celebrations."

"Agreed," replied Horsa.

"Imagine their faces when they see us!" said Aelfhere. "They'll think we are spirits back from the dead!"

"Serve those heathen scum right," said Horsa.

The trek across the moors was long and cold, and the hoard of treasure they carried with them made the journey hard. But with a bellyful of roasted pork each and a burning desire to wet their blades in Hrolfing blood cheered them.

As the rolling moorland swept down to the fens the companions finally set eyes upon the small circle of lights from the village that had betrayed them. The morning mist clouded the palisade but the torch lights of the guards shone out like beacons.

They knew they were vastly outnumbered and so any plan of attack had to be based on subtlety and stealth. Not a tactic any of them were particularly used to. The gold was well hidden behind some rocks, ready to be reclaimed once it was all over. Then, like shadows in the fog, the companions crept silently down the slope towards the village.

Beneath the palisade a guard stood leaning on his spear, his head nodding slowly. He was drunk. Horsa crept around to the side and reached his arm around the man's neck in a headlock. The guard snorted awake just in time to feel the coldness of *Hildeleoma* slide in between his ribs. He fell to the ground without a sound and the attackers swarmed up to the palisade.

Horsa wiped his blade on the dead man's shirt and sheathed it. Beorn knelt down and helped Horsa up over the spiked timbers. One by one, the crew followed, dropping down on the other side and sinking into the shadows.

The village was silent, as if deserted. Only a few chickens clucked out their protests as the raiders darted between the buildings towards the hall of the Hrolfingas, their breath steaming in the chill of morning.

A second guard, more alert than the first, saw them coming and tried to cry out an alarm but it died in his throat as Aelfhere sent a spear whickering through the air, catching him in the chest and hurling him to the mud.

"They all must be asleep in the hall," Beorn whispered to Horsa. "What is your plan?"

Horsa looked around at the surrounding huts and stalls. An idea formed in his mind, a nasty, idea but a fitting vengeance. So strong was the anger within him at the ones responsible for the blasphemous little cave up on the moors that he wanted to see them all burn for it; Ealdorman Herogar who led this heathen cult, Eadgar's mother who had abandoned her own son to a life of wretchedness, all of them.

"Get those barrels," he said, indicating a stack of containers piled up beneath a thatched awning. "Block this door. Beorn, take some men around the back and secure the other entrance."

The men acted swiftly and without question, heaving the barrels down and passing them along in a line to be stacked up against the oak doors of the ealdorman's hall. More barrels and other detritus were found and piled up onto the barrels at both entrances, sealing the slumbering inhabitants within their master's hall.

"Now we have them!" hissed Horsa and he plucked up a flaming torch from its nearby brazier and hurled it high into the air above the hall. It landed on the thatch and rolled down; a cascade of glowing embers that nested amongst the frost-encrusted straw.

The crew watched as the embers caught, slowly at first, melting the ice before spreading into the thatch. The roof began to burn. A large crackling circle widened and soon consumed the entire sloping side in a blazing inferno that wavered and danced, sending sparks up into the grey sky.

Someone inside must have awoken, for there came a soul splitting scream of terror that was quickly taken up by more and more voices, as the inhabitants of the hall discovered the sheet of flame above them that was sucking the air out of the building and dropping flaming pieces of thatch down on them. Fists hammered on the insides of the blocked doors and men and women gave vent to their horror in an awful roar of noise that must have awoken the gods from their slumber in Esegeard.

The men at Horsa's back watched the hall burn in silence. If any of them felt any guilt for visiting such a terrible fate on those within, they did not dare show it. Horsa held *Hildeleoma* aloft, its long blade reflecting the fiery glow of the hall and he called up to the gods.

"Woden! I am Horsa the Jute, son of Wictgils, captain of the *Bloodkeel*. Hear me! I offer you the lives of these heathens as a sacrifice to you! Glory to the Ese! We have destroyed the temple to the Wane-goddess in your honour! Grant us safe passage back to our homelands and protect my brother so that I might see him again!"

His voice was carried away with the smoke and embers that whirled up to the clouded sky.

And Woden turned his single eye upon Horsa, his ravens flapping and cawing madly. Thunder rolled in the distance as the iron-rimmed wheels of Thunor's chariot ground across the sky. Frige's voice whispered on the wind. All the gods were listening, so great and bloody was this sacrifice, the like of which had not been seen since the old times. The flames of the hall and the smouldering flesh of the Hrolfingas would be long remembered by those who had once walked the world as men before men. This young mortal had struck a blow against an age-old enemy of the Ese and they would honour him for it. The Wyrd Sisters spun their yarn frantically, weaving the future; Horsa's future. And it was to be one of great importance.

Angry shouts sounded from behind Horsa and he turned to see several Hrolfingas running towards them, spears lowered. They had been sleeping in one of the other buildings and had been awoken from their drunken slumber by the noise and light of the blazing hall.

"Keep them away from the doors!" shouted Horsa.

The crew of the *Bloodkeel* lined up to meet the ealdorman's men with grim determination. Few had shields and so their only defence was their spears, axes and blades. Steel clashed and blood spurted by the light of the blazing fire. Beorn's axe cut a man down mid stride and Horsa swung *Hildeleoma*, ripping through flesh and mail, his arms powered by a new strength. The half-drunk guards were no match for the brute aggression of the raiders, and spears and saexes did for the rest of them.

The fight was short lived and by now the screaming from within the hall had subsided. The stench of burning flesh reached their nostrils and they stood and watched as the blazing roof finally caved in on itself with a great creaking and groaning of charred timbers.

Horsa watched it burn, saying nothing. His sacrifice was complete. The gods had been honoured. They were all dead. But why then, did the screaming of the women and children ring in his ears like the cries of ghosts, even as their mortal flesh burned black?

Eager to leave the settlement of the slain and return to the *Bloodkeel*, the crew searched for food and drink. Horsa ordered the treasure be brought down from the moors and, after securing their frightened horses from the stables, they set off once more across the marshes towards the coast, leaving the noxious stink of death and roasting flesh in the mist behind them.

By the time they reached the boat, a day and a half later, the weather had turned for the worse. Light snowflakes were whirled around by the bitter wind and the sky was a darker shade of grey than any sea captain likes to see. But the salty tang of the sea caught their nostrils like the familiar smell of home.

The *Bloodkeel* was as they had left it, but furry with frost that cracked and fell away in chunks as they hauled it by its stiff ropes down into the water. The sea was dark and flecked with whitecaps but nothing would stop them from trying to reach home.

They stowed the treasure and every man wrapped himself in the warmest furs they possessed before dropping oars and beginning the laborious task of rowing out onto the open sea. With only ten of the crew left, it was hard going and they barely had the strength to power the boat through the waves.

Horsa watched the coastline of Dane-land vanish behind him as the boat tipped and rolled on the heaving sea. They had got what they had come for, but at a shockingly high cost. Nevertheless, they would rest easy this winter, warm in their halls with their hard-earned gold at their feet.

And now he was captain, surely that was worth more than all the treasure put together? Now, if the gods accepted his sacrifice, he could return to Jute-land and rejoin his brother as he had always planned, rich and successful.

Now the gods had noticed him.

Now he was ready.

Hengest

The beginning of the festivities was marked by the lighting of the Geola log. A fine piece of timber had been chosen by the king, cut down and dragged into the hall. It was placed in one of the hearths and all gathered around to see it being kindled with the remains of last year's log. The Geola log would burn slowly for several days, and never allowed to go out during the festivities, bringing luck and good fortune to the host and his household.

Afterwards, the Frisians and their guests gathered in the nearby grove to the gods to perform a ritual sacrifice that would ensure fertility and blessings in the year to come. The grove was much like the one near Hengest's home only this one was dedicated to many more gods than just Woden. Wooden effigies of Thunor and Frige stood on either side of Woden along with Tiw, the one-handed god of single combat.

A great black stallion was brought forward to be sacrificed. As the magnificent beast sank down to its knees and rolled over, its jugular severed by the knife of the High-Priest, blood was collected in wooden bowls and all in the gathering smeared the warm, dark liquid on their foreheads. The rest of it was splashed upon the faces of the gods and Hengest was reminded of a similar blood ceremony that had been carried out by a young boy twelve years ago in a grove in Jute-land.

That night Garulf arrived in Finnesburg, bringing the king's son with him. He was accompanied by a large company of Jutish warriors; the remainder of Ealdorman Guthulf's thegns who had escaped to Frisia when the spears of the West Danes had slain their lord.

Frithuwulf had his father's features: the dark hair and the strong but gentle chin. Finn grasped him in a crushing embrace on the steps outside the hall.

"My boy!" he exclaimed. "It is good to have you back! Have you learned much? Has Garulf been a good mentor?"

"He is his father's son alright," said Garulf, a youngish man in a cloak of green. "I have never known one so young to be so skilled with bow and blade."

"I have missed you, Father," said Frithuwulf. "And you, Mother." He embraced Hildeburh whose face was streaked with unrestrained tears of happiness at the return of her eldest.

"You have started the celebrations without us it seems," said Garulf, looking around at the feasting and merrymaking as Finn led them into the hall.

"Indeed we have, I am afraid," replied Finn. "We thought you would be here for the lighting of the Geola log and the sacrifice but you must have been detained."

"Yes, a minor dispute between two of my thegns held us up. But no matter, I am here now."

The Danes sat in uneasy, expectant silence as the newcomers entered. Hengest looked at Hnaef. Garulf had not noticed him yet. The Dane's face was grim and he clutched his mead horn tightly, taking small, controlled sips.

"Come and eat, Garulf," said Finn. "You must be starving from your journey here. Besides, I want you to meet someone."

"I thought you might have other guests," replied Garulf, following Finn across to the hearth where meat was slowly roasting on spits. "Else your retinue seems to have doubled in size."

As his eyes scanned the faces of the men on the benches, they froze as he spotted Hnaef. His smile locked in a comical grin as the two rivals stared into each eyes across the fire pit.

"What's going on here?" asked Garulf, turning to Finn angrily. "Is this a joke? Or is my life to be offered up tonight as a second sacrifice?"

"Now look," said Finn. "It is the festival of Geola. Peace between brothers …"

"Peace? This man killed my father! He tried to kill me! He took my lands and forced me into exile. I have no quarrel with your queen for I know that she is Hnaef's sister, but you cannot expect me to share a hearth fire with this man!"

Hnaef got up and walked around to the other side of the fire pit bearing a full horn of mead. "I have no ill intentions towards you, Garulf, son of Guthulf. Let there be peace between us tonight." He held out the mead horn to Garulf.

"Don't you ever say my father's name!" shouted the young Jute, and he bashed the horn from Hnaef's hand, sending it clattering across the floor in a spray of golden mead. Several Danes rose up from their seats and grasped the hilts of their saexes. The Jutes at Garulf's back did the same and for a horrible moment the hall was silent but for the crackling of the Geola log in the hearth.

"Halt!" bellowed Finn. "I am king of this hall and you are both my guests! If I say there is to be peace tonight then there shall be peace! Hildeburh, fetch Garulf a new mead horn. The rest of you Jutes, find seats and eat. There is plenty of food for all."

The Jutes obeyed and began to find places among the Frisians but avoided the Danes like the plague.

144

Garulf accepted a mead horn from Hildeburh but did not take his eyes off Hnaef as he sat down, his face dark and lined by the flickering of the fire.

Conversation resumed and a scop took up a tune on his lyre, but the merrymaking was guarded. There was no singing or wrestling and the Jutes and Danes did their best to ignore each other with the Frisians acting as the go-betweens.

Hengest ate and drank in silence, watching his countrymen on the other side of the hall but refusing to join them. Their Jutish dialect reminded him of home but his loyalty to Hnaef restrained him from conversing with them.

"What did I tell you?" said Guthlaf, leaning over to speak softly into Hengest's ear. "Peace rests upon a thread of sobriety tonight."

"Don't be such a pessimist, Guthlaf," said Ordlaf, reaching over to take some bread from the table. "Not everyone is in the mood for bloodshed all of the time."

"Lad, I've seen more bloodshed than you've had whores," Guthlaf replied. "But still, I'm surprised at you, Ordlaf. Haven't you seen enough of the world yet to know that a king's hall, no matter how big, is not large enough for three tribes to sit elbow to elbow?"

"I suppose I have the optimism of youth on my side," said Ordlaf. "Maybe when I'm as well seasoned as an old oak, I'll know what you mean."

"Less talk of the 'old oak' if you please," replied Guthlaf. "I'm not that much older than you."

"Oh, please," snorted Ordlaf. "Your head is so white it looks like it's been snowed upon."

The evening wore on and Guthlaf's worrying seemed to be ill-founded. The mood softened a little as the mead and ale sank in and spirits lifted. Conversation even broke out between some Jutes and a few of the Danes. Frithuwulf had taken a seat opposite Hengest and was discussing ancient heroes and folktales with Ordlaf and Guthlaf.

"None can be greater than Sigemund," commented Guthlaf, reeling on the bench drunkenly. "A man who can bite the tongue out of a she-wolf's mouth and escape unscathed cannot be beaten."

"You should hear some of the tales concerning Jutish heroes, Dane," replied Frithuwulf. "During my stay with Lord Garulf I heard such stories that would make your beard curl."

"It is true," said Guthere, an elderly Jute who had been a close friend of Garulf's father and was something of a mentor to his surviving son. "We are a people not to be bested at drinking, eating or fighting. You, Hengest, you know this surely, for I detect a Jutish twang to your voice."

Hengest was on the verge of answering the old man when Garulf approached. "Of course, our people have lessened somewhat since the days of great heroes," the exiled nobleman said, fixing an eye on Hengest. "With the sons of ealdormen forsaking their tribes and taking up arms with Danes …"

Hengest looked up from his mead and stared straight at Garulf. He had not expected to be recognised by the son of his father's friend and it took a while for the insult to sink in. He nearly reached for his saex but caught Finn's eye on the other side of the hall and thought better of it. He planted his horn on the table and stared at Garulf who gazed at him with an expectant expression.

"I would curb your tongue, Garulf," said Guthlaf, speaking for Hengest. "What does an exile know of heroic deeds?"

"More than a traitor to his people, and more than a Dane who takes lands that do not belong to him and sends his men to butcher whole families who speak out against him."

Garulf spoke this part loud enough for all the hall to hear. The tension that had been bubbling beneath the surface all evening finally erupted.

"You dare insult me in front of our host?" demanded Hnaef, storming across the hall towards Garulf. People stumbled out of the way as the large Dane strode towards the table. Jutes rose up as did Danes, ready to fight for their lords if it came to it.

"Be silent, all!" demanded Finn, his hands upraised and his voice spiked with anger. "Whilst you are guests in my hall, you will not threaten or goad each other! What has passed has passed and it will remain so whilst I am King of Frisia."

Frithuwulf rose from his seat. "Father," he exclaimed, "you cannot expect our good friend Garulf to sit here alongside the man who destroyed everything to his name."

All in the hall looked to the young Frisian. They were shocked. The boy was standing against his own uncle. It was clear that he had developed a close bond with his Jutish foster-father and there was no question as to where his allegiances lay.

"I will not have violence or harsh words this night," said Finn, regarding his son reprovingly.

"Nevertheless," said Hnaef. "This Jute has insulted me."

"Then you will bear it!" yelled Finn.

There was an uneasy silence. The king had spoken. All parties – Danes, Jutes and Frisians – glared at each other and made moves to sit down quietly and continue with their eating. It was the end of hostile talk that night. Only sour glances and silent looks remained, and it was not long before the feast ended and all began to talk of bedding down for the night.

King Finn's plans for peace between Jute and Dane did not extend to forcing them to sleep in the same hall, so once Hnaef had led his men to their hall across the bridge, the Jutes were shown to their own hall on the opposite side of the river. The symbolism was lost on nobody; one side of the river housed Danes and the other Jutes. And right in the middle, on the island that linked the two sides, sat the household of Finn; a peacemaker and broker for unity between tribes.

Hnaef grumbled all the way across the bridge. "If I had known that Finn was the type to shelter my enemies, I may not have been so hasty to see him married to my sister," he said to Hengest. "And to think, he sent my nephew to live amongst them so that his words have become as knives to me!"

"The boy has hardly known you during his short life," replied Hengest. "It is only natural that he feels a closer bond with the man who has been his foster father these past few years."

"No bond can be stronger than blood!" snapped Hnaef. "In seeking to bring two enemies closer together, Finn has only succeeded in driving a wedge between me and my own kin."

"Frithuwulf is young," maintained Hengest. "All young boys speak foolishly at times. Don't think too much on it. Perhaps in the coming weeks you and he will grow closer."

"Gods, weeks!" said Hnaef. "How am I to suffer the insults of Garulf and his men for weeks? I warn you that my brother-in-law is a foolish man. There shall be bloodshed this winter, I guarantee it!"

Several hours later, all was silent over Finnesburg. The roofs of the settlement were dusted with snow and illuminated by the yellow moon that drifted across the night, pursued by the wolf of darkness. A figure etched in silver crept out of the hall where the Danes slept and made his way around to the side of the building to relieve his bladder.

The crystals of frost melted on the timbers as he urinated, steam rising up in the cold night air. The front of the hall faced east and Earendel – the morning star – was winking at him from the bow of the ship that carried him ever on across the night. With morning the first hint of the dawn would creep over the horizon and flood the plains with its golden light. Dawn was several hours away and yet there was a faint glimmer of light rising in the east.

The man shook himself dry and fastened his breeches as he squinted into the night. Beyond the bridge lay the gables of King Finn's hall and beyond that he could make out the approaching light. It was a dull gleam like fire beneath heavy clouds.

The man's mouth was dry and his head pounded with the mead he had drunk. In his befuddled state he imagined the scorching breath of a great fire-drake approaching; panicking, he scampered back into the hall.

Hengest was awoken by the man shaking his shoulder violently.

"Lord Hengest! There is something amiss!"

Hengest heaved himself up onto his elbows and rubbed his face with the palm of his hand. The hearth had burned low and the Danes slumbered around it, showing no movement.

"What's the trouble, man?" he asked. "Gods help you if you've woken me for nothing."

"There is a light in the east, but it is too early for dawn. It looks like a fire drake come to destroy us!"

"You're drunk, man. Get some sleep, and if you wake me again, I'll stick my saex in you."

"There is a light, I tell you! A fire! Something burns in Finnesburg!"

Hengest sat up and stared into the Dane's frightened eyes. "Show me."

By the time they got to the door, the light was so close that it was clearly no fire drake. It was torches. Many of them. Their flickering flames reflected off iron helms and wavering spear tips as a column of men made its way across the bridge with all the intent of a warband marching to battle.

"Wake the king," said Hengest, his voice low and alert.

By the time Hnaef reached his side, his face groggy, the front line of the approaching warriors could be seen. Garulf and Guthere led them, their faces set with grim purpose.

"It's the Jutes!" hissed Hnaef. "They have come to kill me! Even the Geola peace won't stand in the way of Garulf's lust for vengeance. King Finn will never allow this to pass! And neither must we!" He turned and shouted into the hall, "Awaken now my warriors! Grasp your coats of mail, take up your spears and shields! Think of valour and bear yourselves proudly, for evil comes our way!"

In an instant the hall was alive with activity. Men leaped up from their beds and seized their arms. There was a fury of buckling and fastening as the thegns of King Hnaef armed themselves for battle.

Hengest peered out at the rapidly approaching faces of his countrymen. There was a face out there that was not that of a Jute; a youthful face framed by dark locks of hair. "Hnaef!" shouted Hengest. "Your nephew is with them!"

Hnaef thrust his head out of the doorway to get a better look, his eyes alive with angry passion. A short-handled throwing axe spun through the air and embedded itself in the doorframe, a few inches from Hnaef's face. The king of the West Danes ducked his head into the shadows and called for the door to be barred.

"My own nephew taking up arms against me!" he cried. "Mark my words, woeful deeds have begun this night that will bring a bitter end to the enmity between our peoples! Sigeferth! Eaha! To my side! Hengest, take Guthlaf and Ordlaf and look to the other door in case they come around!"

The thegns set about their task. The long oak tables were flung on their sides and heaved up against the doors, and the floor was cleared of bedding and benches to allow the defenders more room.

Hengest took up position at the west door, flanked by Guthlaf and Ordlaf. The Jutes had indeed come around, circling the hall and pressing from both sides. Axes and hammers chipped away at the oak, whilst a bench that the Jutes had brought with them was slammed repeatedly on the east door, again and again like the tolling of a bell.

Hengest and the Danes, gripping their swords tightly, stared wild-eyed as the axe heads of the attackers worked their way through. A large chunk of wood burst from the door and skittered along the stone flags to rest at Hengest's feet. He looked up and saw a fierce Jutish face peering through the hole he had made with his axe.

The man only caught a brief glimpse of Hengest's snarl as he ran forward and thrust his sword through the hole, piercing the attacker in the throat.

The defenders had won first blood but, spurred by the death of their comrade, the Jutes continued their attack on the west door with renewed energy, pulling, wrenching and tearing at the doors. Soon they would be through.

"Once the doors come down," said Hengest to his comrades, "we rush them. Give them no chance to set foot within the hall. Hack them to pieces!"

The Danes around him nodded and watched, unblinking as the doors wavered and crumpled under the assault. Finally, they fell away revealing the helmeted heads of the Jutes against the starry night sky.

"Now!" cried Hengest, and they charged.

Spears and blades met flesh, and iron slid off leather and wood as the shields of the two sides slammed together. Caught off-guard by the sudden rush, the Jutes fell back. Hengest swung his sword and clove a man from shoulder to chest. He briefly recognised the face of Frithuwulf as he battered aside the body, but it was too late to do anything as the Frisian heir fell beneath the trampling feet of the Danes.

Finn

The king was awake and sitting up in bed even before his theow came hurrying into his chamber to bring him the disastrous news. The unmistakable sound of sword blows and shouting from across the river had reached his ears, stirring him from his slumber.

"My king!" said the theow, in a state of great excitement. "There is violence in your household! The Jutes are attacking the Danes!"

"What?" bellowed Finn. "They dare to attack my guests? I'll have their heads upon the gables of my hall for this!"

Hildeburh was awake next to him and she sat up, her eyes orbs of white in the darkness. "Why were they not stopped?" she demanded. "They must have walked straight past this hall on their way."

"There were too many of them for the guards to halt, my lady," stammered the theow. "They are drunk and filled with a lust for bloodshed. Besides, your son is with them."

"Frithuwulf?" bellowed Finn. "My son is involved in this folly?" He leapt out of bed and hurriedly began to strap his armour on over his bedclothes.

A side door to the chamber opened and little Frealaf emerged in his nightgown, his face frightened. Hildeburh flung the bedclothes aside and scooped him up, whispering words of comfort to him.

"Arouse every thegn on the island," Finn told the theow. "Have them ready and armed outside the hall as soon as possible. By the gods, I'll carve the lungs from each and every one of those traitorous dogs if any harm comes to Frithuwulf!"

Garulf

The east door of the hall was buckling beneath repeated blows of the mead bench. The Jutes clamoured around it, cheering and chanting battle-cries, eager to get in at the Danes who held the hall.

"Frithuwulf must have got in on the other side," said Garulf to Guthere, shouting over the noise of the slamming bench. "Else there would be more Danes guarding this entrance. Come on men! Bring it down! Within lies the murderer of our kinsfolk and the cause of our exile! Vengeance is within our grasp!"

Finally, the doors tumbled inwards and with a mighty cheer the Jutes fell in upon the Danes. Garulf made to charge with them, but Guthere placed a heavy hand upon his shoulder and restrained him.

"My lord, do not risk your life in attacking," he warned him. "You are the last of your line and your life is too precious to waste."

"With that Dane-bastard in there taunting me?" Garulf demanded.

"He is waiting for just such an opportunity to take your life," replied Guthere. "Don't make it so easy for him!"

"This is the hour of my victory, old friend," said Garulf. "Not you, not Woden, nor the ghost of my father can stop me from claiming my vengeance!" He shook himself free from the old man's grasp and ran into the fray, chopping and slashing at the Danes with his father's sword.

The figure of Hnaef was visible beneath the arch of the door, surrounded by his thegns. Blood was spattered on his helm and his beard was clotted with red. Garulf desperately fought his way towards him, hoping that no Jutish spear might fell his enemy before he had a chance to kill the Dane himself.

He let his eagerness distract him and nearly didn't have time to raise his shield against the blade of the aetheling called Sigeferth, who swung at him from the darkness like a phantom. The blade sliced through the iron rim and bit deep down into the wood, splitting the shield down to its boss. Garulf heaved the useless object aside and, as the Scegan aetheling lifted his sword for another deadly stroke, he ducked in low and thrust his blade through Sigeferth's chest.

But the power behind the Scegan's blow was only slightly lessened by the mortal wound and the sword swung wildly, catching Garulf on the helm. His ears rang with the bells of Waelheall and he clutched at his dented helmet. Dazed and confused, he barely registered the war cries of Hengest and the remainder of the Danes as they charged around the side of the hall and slammed into the right flank of the Jutes.

Blood spattered from open wounds, shields were dashed and swords rang together in a ferocious cacophony of slaughter as the Jutes suddenly found themselves fighting on two fronts. Frithuwulf and his company had been slaughtered and now Hengest led the Danes to the aid of their king.

Hnaef was hopelessly unreachable now and Garulf cursed. It was as if a tide of Danes had swept him away from his goal. And at the tide's head was Hengest.

Garulf fought his way towards the traitorous Jute; content for the time being in an opportunity to wet his blade in the turncoat's blood. Hengest had seen him and their two blades clashed and slithered together. There were no restraints now, no stern voice of authority to pacify them and both Jutes swung at each other in a ferocious volley of blows. Garulf found a stroke parried and felt Hengest's blade sink deep into his belly. He tried to let out a cry, but words would not come to him as he sank down to the ground, blood rising up in his gullet to choke him.

Guthere

From the rear lines of the battle, Guthere saw the son of his old friend fall, and cried out in anguish. Forcing his way through the throng of Danes and Jutes he fought his way towards his lord. Garulf sank from view, his killer moving on into the fray. Bashing aside friend and foe alike, Guthere made his way to Garulf's side. The young exile clung to life upon the frozen mud, clutching a gaping wound in his abdomen from which blood pumped.

"Garulf, my boy," said Guthere, cradling the head of the last of Guthulf's line. The battle raged around them, unheeded. "I shall avenge you. It was that traitor, Hengest …"

"Leave him," coughed Garulf. "Avenge my father instead. Do that which I failed to do … kill the Dane!"

His coughed some more and the effort killed him. His eyes glazed over and Guthere let his head sink back down to the mud. He rose, gripping his sword tightly. His eyes stinging with tears, he looked about, scanning the seething mass of warriors for the face of the Danish king.

Hnaef's sword arm was red and wet to the elbow; his shield had long been discarded for the repeated blows had tired out his arm.

Guthere was tall and his helmed head rose above the carnage that surrounded him as he strode towards Hnaef like an ettin in the old tales. His grey features blazed with rage held in check by determined purpose. His sword swung through the air, droplets of blood flying from its tip.

Hnaef saw him in time and blocked it. A circle formed around the two battling warriors. None could intervene. Hnaef was tired and already wounded in a score of places. His sword weighed heavily in his hand as he swung it, making him slower than the older man who faced him.

A wrong footing, a misjudged stroke was all Guthere needed; and with a mighty heave of his blade, he batted the sword from Hnaef's hand and slashed his unguarded neck in the backswing.

The Dane-king, his head half severed and blood spurting between exposed tendons, tumbled backwards to the sodden ground and lay still. The Danes cried out at the death of their lord. The Jutes yelled in triumph for the tyrant was dead and their lost ealdorman and his son had been avenged at last.

Hengest

Hengest had seen Hnaef fall and shared the anguish of the Danes. With Hnaef died all the dreams and hopes for a united north. A moment like this could break their spirit and not only cost them the battle, but their lives too. He saw no option but to seize the moment as a rider might seize the reins of a panic-stricken horse.

"Danes!" he cried. "Rally to me! Form as one!"

There was little hesitation. Leaderless and frightened, the Danes blindly followed him in place of their king. The two factions of Danes forced their way together at the open archway of the hall. Guthere, his purpose fulfilled, allowed himself to fall beneath the vengeful blades of his enemies who hacked and trampled him underfoot in their rage.

Horns bellowed from somewhere and many heads turned. Across the bridge came a troop of Friesians with King Finn at their head.

"Back inside the hall!" shouted Hengest. "Block the doors!"

The Danes forced themselves in, holding off the Jutes. Shattered furniture and the remains of the doors were piled up to bar the entrance.

The Frisians ploughed into the rear of the Jutes who found themselves pinned against the eastern side of the hall. Finn showed no mercy and Jutish blood ran freely as punishment for their outrage.

Inside the hall Hengest gasped with exhaustion as the sounds of the Frisians finishing off the traitors seeped in from without. His arms were red and sticky with blood and he had a deep gash on his forehead that was still bleeding. He had never seen a real battle before. He had been trained for it by his father's tutors since childhood and he had killed several men in small disputes, but nothing could have prepared him for the surreal mixture of emotions that battle brought. Fear and exultation, disgust and joy, all fought for space within him so that he felt like he might burst apart.

Bodies littered the floor of the darkened hall, both Jutish and Danish. The walls and pillars were splashed with blood and the stench was sickening. The Danes looked to Hengest. Their king was dead and all had seen how heroically he had led the attack on the right flank of the enemy.

"What now?" Ordlaf asked him.

"The gods alone know," replied Hengest. "Did you see Frithuwulf out there?" His stomach shrank at the memory of the young boy's face as he had hacked him down. "Finn will show no mercy on the killers of his son.'

"But the king's son was one of the attackers!" said Ordlaf

"I'm not sure that Finn will care. The peace of Geola has been broken and his household shamed."

He gave orders for the bodies of the fallen to be piled up around the walls and was surprised at how readily the Danes accepted his command. Guthlaf walked over to Hengest and Ordlaf, his feet splashing on the floor which was awash with blood.

"We can't stay in here," he said. "Not with all these dead."

"Agreed," said Hengest, peering out through the broken doors at the Frisian warriors. "And there are not enough of us to withstand a second attack." He felt Guthlaf's hand on his shoulder.

"Hengest, the men are leaderless and their spirits are broken, but they will follow you if you can promise

160

them a glorious end. Let us charge out now, cut down as many Friesians as we can and die the deaths of true warriors worthy of Waelheall!"

"No," replied Hengest. "We don't know where Finn stands in this. It may be that he will not attack but will seek a truce."

"There is no honour in that!"

"No, but it may be the only way we can get out of here with our lives."

Somebody was hailing them from outside. It was Finn.

"Danes!" the Frisian king cried. "Does King Hnaef still live?"

Hengest walked up to the doorway and answered him, shouting through the gap in the furniture, "He does not. His life was taken in a cowardly attack by the Jutes."

"Is that you Hengest?" called Finn. "Do you lead the Danes now?"

Hengest looked to the men at his back. Nobody spoke. "For the time being," he replied.

"Is my son in there with you?"

Hengest's heart sank. There was no dancing around this matter. He would have to tell the truth. "Your son was one of those who led the assault," he said. "I am sorry to tell you that he is dead. If we could have prevented it in any way we would have."

There was a silence outside. Then Finn spoke in a strained voice, "Will you come out at least, so that we may speak as men. There will be no violence towards you on the part of me or my men, I give you my word."

"It could be a trap," warned Ordlaf.

"We have no choice," said Hengest, unbuckling his sword belt. "Either we face him or we stay in here and

161

die of starvation and disease. Help me move this barricade."

They began heaving aside the furniture, clearing a way for their new leader. Hengest stepped out of the hall to face Finn and felt the eyes of every Frisian upon him as he did so. The light of dawn was finally creeping up over the gables of the hall beyond the bridge; no illusion this time.

The ground before him was littered with the many bodies of the Jutes. Not a single one of them had been left alive. Among them was Hnaef's corpse which Hengest stepped over as he spoke to Finn.

"My lord, this quarrel was none of our doing. I feel for your loss but there have been many losses this night. My men are without their king and we have lost many good friends to the treachery of the Jutes."

"I could have you all executed right now if I wished it," said Finn bitterly, but Hengest could see in his eyes that it was an empty threat.

"My Dane-friends and I will make a final stand in this hall if we need to, and we will take many Friesian lives before we lay down to die," said Hengest. "The gods will know that we died honourably and untarnished by guilt. But I offer you our surrender in exchange for safe passage to our homelands."

A silence followed and thegns on both sides gripped their weapons.

"Very well," said Finn at last. "I accept your surrender. But here are the terms: all of the men under your command are free to leave as of their own choosing, but in exchange you, Hengest, must remain here and pledge your eternal allegiance to me as you once did to Hnaef. You may keep whatever followers you choose here with you, and I give you my word as king that you will not be harmed or insulted by any Frisian."

The words of Hildeburh flashed through Hengest's mind. Here was an oath that could very well be a prison. His presence in Finnesburg might be a token of trust and insurance against any threat from Dane-land. But, was that all there was to it?

It was a hard bargain. Hengest had no desire to remain in Finnesburg a day longer, let alone indefinitely. But the lives of his men depended upon it and he could see no other choice.

"Accepted," he said finally.

"Good," replied Finn. "Now, if you would be so kind, I would like to see the body of my son." His voice was beginning to crack with emotion.

Two Danes went to the western door and searched the corpses for the body of Frithuwulf. All were silent as the young aetheling was brought through the hall and carried out to the line of Frisians. It was a shattered ruin of a man. His face was plastered with mud and the ghastly wound inflicted by Hengest's sword gaped at them all. Hengest stared at the ground uneasily as Frithuwulf was placed at the feet of his father. Finn looked down with controlled emotion, but a hand went up to his mouth. Tears fell from his steely eyes as he struggled to maintain his authority.

There came a screaming from the back of the Frisian host and Hildeburh pushed her way through to the front. Finn's thegns moved aside to make way for their queen and she flung herself upon her son's corpse, wailing and cursing all present for the hideous crime. Her pale nightdress fluttered in the cold air of morning as she kissed the blood-streaked face of her boy. All stood in respectful silence as a mother grieved for her fallen son.

Hengest could not look at her. He turned his face to the coast. A chill wind blew in on the dawn. It brought promises of a very long and cold winter.

There was much discussion in the following days as to whether the funerals of Jutes and Danes would be held separately or together. Naturally, some of the Danes were repelled by the idea that their fallen comrades would be cremated alongside their murderers and cried for separate funeral rites. But most agreed that enough hostility had passed and, since the leaders of both factions were dead, the enmity between the two peoples should be ended once and for all.

Construction began on three enormous pyres on the outskirts of Finnesburg and the maimed and hacked bodies of the slain were cleaned and tended to by Finn's theows. A gealdricge was brought in from one of the nearby settlements to preside over the funeral rites.

She was dressed entirely in black and many ornaments of bone, feathers and twisted animal parts hung from her cloak. The priests of Finnesburg treated her with a guarded respect. These 'yell-women' played an important part in funerals. Their wailing laments accompanied the fallen to Waelheall in the arms of the Waelcyrie – Woden's shield maidens.

A young slave girl was chosen to accompany the dead on their journey. It was the custom to sacrifice somebody at costly funerals in order to relay messages from the living to their deceased friends. The young girl was kept in a chamber within Finn's hall whilst the other matters pertaining to the funeral were seen to. She was plied with mead and strong ale day and night. Several of the Danes visited her in her confinement to give her messages they wished her to pass on to friends beyond the veil of death; although Hengest wondered if the drunken girl would remember any of the words they spoke to her at all, so intoxicated she was.

The funeral was a magnificent affair. The bodies of the slain were placed upon the pyres along with many gifts from their living comrades. Gold was heaped up on the wood along with rings, armbands, belt buckles, knives, religious talismans and items of clothing that the dead might require once they passed from this world. Three of Finn's magnificent black stallions were ritually sacrificed and their meat was cut up and thrown steaming onto the pyres as food for the dead on their journey to Waelheall where Woden and his groaning boards of meat and drink awaited them.

Queen Hildeburh had not been seen since the day she had cradled her son's corpse in front of them all. She kept herself confined to her bedchamber in mourning. Her handmaidens brought her food and drink, and she would see no one.

Upon the day of the funeral she finally showed herself. She had dressed herself in her finest clothes and showed not a bit of the crushed anguish they had all seen the night of the massacre. In fact, she had summoned a steely resolve of staggering proportions. She was their queen and she would make sure that everybody knew it. She had mourned her son and now she was ready to see him depart Middangeard with honour.

At her insistence Frithuwulf's body was placed next to Hnaef's. There were some mutterings at this as bad feelings were still held by many towards Finn's son for betraying his own uncle, but others agreed that, at least in death if not in life, uncle and nephew would be united once more.

The entire settlement turned out and assembled on the outskirts where they could get a good view of the pyres. The slave girl was carried out of Finn's hall by two thegns and placed atop one of the pyres. She was so intoxicated that she barely seemed to register where she was and her head lolled about drunkenly on her slim shoulders.

The old gealdricge clambered up next to her and muttered a few incantations beneath her breath whilst placing her palm on the young girl's forehead, preparing her soul for its journey. Then, swiftly, the old woman drew a short bone-handled knife and slashed the girl's throat with one quick jerk. The blood flowed out so quickly to darken the white garment she wore, that her already weak strength was further dampened and she did not even cry out. The seeress clambered back down from the platform and the pyres were lit.

Black smoke coiled up into the sky and the stench of burning flesh grew strong, blown about by the cold wind. The gealdricge began to sing in an archaic dialect, her voice carrying over the sound of burning wood and crackling body fat. Hengest was surprised that such a frail looking woman could have such a powerful voice as the words drifted and mingled with the smoke; prayers to help the slain on their way.

It took nearly two days for the fires to die down. Nothing was left of the corpses and offerings. Meat had roasted to ash, bones had crumbled and gold had melted. Woden's shield maidens had snatched all away during the inferno, leaving only ash and blackened cinders. A mound was reared nearby and the ashes were interred in ceremonial urns within. A wooden pole was raised atop the mound carven with runes that related the dreadful events that had taken place. It would serve as a reminder for generations to come of the folly of men and the untended hatred that leads to such bloodshed.

Several days of drinking followed in honour of the dead. This ritual was usually a joyous affair; a celebration of those whose wyrd had been fulfilled, but these celebrations were marked by the tragic futility of the events that had caused the deaths of so many good men. There was no dancing and precious little singing. The Danes sat on one side of the hall and the Frisians on the other. Without Hnaef to bring the two peoples together, there seemed to be little point in being friendly to one another.

Finn and Hildeburh sat on their thrones at the head of the hall in silence. Hengest watched Hildeburh closely. Her face was rigid and devoid of emotion. He marvelled at her strength. If it had been one his own children who had been killed – little Aesc, or Hronwena – he knew that his own emotions would have known no bounds.

Aesc.
Hronwena.
Halfritha.
Horsa.

Would he ever see any of them again? He had bought the freedom of his men at the expense of his own. It had been the only choice, and yet he hated himself for it. It was as if he had been sacrificed along with the three stallions and the slave girl, burning on the funeral pyre of others so that they might fulfil their own destinies.

But what of his own?

He prayed to the gods for wisdom that night, and many nights after, as winter gripped Frisia in its vengeful fist.

PART IV

(Hægl) "Hægl byþ hwitust corna;
hwyrft hit of heofones lyfte,
wealcaþ hit windes scura;
weorþeþ hit to wætere syððan."

(Hail) "Hail is the whitest of grain;
it is whirled from the vault of heaven
and is tossed about by gusts of wind
and then it melts into water."

Halfritha

Winter's icy reign was passing. Jute-land, weary with frost and heavy with snow, was picking itself up and stamping its feet to shake off the cold. Some of the trees prematurely showed green buds and the weather was gently softening. But every so often, a day would come so harsh and fierce that it would knock spring back a bit, and remind the land that winter was not quite ready yet to relinquish its grasp.

Today was such a day.

The hailstorm showed no signs of abating. The small white stones drummed down on the thatched roofs of Brand's farm, rattling on frozen puddles and skittering across the wooden timbers of the buildings. Cows lowed inside the houses and smoke drifted from the homes of the theows. All were indoors, tending their hearths.

Halfritha gazed across the flames at the two men who sat opposite her. She was speechless. Words seemed to catch in her throat. What they were saying to her was inconceivable. The elder of the two – Guthlaf, he had said his name was – had a short white beard and a kindly face. The other – Ordlaf, who was considerably younger – sat in silence watching her reaction. Brand, her husband's trusted thegn, sat nearby whilst his wife prepared their evening meal.

"Had there been any time to prevent Hengest from swearing the oath to Finn, we would have seized it," said Guthlaf. "But he spoke without consulting us. There was no other way he could ensure the safety of the Danes. Finn demanded it. Your husband was a great hero."

Halfritha nodded, noting the old man's use of the past tense when referring to her husband. They had both come all the way from Frisia to tell her this, sent by Hengest as messengers in his stead. Crossing the northern sea in winter was dangerous and their faces showed the strain of their voyage. Their beards were frosted with salt and their eyes wore dark circles showing that they had not slept much during the trip.

She looked down at the bag of gold and silver the two warriors had brought her. It was enough for her and the children to live comfortably for the remainder of their years, but the very sight of it tore her heart out of her breast. Hengest's intention was clear; he was not returning.

Their days together had been happy following their marriage. Their two children had grown up healthy and strong and Hengest's respect and influence had grown amongst the nobility. People often brought their problems to him instead of to his father and he had developed a reputation as a fair and just lawgiver and a man of his word. His father did not begrudge him this and showed pride in his son's reputation. There had even been talk of Hengest succeeding Wictgils before the old man passed from Middangeard to his seat in Waelheall.

But then Hengest had sworn that damnable vow to Hnaef of the West Danes and banishment had followed. They had been forced to give up the farm – *her* farm and childhood home – but that was not what had pained Halfritha the most. They had lost all of their friends, never to see them again. They had uprooted Hronwena and Aesc; but even that was tolerable. No, what truly worried her was the thought of losing her husband in battle, for this Hnaef was a dangerous man

172

by all accounts and not well-liked throughout the northern world. Any number of things could happen to Hengest whilst he was away proving his allegiance to this warlord. And if he should be killed, then she and the children would be left to fend for themselves, in a strange part of the land that was unfamiliar to them.

How she had worried about him in the weeks he had been away! How she had hated this Hnaef, a man she had never met! But, she had respected her husband's decision, for she loved him and wanted to be a dutiful wife. Now these men told her that Hnaef was dead and Hengest was sworn to another lord. A lord that would keep him in Frisia; keep him from his family. How pointless it had all been! Halfritha nearly wept, but she remained strong in the face of her guests.

"Did my husband have any instructions for me?" she asked, a little hopeful. Surely Hengest did not mean for her and the children to simply forget about him and move on with their lives?

Guthlaf shook his head. "He will be in Frisia for the foreseeable future. He expressed his hope that his loyal friend, Brand, would continue to safeguard his family."

"He need not worry on that count," said Brand from across the hearth, his massive forearms resting on his knees. "Halfritha and the children are as my own family to me."

Brand was a large, kindly man who did not look like much of a warrior, but Halfritha knew from her husband's stories that he was formidable in battle. He had accepted her and her children without hesitation when Hengest had brought them to him, providing for them and sheltering them during the months Hengest had been away and for that Halfritha would be eternally grateful.

The door that connected the barn to the house banged open and Hronwena and Aesc ran in laughing, joined by two enormous hounds that bounded and capered about in excitement. They had been playing in with the cows as they often did now that winter had confined them indoors. Hronwena was nearly a woman and looked every bit her mother's daughter. Her hair was golden and her face showed a maturity that made her seem older than her years. Aesc on the other hand was a playful scamp, barely nine and extremely energetic. Winter did not agree with him and he hated being cooped up indoors.

Their laughter stopped abruptly as they saw the guests and their mother beckoned them over to her. They knelt down on either side of her and she hugged them close.

"What's wrong Mother?" asked Hronwena. "Is it Father?"

Halfritha could have smiled. Her daughter had such a keen wit and rarely let anything slip past her. "He's fine but he is still in Frisia," she told her.

"Is that far away?" asked Aesc, thrusting his head underneath the loop of her arm.

"Yes, it is," Halfritha replied.

"Won't he be coming home in the spring?" Hronwena asked.

Halfritha's heart ached for her children. "No, dear. He serves a new lord now but he wants you both to know that he loves you very much."

"A new lord?" complained Aesc. "I thought he went to serve King Hnaef after grandfather banished him."

"King Hnaef is dead. Your father serves King Finn of the Frisians now."

"Who?"

"When *will* he come home then?" Hronwena asked.

Halfritha looked at Guthlaf. "Will you be going back to Frisia now?"

Guthlaf nodded. "We shall leave in the morning if you would be so kind as to offer us hospitality for the night."

"You can stay as long as you like," said Brand. "For surely, you will not be attempting the journey back to Frisia until winter has fully passed?"

"We are honour-bound to our lord Hengest," said Guthlaf. "If he is to remain at the hall of King Finn, then so shall we. We owe him that much."

"Is there a message we can take back to him from you?" Ordlaf asked Halfritha.

Halfritha thought for a moment. There was so much she wanted to say to Hengest, but she could think of nothing to tell these men she had only just met. She must send them back with something. She hated to see them leave, knowing that they may be her last and only chance to contact her husband. If only there was something she could do, or somebody she could ask for help. But there was nobody. Only Brand, who commanded no men other than a few theows. But then a thought struck her.

Horsa.

She had only met her brother-in-law once and her memory of the charming but cheeky youth who had approached her at the ealdorman's feast twelve years ago did not inspire great confidence. But Hengest often talked fondly of him and loved him dearly. He had told her about the oath Horsa had sworn to him and about his taking up with a band of raiders.

Could he help?

Surely if he took his oath seriously at all, then now was the time for him to fulfil it, for Hengest was sorely in need of assistance now. But she had no way of contacting him, and she did not know what position he was in with the raiders, or how many men he commanded. But maybe these two seafarers could get word to him, wherever he was. It was worth a try.

"Hengest has a brother," she said.

"Yes, he mentioned him," said Ordlaf. "Horsa, I believe."

"He is in with a band of raiders. Angles. If you could get word to him …"

"And if we did?" interjected Guthlaf. "Finnesburg is too well fortified for a bunch of raiders to achieve much if rescue is what you're thinking of."

"Horsa has sworn an oath to Hengest that he will come when he is in dire need," insisted Halfritha. "I don't know what he could do but he must surely think of something. Will you notify him for me?"

The two thegns shifted uneasily. The sea lanes were rough enough as it was and the journey back to Frisia was paramount in their minds. Seeing their hesitation, Halfritha said; "My husband's freedom and his life hang in the balance. Would you please do it for your lord if not for me?"

Guthlaf and Ordlaf glanced at each other. Then Ordlaf said, "We will try, lady. Hengest gave his freedom for ours and we owe him our lives. In the morning, we will set out for the Angle lands and see if we can find Horsa. Though there are no guarantees of our success. The raiders are a violent, honourless lot.

Finding your husband's brother will not be an easy task."

"I would be most grateful if you would try," said Halfritha.

They ate their meal together before Halfritha and the children retired to their own quarters, screened off from the rest of the hall. The two thegns slept by the hearth and left early the next morning after breakfast. The wind and tide carried them back out to sea taking Halfritha's last remaining hope for her husband with them.

Horsa

Beorn's farm was a small holding with only a few families living together in a collection of thatched huts surrounded by pastures. A slim bay fronted the settlement where fishing boats lay on the sand, covered in hides for the winter. Children wrapped up in warm furs ran in between the buildings, and several mangy grey dogs barked and capered about them.

Horsa looked out from the doorway to where Beorn was chopping wood. The loud cracks of his axe splitting the wood rang out above the squealing of the children and the clucking of the chickens in the nearby coop.

Horsa hated winter. It always reminded him of the long cold seasons he spent in his father's hall, utterly bored and eagerly awaiting spring so that he might be out and about again. This winter had been worse than the others. The *Bloodkeel* called to him from beneath its greased coverings like a ghost on the tide. He was its captain now and winter had grounded them before he had a chance to flex his new authority.

There was much to prepare come spring. He had to find several crewmembers to replace those they had lost over the summer. The *Bloodkeel* would probably need re-caulking and several strakes were damaged, needing to be replaced before he could think of putting out to sea.

Roll on spring.

He froze as he spotted the strangers walking towards the settlement. They appeared to be armed, but there were only two of them. Several other men from the settlement had seen them also; they were retrieving weapons and walking out to meet them.

Horsa caught Beorn's attention and nodded in the direction of the strangers. The big man turned to look at them, his axe resting on his massive shoulder. Horsa ran indoors to fetch *Hildeleoma* and jogged over to join the other men who stood expectantly at the edge of the settlement.

"What is your business here?" asked Beorn of the strangers, his voice edged with warning.

"Is there a man amongst you who answers to the name of Horsa, son of Wictgils?" asked one of them, a tall man with long, grey hair spilling down from the rim of his helm.

"What if there is? And who are you to ask?"

"I am Guthlaf, son of Hunlaf," the man said. "I am a thegn to Hengest of Jute-land."

"What news have you of my brother?" Horsa broke out, stepping forward.

The grey-haired man looked him up and down as a farmer might assess the usefulness of a farmhand before hiring him. He removed his helmet and bowed his head slightly as if in cautious respect. For a moment Horsa was reminded of the days when everybody had paid him the same kind of respect. He rarely came into contact with nobility these days and by the cut of the man before him, he now had no doubts that he was acquainted with his brother.

"My lord Hengest is a prisoner of Finn of Frisia," Guthlaf said.

"A prisoner?" asked Horsa. "Is he harmed?"

"No, but he was forced into an oath that binds him to King Finn. His wife sent us to fetch you; said something about you owing him a favour."

Horsa could have laughed if the situation had not been so serious. The Wyrd Sisters had a funny sense of timing. Sometimes they chose the worst possible time to throw a fork in the path of a man and at others, they could choose the perfect time. On this occasion, their timing was impeccable.

They went indoors and sat down by the fire, whilst Beorn ordered his theows to bring mead and food for the guests. Guthlaf related the tale of the fight at Finnesburg and how Hengest had assumed command of the Danes on the death of Hnaef. Horsa listened intently without interruption until the Dane was done.

"How many of the Danes remained with my brother at Finnesburg?" he asked.

"Not many," admitted Guthlaf. "Only Hengest was required to pledge the oath so that his men could go free. Most returned to Dane-land but a few stayed with him out of thanks and loyalty to him for arranging their pardons."

"What are you planning?" Beorn asked Horsa.

"I think it is time we prepared the *Bloodkeel* for her first voyage of the year," Horsa replied.

"This early? But the sea lanes are too rough! I know that you are restless here, Horsa, but …"

"These men braved the sea to bring me news of my brother," Horsa replied. "And Thunor kept them safe. And the Ese are surely on our side after our sacrifice to them."

Beorn stared into the fire. The massacre of the Hrolfingas had not been mentioned by any of them all winter. Horsa was haunted by the screams of the dying and knew he was not alone in that. But what was done was done and the gods had been honoured.

"Besides," Horsa continued, "I need to fit her out with a new crew and make the necessary repairs first. That will take time."

"Then you are the captain of your crew?" asked Ordlaf. "We were led to believe that you were the first mate."

"There have been some changes," Horsa replied with a smile. "Beorn, can you get word to Aelfhere and the others, and have them ready to sail in a week? I shall oversee the repairs if you can lend me some theows to do the work."

"Of course," said Beorn. "The theows are yours and most of the crew are likely to be drinking away their fortunes in some tavern in Reddasporth, but I'll drag them out by their heels if I have to."

"As soon as she is sea-worthy, we shall row down to Reddasporth and recruit new oarsmen. And then, westwards! I'll have that Frisian bastard at my knees for keeping my brother a prisoner!"

Beorn and the others watched Horsa as he paced back and forth, making plans in his head. He was excited at the prospect of new adventures and bloodshed further west. The time had come for brothers to be reunited. Once again he would stand by Hengest's side.

But caution was required. The two Danes had been in Thunor's favour on their journey here. Perhaps it would be the same with them. He made a mental note to sacrifice an extra plump chicken to the thunder-god before they set out for Reddasporth.

Hengest

Winter had been an ordeal for Hengest and a great test of his pride. He and the few Danes who had remained with him had not been mistreated. On the contrary, Finn had remained an impeccable host and none of the Frisians had shown them the slightest discourtesy. But his oath to Finn burned like a brand pressed deep into his flesh. It remained unspoken, but Hengest could see the derision in the eyes of the Frisians and he could feel their antipathy, like vipers who would not strike simply because they did not have to.

The hall where the fight had taken place had been scrubbed clean, and new doors had been hastily built to replace the shattered remnants of the former ones, before the building was placed once again at the disposal of the Danes. Hengest made a point of posting two guards – one at each doorway – every night. Not that he feared a reprisal from the Frisians, it was more for peace of mind for he and his men felt the ghosts of the slain in the timbers of that hall, reminding them of the treachery that had taken the lives of their comrades and their king.

Hengest and his small group of followers spent most of their days within their hall, huddled around the hearth, talking and sleeping whilst the snow whirled about outside. Each evening they were summoned across the bridge to Finn's hall where they ate their evening meal, sitting well apart from the Frisians. None openly blamed the Danes for the death of Frithuwulf, but the Geola celebrations had been soured irrevocably by the young aetheling's death.

As the days passed, the Danes greatly looked forward to the first signs of spring which would herald an end to the long, hard winter that had taken the life of their lord. What they would do when the sea lanes calmed, Hengest did not know. He supposed that their loyalty to him would wane as fresh buds appeared on the trees and thoughts of homes and families would begin to stir in their minds. He could not blame them if they departed; after all, they were free to go, whilst he must remain in their stead.

As the weather warmed he began spending a lot of time down by the coast, scanning the grey waters for the sign of the boat carrying Ordlaf and Guthlaf back from Jute-land. He kept his thoughts of Halfritha and the children close like a talisman as he bided his time. He had barely known Guthlaf and Ordlaf six months yet they had agreed to go on this mission for him and to return, even though the journey was treacherous. Such loyalty could not be bought and every day Hengest prayed to Woden and Thunor to safeguard the two men he had sent to Jute-land; hoping that they had not been sunk by a storm or attacked by raiders, or had simply betrayed his trust and taken the money he had meant for his family and gone off to enjoy their freedom.

The other thing that caused worry in his life was Hildeburh. The Frisian queen was colder than ever in the wake of her son's funeral. And there were rumours doing the rounds of the town that it had been Hengest who had dealt Frithuwulf his mortal blow. Hengest did not know if these rumours had reached the Queen's ears. Before the disaster that had befallen Finnesburg, Hengest had felt that he and Hildeburh had enjoyed a small trust; two pawns in this game of kings. But all that had been swept away by the violence that had followed. They had not spoken since the battle and she spent all of her time in her chambers, tending to her sole surviving son.

Each night Frithuwulf's face visited Hengest in his dreams; that frozen mask of terror and pain as his blade cut through mail and bit into his flesh. Hengest could hear his screams as he went down beneath the trampling feet of the Danes, his body smashed and trodden into the mud.

At last, one windy morning, word spread throughout the settlement that a boat had been sighted and the people marvelled at the courage of those who had dared an expedition so early in the year. When it was rumoured that it was captained by two Danes returning to Finnesburg, Hengest ran all the way to Finn's hall where he found Guthlaf and Ordlaf at a meal of stew by the hearth.

"Thunor himself would be impressed by the courage of you two!" he said, embracing his two thegns tightly and pounding them on their backs. "And I thank you from the bottom of my heart. My family, are they …"

"They are well," replied Guthlaf. "They were grateful for the silver and your wife was bitterly sorry to hear of your predicament. But we have some other news for you." He looked around to make sure that no Frisians were eavesdropping. The hall was nearly empty and the few of Finn's men that were present were engaged in a high stakes dice game in the corner and paying no attention to the Danes and their Jutish lord. "Your wife wishes you to return to her."

Hengest looked at him with bitter reproach. "I cannot leave, Guthlaf. I gave my word to Finn."

"Under the circumstances, that word can be broken with your honour held intact. You sacrificed your own freedom so that your men could go free. Woden will recognise this."

Hengest was unsure. Oath breaking was one of the highest crimes a man could commit in the eyes of the gods. The misty lands of the dead were full of men who had gone back on their word, forced to wander endlessly, forever denied the warmth and splendour of Waelheall.

Ordlaf took another cautious look around. A cheer went up from the dice game as fortune favoured one of the players. "Your brother is here," he whispered.

Hengest's eyes lit up. "Horsa? Here? But how?"

"After visiting your family, we went in search of him. It was the lady Halfritha's idea. She could not bear to hear of you left in the company of these Frisian bastards. Your brother commands a ship of raiders and waits behind the headland for your signal."

"My brother!" exclaimed Hengest, barely stifling a whoop of joy. "And he commands a ship, you say? But what would he have me do? There are too many of us here to sneak away undetected and too few of us to fight our way out."

"Perhaps a combined assault then," Guthlaf said. We could organise a diversion within Finnesburg while your brother leads the attack from without."

Hengest considered this. Admittedly, it was a pleasing prospect to wet his blade in Frisian blood before fleeing Finnesburg for good.

"Your brother also sent you a gift," said Guthlaf. He produced a long object wrapped in otter furs and handed it to Hengest.

It was heavy and hard. Hengest unwrapped it and gasped at what glinted within. A golden hilt and shimmering blade twinkled at him. As he read the runes, he felt as if his ancestors were calling to him, calling on him to act and save his honour. "Woden's eye …" he whispered. "*Hildeleoma*; the lost sword of the Jutes!" He quickly wrapped up the legendary sword, looking around to make sure nobody had seen it. "How on earth did my brother come by this?"

"He said something about raiding a troll's nest," replied Guthlaf. "We didn't ask further."

"Ha!" laughed Hengest. "Raided a troll's nest! Either that is a tall tale or my little brother has got bigger balls than I ever gave him credit for! But I'll get the truth from him once we are reunited." Passion surged within him; a passion and a lust for life that had been dampened by the cold winter. The shimmer of gold from the ancient sword and the news of his brother – whom he had not seen in twelve years – had rekindled a flame within his soul that was determined to burn free, oath or no. "Return to my brother," he told his Danes. "Tell him that we act tonight and to have his men ready for my signal."

"Will you order them to storm the town?"

"No, that would be useless. The palisade is too well guarded. However, if we get rid of a few guards from the inside, then Horsa and his raiders have a chance of slipping in undetected. I shall have our men on the move when the moon is at its highest. You both remain with Horsa and stay hidden until I give the word."

"We'll be off then, my lord," said Ordlaf. "Best of luck."

"And to you, my loyal thegns." He watched the two Danes depart the hall leaving him holding the hard shape of *Hildeleoma* in its fur coverings. He gripped it tightly. It was a bold plan and could fail in many ways, but he was determined now to finally rid himself of the wretched oath and sink the sword of the Jutes into the body of Finn whilst Finnesburg burned around them.

That night darkness fell quickly, bringing with it portents of doom. The king and his wife lay in their bed. Their thegns slumbered in their hall, the waters of the river silently slipping by beneath the crust of ice that had formed around the island. The settlement was silent. Ceorls and their families slept in their homes and theows in their hovels warmed by the dying embers of the forges and ovens.

Atop the palisade a ring of torches flickered, each one indicating a guard at his post. Their faces were turned outwards at the black and silent land surrounding the settlement and none of them saw the group of Danes that crept between the huts behind the wall, shadows within shadows.

No torchlight lit their way, only the occasional pinprick of light reflected from a blade would have given them away, had any of the Frisians cast their eyes inwards upon the town they were defending.

Below the wall a barracks had been constructed for the guards who were not on duty to eat and sleep. No sound came from within and the Danes halted just outside its large doorway. Hengest gave a silent order to two of his men and they ran forward carrying a thick length of rope between them. This they fastened around the iron handles of the oak doors, sealing the slumbering thegns within their barracks. This task complete, the Danes moved to the wall and began to scale the ladders to the top of the palisade.

One by one, the guards who stood by their torches felt the cold fury of the Danes. Using only saexes, the thegns of Hengest spilt Frisian blood by opening throats, slashing jugulars and driving deep into kidneys and other vitals. Bodies were hurled from the palisade to shatter on the frozen ground below. The killers did their silent work well and no alarm was raised. All along the wall torches were extinguished, plunging Finnesburg into blackness.

All torches except one.

Hengest took the single blazing brand from his thegn and ordered two of his men below to open the gate. He waved the torch to and fro, its roaring filling his ears, its light a beacon for those who lay in wait somewhere out there in the darkness.

Horsa

"That's it!" said Horsa. "That's the signal!"

He, the two Danes and the crew of the *Bloodkeel* had been waiting in a wooded area not far from the paved trackway that led into Finnesburg. It had been a long, cold wait, half buried in the snow. Their stiff limbs screaming, they rose as one and quietly left the thicket, spears and swords held in numb hands. The gate stood open to them and the shadowy figures of Hengest and his Danes stood above it, their faces illuminated by the light of the single torch.

They swept through the streets of the doomed settlement and the Danes came down from the palisade to join them. Horsa flung himself at Hengest and the two brothers embraced, separated for so long, brought together at last by an oath and a brother's loyalty. They stood apart and looked at each other, each taking in the changes time had wrought on their brother.

Hengest was little different in Horsa's eyes; still the tall, lanky man with the noble bearing who had so often berated him in his youth. His eyes were a little more lined perhaps, his face a little gaunt. But Horsa knew that he was the one who had changed the most. When Hengest had last seen him, he had been a scrawny thing, a full head shorter with arms as thin as reeds. Now he was a stout, strong man nearly equal in height to his brother and bulkier by far. His arms were muscular and his hands were callous from years of rowing. The scars that marked his body hinted at the violent life he led.

"By the gods, it's good to see you, little brother," said Hengest, slapping Horsa's arms.

"I told you that nothing could stop me from fulfilling my oath to you," Horsa replied. "Not a king or a demon or a god."

"And thank you for the gift." Hengest lifted *Hildeleoma* in gratitude.

"It fits your hand better than it does mine," replied Horsa. "I prefer my weapons simpler with less fancy ornamentation."

"I want to hear all about how you got it, but first, let us deal with my Frisian problem."

Already the Danes and the raiders were seeking out Frisian thegns where they slumbered and were butchering them with unrestrained violence. Blood ran in rivulets on the ground, thawing the frozen mud with its dying warmth. Few Frisians had even the chance to awaken properly, much less put up any resistance before a sword or an axe plunged into their flesh. Screams were taken up by the women who had awoken to find strange enemies ransacking their homes and butchering their husbands. Some tried to fight back and were cut down where they stood. Soon buildings began to burn. Flames from flung torches ate into thatch and wood, sending up embers and thick smoke as Finnesburg was consumed by fire and slaughter.

The guards in the barracks had been awoken by the screaming of the people they were sworn to protect and were now hammering on the doors, the rope straining to contain them. A sword was wedged in through the crack and sliced downwards, cutting the rope in two.

"At our backs!" cried Hengest. "Shield wall!"

Several Danes ran to form a hasty barrier in front of him to meet the oncoming Frisians. The two sides slammed together and the sound of battle filled the streets.

Elsewhere, Horsa and Beorn fought off another group of Frisians who had emerged from the un-ransacked buildings. Beorn swung his massive axe around in a welter of blood and innards, yelling his war cry whilst Horsa ducked in and out, cutting open bellies and stabbing groins with his sword.

Something twanged in Horsa's mind; some little ripple of warning, and he spun around, just in time to raise his shield against the sword blow of a man who had made his way around Hengest's shield wall. The blow glanced off the iron boss but shattered the wood and knocked him to the mud. He tried to bring his sword up to defend himself but could see that it would be too late, for his attacker was already swinging his sword down in a chop that would split his head.

There was a flurry of black feathers.

The sword stroke did not fall.

The attacker screamed and stumbled backwards, clutching at something attached to his face. It was a large, black raven. Its sharp talons clawed at the man's face and its polished ebony beak pecked at his eyes, making his face run with blood.

And then, it was gone, winging its way high up into the sky upon sails of midnight, vanishing almost as quickly as it had appeared.

Horsa was on his feet in a second, charging at the stricken man who still pawed at his bleeding face. He drove his sword deep into the man's side and twisted it before wrenching it out and hurling the man from him. He looked up into the grey sky but could see no sign of his mysterious winged helper.

Once the Frisian guards were defeated, Hengest led a small group of his men towards the bridge, *Hildeleoma* gripped tightly in his hand, red to the hilt.

King Finn had been alerted to the attack and had ordered the bridges to his island burned. The outline of the timbers were visible in the roaring inferno that crackled and blazed on both sides of the island.

"He must be planning to hide in his hall and hope we go away," said Horsa, rejoining Hengest on the riverbank. "Does he have many thegns left on the island?"

"Can't have," replied Hengest. "Otherwise he wouldn't be so desperate as to burn his bridges."

"We could starve him out," said Horsa. He ducked suddenly as an arrow whistled overhead, shot by somebody on the opposite bank. A small group of Frisians stood there in war gear, sending projectiles across at the attackers.

"There's no honour in a slow victory," Hengest said. He watched the embers sent up by the blazing bridge fall in the cold air and settle on the ice. "There is one bridge still open to us. Guthlaf! Get down to the river and check where the ice is thickest!"

Guthlaf followed the river around, tapping at the ice with the tip of his sword. Confident that the ice would hold their weight, the attackers began crossing it in small groups of two or three, shields upraised to deflect the missiles sent by the Frisians on the other side. The frozen armour of the river groaned and cracked as they trod its surface, but it held fast.

As soon as the attackers set foot on the island, sword blows rang out across the frozen water and the rest of Hengest and Horsa's men hurried across to reinforce their comrades. The Frisians on the far bank were soon overwhelmed and were cut to pieces on the shore.

Finn and the rest of his retainers had barricaded themselves within their hall. The attackers tore down one of the pillars supporting the overhanging roof and began to use it as a battering ram. A great cheer went up with each slam of the pillar against the door. Sword hilts and spear butts drummed on shields rhythmically with each stroke. The sound of cracking and splintering oak could be heard. Eventually the door fell in on itself and Hengest and Horsa led the attack into the hall.

The scene inside was pitiful. Only three or four thegns still guarded their king. The rest of the inhabitants were terrified women and a few children who had sought refuge in the last safe place in Finnesburg. Finn himself stood defiantly at the head of the hall, his sword in his hand, ready to fight to the death against those who had destroyed his settlement.

"Why did you betray me, Hengest?" he cried. "I gave your people their freedom. All I asked of you was to stay as a surety against any further violence! And now you turn on me like some rabid dog?"

"You gave my people their freedom?" roared Hengest. "Who are you to grant such things? My people committed no crime. They were attacked by your friends and their king was murdered by your own brother in law! And you think we owe you recompense because we fought back? We owe you nothing! *I* owe you nothing!" He advanced, *Hildeleoma* dripping in his grasp.

Finn's thegns rushed forward but encountered Horsa and his men who cut them down and sent their blood spurting across the stone flags.

Hengest swung at Finn and the Frisian held up his blade in defence. The sword the Jutes shattered Finn's blade into several pieces which skittered across the floor, just as the staff of Woden had shattered Sigemund's sword during the great hero's last battle. The doom of that great warrior, whose tale was told in the tapestry upon the wall of that very hall, was the last thing Finn thought of before Hengest struck off his head.

The victorious attackers began ransacking the chambers of the hall, looting whatever gold and silver they could find. The screams of the terrified women and the wailing of their children filled the place. From one of the rear chambers a noble woman was brought forth, her pale arms held tightly between two Danes. Her face remained impassive, but her eyes watched Hengest with a hatred that made Horsa feel cold. Who was this woman?

"What shall we do with the Frisian queen?" asked one of the Danes. "Put her to the sword?"

"No," Hengest replied. "Her and her son are not to be harmed. Take her back to her chamber and guard her well. A boat shall leave for Dane-land in the morning. She is to be taken back to her people."

Hildeburh looked like she was about to say something but instead she spat viciously into Hengest's face. The Danes roughly dragged her away. Hengest watched her leave before wiping the spittle from his face.

"You're too soft with women," said Horsa. "I would have knocked the teeth out of the bitch for that."

Hengest continued to stare at the doorway through which Hildeburh had been dragged. "If I had she wouldn't have cared," he said. "Her heart is shattered. There is nothing I, nor any man, can do that will harm her now."

As the sun rose over Finnesburg, the settlement was eerily silent. Much feasting and looting had gone on the night before and the drunken victors slept off their stupors within its smoking ruins. Many of the former residents of the town had fled during the night taking what valuable possessions they could carry to seek new homes. The ones who had stayed – too old, sick or young to flee – now found themselves theows to Danish warriors.

As noon approached, Horsa was awoken by a kick from Hengest. He pushed away the naked limb of the woman next to him and sat up. His mouth felt dry as ash and he searched for the clay flagon of mead by his pallet. It was empty.

"Come down to the wharves with me," said Hengest. "There's something you'll want to see."

Horsa mustered the strength to stand up and follow his brother down to the river where the Danes had commandeered a boat; they were piling as much loot and slaves into its hold as possible.

"I hope your boys left enough loot for my men," said Horsa.

"I set your share aside, Horsa. They won't be disappointed. Anyway, this is your real reward." He pointed to a large vessel tied up at its own mooring.

The ship had been the pride of King Finn's fleet. It was at least twenty metres long with enough oar benches for thirty men. Its smooth strakes curved up high in the prow and stern and were topped with a drake's head in the former and a tail in the latter. But the most flabbergasting thing to Horsa's mind protruded from the centre of its hull.

"It's got a mast!" he exclaimed. He had heard of longships fitted with masts and sails – the Romans were said to have used them extensively – but he had never seen one with his own eyes. The only sail-carrying boats he had seen were river-going vessels and small coastal traders. The idea of a twenty or thirty-man longboat like the *Bloodkeel* carrying a sail was unheard of for its shallow draught would topple it. "It must have a deep keel to support a mast of that height," he said.

"Apparently so," said Hengest. "You know I'm no sailor so it's up to you to figure out the ropes and rudders, so to speak. The Frisians call her the *Raven*."

Horsa's grin faded somewhat. "Brother, I would love nothing more than to captain such a vessel for she is truly a queen among ships. But I have only enough men under me to crew one ship and most of them are newly recruited from Reddasporth. They are not battle-tested. And I should hate to abandon the *Bloodkeel* for she is the first boat I have commanded."

He also hated to leave such a treasure as the *Raven* in Frisia, or give her to the Danes to take back with them, but there was nothing to be done. He couldn't take on another vessel.

A solution to his dilemma presented itself later that afternoon.

"Come back with us," said some of the Danes to Hengest. "You led us well against the Frisians and you could win lands for yourself in Dane-land in the coming wars amongst our people."

Hengest shook his head. "My way lies with my brother. And I tire of foreign kings and their wars. I have a family to return to."

"Well, I have no desire to see my homeland torn apart by war," said Guthlaf. "Let younger men choose a new king, I'll have none of it. I follow you, Hengest.

I've never seen a man, Jute or Dane, with more honour, and I'd follow you to the Mistlands and back."

Ordlaf sighed. "Well, I suppose you can count on me too, Hengest. Guthlaf is right. It will be a rough few years for the West Danes. Either I die fighting for some new king I've never heard of, or I return to my father's forge. I've a desire for neither, so I'll pledge you my sword, if that's alright?"

"You do me great credit, my loyal warriors," said Hengest. "Hnaef was served proudly by such Danes as you two and I bear the greater honour in accepting your oaths."

There were many Danes who shared the sentiments of Guthlaf and Ordlaf so Hengest found himself a leader of a war-host that rivalled his brother's in size.

"Here's your crew for the *Raven*," Hengest said to Horsa, as dusk approached.

"But who'll captain her?" said Horsa. "I'm needed aboard the *Bloodkeel* with such a fresh crew, and you are no sailor as you've already admitted."

"Guthlaf and Ordlaf got me to Frisia," said Hengest. "They can get me out of it. They've many years riding the whale-road between them. I'll be captain in name only and they'll be the ones giving the orders."

"So your heart is set on joining forces with me then?"

"You have the boats, I have the men. We'll be a force to be reckoned with!"

"That we will."

On the third day a fine westerly wind was blowing and Hengest and Horsa accompanied the Danes who would depart down to the wharves.

Hildeburh and her sickly son, Frealaf, were brought down from the hall and placed in the hold with the slaves and treasure. The former queen of Frisia said nothing and bore herself proudly. Her eyes were as coals, not glowing with flame, but black and cold. Her time in this land was at its end. She was being taken home.

The Danes pushed off, their oars splashing in the water, shoving their loaded vessels towards the ring of islands in the distance. Hengest and Horsa watched them from the shore until they were dots on the horizon.

"What now, Brother?" asked Horsa, turning to Hengest. "There is much plunder to be had in other lands. Or are we to return to Jute-land to confront our father and persuade him to rethink your banishment?"

"I'm sure the arrival of our combined warband on his wharves would be enough to convince the old bastard to hand over his title," said Hengest. "But I feel the Wyrd Sisters weaving a grander path for us, Horsa. No, we shall return to Jute-land but only to collect Halfritha and my children. You'll love your niece and nephew and it's time they met their uncle."

"A warband is no place for women and children," said Horsa.

"That's why I want to set about finding a new home for us. All of us."

"As an ealdorman?"

"Perhaps."

"Sounds ambitious. All land is owned by somebody and every ealdorman and king guards his territory jealously. It may be a hard fight."

"The world is changing. We have seen the downfall of one king, and were it not for the fierce reprisal Finn's kin will bring, I would stay here. But the changing world will provide us with an opportunity, I am sure of it."

Horsa smiled. "I'd better see about outfitting my two vessels, then. We'll make a sailor out of you yet, Hengest!"

PART V

*(Sigel) "Sigel semannum symble biþ on hihte,
ðonne hi hine feriaþ ofer fisces beþ,
oþ hi brimhengest bringeþ to lande."*

(Sun) "The sun is ever a joy in the hopes of seafarers,
when they journey away over the fishes' bath,
until the courser of the deep bears them to land."

Halfritha

The weeks had passed slowly for Halfritha since the two Danes had left in search of Horsa. The weather had improved, and that meant the children could play outside, which was something at least. The sounds of their carefree playing, wholly untainted by the worry she felt, brought her some peace.

She helped out around the farm as much as she could in an attempt to keep her mind from dwelling on Hengest, but it was not easy for her. She found her eyes constantly drifting away from her work towards the horizon, scanning the flat fields for any sign of her husband returning to her. She would then chide herself for daring to believe in such a frail hope when all the odds were stacked against it.

It was early one morning when the strangers came, appearing as a black line on the nearby rise. Aesc saw them first and called out to his sister and mother who were washing some clothes beneath the overhang of Brand's hall.

"Get inside the house, both of you!" she snapped to her children.

The line of men were advancing as one, the low sunlight glinting off axe heads and shield rims. These were no peaceful visitors. She called for Brand and the loyal warrior came running out with his spear and several theows in tow, each brandishing a tool or a knife as a weapon.

"Close the gate!" shouted Brand. "Every man take a spear or bow and make for the palisade!"

The gates were drawn shut and braced with timbers. The entire holding was in a flurry as women and children were hurried into the buildings and men, young and old, theow and ceorl, took up weapons and positions along the low wall of wooden stakes that served as the holding's only protection.

"Who do you think they are?" Halfritha asked Brand, her face pale.

"I've no idea," he replied. "But they carry weapons and do not wear their shields on their backs. Get inside, and do not come out until I say so!"

Halfritha nodded and chased Aesc and Hronwena to the doors of the hall where Brand's wife was helping the women and children indoors. As she entered the hall she turned and saw two men at the palisade struck by spears fall backwards. There was a great whooping and yelling as the attackers came upon the little settlement, circling the wall and shouting taunts.

"Come on, Halfritha!" said Brand's wife, drawing the doors closed on the scene. "Brand will fend them off, you'll see!"

Halfritha could sense the terror in her voice, although the good woman tried to mask it with confidence. Brand may be a warrior but there were far too many of the raiders for him and his small group to hold off.

They retreated into the confines of the hall and huddled around the hearth listening to the sounds of slaughter without. Women wept and children bawled in terror.

It was quick work for the attackers and soon the sound of victorious shouts could be heard in the grounds outside the hall. A heavy blow caused the door to shiver, straining against its bolts. All within screamed. Halfritha drew Hronwena and Aesc close to her and marvelled at their courage. Neither of them wept, but she could feel Aesc's tense body beneath her arm.

Another blow.

The door rattled like thunder rolling across the plains. People began to pray, calling upon the gods, for surely death was at hand now. A third blow cracked the bolts and the doors tumbled inwards.

The leader of the raiders was a fearsome looking man. Flame-red hair fell to his shoulders and a square-cut beard framed his ruddy cheeks that glowed as he strode into the hall. His clothes were colourful and of finely spun wool; a sure sign of a wealthy but vain man. Gold armbands and other decorative items ornamented his massive body.

"Your menfolk are dead and that could not be avoided," he said, as he strutted about in front of the terrified women and children. His accent was strong and Danish. "But I would like to spare your lives if I can," he continued. "I am here for only three of you and if those three come forward, the rest of you may live."

All in the hall watched in terrified confusion as this brute swaggered about making his demands. *Only three?* thought Halfritha. This was not how raiders acted.

"Among your number is a woman called Halfritha," said the man. "I wish her and her two children to come forward."

The hall was silent. Halfritha tensed at the mention of her name and clutched Aesc and Hronwena close. Who was this man? And why did he want them?

The leader of the raiders watched his audience in silence and then, in one sudden movement, grabbed a nearby theow by her long, blonde hair and slashed her throat with his saex. There was screaming as the young girl clutched at her wound, the blood pumping between her fingers. Life drained away and she slumped forward to lie still on the floor of the hall.

"Now that was unnecessary," said the raider, wiping the blood from his knife. "But many more of you will die if Halfritha and her children do not come forward."

Not a single person in the hall looked at Halfritha, every one of them staring at the ground, refusing to give her away. She was awed by their resolution and their loyalty but things had gone far enough. Whatever this man had in store for her and her children, she could not sit by and let innocent people be slaughtered on her account. In any case, this man would continue to butcher them one by one until it came to be her turn.

"I am Halfritha," she said, rising on shaky legs.

He looked at her with satisfaction. "And these are your children?" he asked, looking to Aesc and Hronwena.

"They are. What business have you with us?" She tried to keep her voice steady and clear but the terror for her children's safety caused it to crack and waver uncontrollably.

He did not answer her. He turned to his men and said, "Take them outside and bind them."

As men came forward to lay rough hands on Halfritha and her children, Aesc broke away and kicked one of them hard in the groin. Another tried to restrain him but the young boy sunk his teeth deep into the man's hand. It was a noble effort, but was little more than the foolishness of youth, for there were far too many for it to make a difference. All Aesc earned for his efforts was a black eye.

They were dragged outside and bound with a length of salty old rope. The leader followed them out and inhaled deeply, his eyes closed as the morning sun fell on his face. "Finish them off," he said to one of his men. "Leave none alive."

"But we need slaves," said the man.

The leader shook his head. "Leave no witnesses."

"No!" protested Halfritha. "You said you'd let them live!"

Again she was ignored and the sounds of slaughter seeped out from the open doors of the hall; axe blows, screaming and the spatter of warm blood.

Once all was done, the group of men set off amidst laughter and singing, tugging their three prisoners along with them.

They followed the river west towards the coast. Halfritha got no answers from their captors that day. She and the children were treated as little more than cattle as the men marched; dragging them along by the rope which chafed at their wrists cruelly.

Halfritha wanted to weep for the deaths of Brand and his family but she refused herself this indulgence. Aesc and Hronwena did not weep, and she must stay strong for them. She could not let them down by succumbing to hysteria.

No matter how much she thought on it, no reason came to her as to why she and her children had been spared the terrible fate that had been inflicted upon the rest of Brand's household. The men, these Danes, were seafarers – their salt-matted beards, oily breeches and fishy breaths were evidence of that. But what business did a bunch of sea-roving Danes have with her and her children? Was it something to do with her husband; some dispute that led to their being taken hostage? But

Hengest did not know any sea-raiders personally. That was his brother's area. Was it something involving Horsa then? The idea of some rival raiding crew exacting vengeance on members of Horsa's family was not too unreasonable but who knew where to find them? Nothing she could think of made any sense.

The children were coping remarkably well. She wished that Hengest had been there to see their son's defiant but futile fight against their captors: and Hronwena had also made her mother proud by spitting in the eye of one of them as he leered at her in passing.

The journey to the coast used up the rest of the day, and as dusk fell they made camp on the banks of the river they were following. Halfritha's feet were blistered and bloody from having walked all day in her soft fur boots. Her hands ran with blood from where the rope chafed and yet Aesc and Hronwena had not complained once. How proud she was of them!

Some water skins were passed around and Halfritha made sure that the children were fully replenished before taking some for herself. It had been a long and exhausting day for all of them. Dried meat and fish was passed to them and they chewed ravenously. A guard was placed over them while the main body of men ate and rested several paces away. After a time, three of them broke away to come and inspect the prisoners, cruel intent written on their faces.

Halfritha watched as they ran their eyes over Hronwena's slender neck and young body. One of them reached out to touch her golden hair. Aesc leaped up to his sister's defence. The man's comrades were ready for this and one of them seized him and pinned him to the ground. Halfritha scrambled to her feet in protest but another of the men landed upon her and pressed down, grasping one of her breasts with a filthy hand.

Halfritha's eyes were frozen upon Hronwena's who sat immobile as the first man stroked her hair. Her daughter's face was set with the same steely determination Halfritha had seen in Hengest's eyes when he was angry. She could see that her daughter was scared but she could see also that she would not give this man the pleasure of seeing her cower from him. Halfritha struggled against her captor's grasp, not caring about his hands sliding up her bare leg beneath the folds of her dress.

Beyond them, the other men carried on oblivious to what was going on with their prisoners. Laughter and merry talking carried on the wind. Halfritha watched as the man who was fondling her daughter drew his knife and began running it along Hronwena's jaw line, pressing the skin but not breaking it. Down, down, the knife went, tracing the quivering outline of the girl's neck and further, down to her small breasts.

"She's just a child!" Halfritha cried out. "Only twelve winters!" She struggled harder against the man who lay on top of her, but he pressed down, chuckling under his breath – his hot, stinking breath that seeped in through her nostrils.

She willed someone to come, some fight to break out amongst the other men, a distraction, a thunderbolt, a divine intervention; anything to stop what was happening to her daughter.

"Leave the prisoners alone," bellowed a deep voice, and a large shadow fell over them. It was the captain of the raiders, whose name Halfritha had learned was Halga. "Wait until we reach port and then you can have all the whores you can manage, but these ones are not to be touched."

The man rolled off Halfritha and he and his comrade seemed ready to move off. But the one who held a knife to Hronwena stood up in defiance. "We've come all this way and risked our lives for these three," he said. "Why shouldn't we have a little fun with them while we can?"

It was a small act of defiance, a minor insult, but in the world of the sea-rovers it was enough, and Halga was a stern captain. Without a word the big man's fist crashed into his subordinate's jaw, nearly lifting him off his feet. The knife fell from his hand, and he slumped to the ground, his senses knocked out of his head.

"If you want to challenge me, then do so like a man and we'll fight it out in the proper manner," said Halga.

The man at his feet rolled over and spat out a glob of blood within which shone a yellow tooth.

"If not, keep your mouth shut and obey my orders. No man here touches these women, I say."

The captain had spoken and he strode off back to the campfire. The two men helped up their comrade and drifted away, muttering curses, their prey forgotten for the time being.

Halfritha scrambled over to Hronwena and held her tightly as the girl began to weep.

"What ... what was he going to do to me?" Hronwena asked; tears streaming down her face for the first time since the raiders had come.

The poor girl, thought Halfritha as she rocked her distraught daughter. *She doesn't even understand. So young ... so young.* Rage boiled inside her at the men who had come so close to violating her daughter. And yet, of all people, it had been Halga who had prevented it.

But why? What was in store for them once they reached port, wherever that might be? It was all such a mystery but she knew that, for the time being, her day to day existence was tasked with ensuring her children's safety. Halga had protected them tonight but there was no telling how long he would be around to do so, or how far his influence over his men stretched. Supposing his back was turned for just long enough … it did not bear thinking of.

As she clutched her children close, Halfritha swore that she would do anything, whatever it took, to keep them safe from the hands of these brutes. She herself had been in a similar situation before when her uncle had kidnapped her and tried to marry her by force, but by the gods she would not allow her children to be treated with such brutality. Hengest had saved her from that mess but Hengest was not here for them now. She was, and by all the souls in Waelheall, she swore that she would protect them.

They were on the move again at daybreak. The coast was near now and the salty smell of the sea was on the air. Gulls could be heard and the men began to grow more cheerful. They sang songs of the sea and rude little ditties about whores in coastal villages. They were clearly eager to be back in more familiar surroundings. They crested a sand dune and Halfritha saw for the first time the boat that was to take them on to their unknown fate.

It was a huge affair; a forty-manned craft at least, with a great curving dragon's head at its prow. Its bulwarks had been painted black and its vast belly rolled on the surface of the sea like a sleeping whale.

Only half of its crew had ventured inland it seemed, with the remaining twenty or so encamped on the beach below in hide tents. There was a great cheering from the camp as the raiders returned, dragging their prisoners in tow.

They were led to a corner of the camp and pushed to the damp sand while two men were set as guards over them.

"Where are you taking us?" Halfritha asked the nearest guard.

The man spat on the sand and grinned at her. "East," he said. "To the slave markets."

Halfritha felt sick. She had dreaded that this was to be their fate. Sold into lives of slavery; endless toil and hardship in foreign lands, their freedom forever lost to the wind and not a whisper of an explanation for it.

There was drinking that night. Happy to be leaving land behind them upon the morning tide, the raiders fell into celebration. The mead and ale (stolen from some merchant, no doubt) was passed around and freshly killed meat was roasted over the campfires.

Halga could be heard roaring and singing and Halfritha flinched every time one of the men walked close by, thinking that in his drunkenness, Halga had relaxed his rule about the prisoners being off limits. But although many of the men eyed her and Hronwena hungrily, none approached and so Halfritha was encouraged to believe that Halga's authority was still in effect.

But, as the darkness grew deeper, Halga approached them. He swayed and reeled from the drink. He carried a bowl of meat in his hand which he dropped down on the sand. None of them reached for it; Aesc simply stared up at him with hate in his eyes,

Hronwena looked away at some point in the far-off darkness.

"You should eat," he said, slurring his words. "Keep your strength up. We have a long journey ahead of us."

"How long?" asked Halfritha.

He looked at her but did not answer. Then she caught his gaze as it fell on Hronwena and it was the same look she had seen in the eyes of most of the raiders that day and the one before it. It was a look of carnal lust made all the more apparent now he was in his cups. He squatted down next to her and reached out his hand. Hronwena shrank from his touch but did not move away.

Halfritha was gripped by panic. None of Halga's men dared incur his wrath by laying a hand on Hronwena, but what of Halga himself? The man was drunk and clearly aroused by her daughter.

She shuffled close to his other side not letting her face show the pain this caused her for her wrists were still bloodied and blistered from the rope. "You are the captain of this band of men, so I know that your wish is law," she said. "But is a young girl really a suitable prize for a strong sea-captain such as yourself?"

He took his eyes off Hronwena for a brief moment and glanced at her in some confusion. She placed a hand on his stained breeches and leaned close, her breath in his ear. "I would have thought that a man of your stature would be more interested in a woman who knows how to please a man in bed, not an inexperienced girl."

The gods knew he wasn't much to look at, but she had to try and hook him somehow, to distract his attention from Hronwena at all costs. She reached her hand to the crotch of his breeches and cupped him.

Halga looked dumb. He looked into her eyes and ran his dirty, thick fingers through her hair.

She had him!

With some difficulty he staggered to his feet and pulled her up with him. Aesc leaped to his feet and Halga knocked him back down with a boot to his chest. Halfritha flinched at this treatment of her brave son but remained placid in Halga's arms.

"Stay with your sister, Aesc," she told him. "Look after her. I'll be back soon. I promise."

"Mother?" Hronwena asked, her voice filled with alarm.

"It's alright, Hronwena," she told her. "You've both got to be brave, now. I'll come back to you."

"Mother!" cried Hronwena, rising to her feet.

Halfritha tried to say more to her daughter but Halga was already hauling her off in the direction of his tent. Hronwena tried to follow but the guards held her and Aesc in their place. Halfritha nearly wept to hear her daughter's panicked cries. "Be brave, my children!" she called out.

Halga's tent stank of sweat and pork grease. His bed was a pile of matted furs and he slung Halfritha down upon it. He unbuckled his belt and tossed it aside before clambering on top of her, a meaty fist planted on either side of her head.

His breath was sour and Halfritha did her best not to cringe from it but she doubted he would notice as he was preoccupied with nuzzling her breasts and running his calloused hands up her dress.

She tried to think of Hengest, but her memories of his soft touch and gentle ways only served to make the drunken fumbling of this raider all the more awful. He licked at her neck like a wild beast and grabbed great fistfuls of her quivering flesh that made her writhe in pain.

She looked over to where Halga had left his belt beside the furs. His saex lay well within her grasp. How easy it would be for her to pluck it from its scabbard and thrust it deep into this foul beast's neck! She had killed her own uncle when she had been a mere girl and she knew she had the courage and strength to dispatch this drunken letch with ease.

But what then? Halga's wrath was all that kept his men from ravishing Hronwena. With him dead, she doubted any of them would reach the slave markets alive. *Gods, what a choice!* To pick between a brutal death and a life of slavery for her children! But she must hold on. The future was not set. The Wyrd Sisters had not yet woven their fates. She must buy them more time!

She closed her eyes and let her body relax, trying to transport her mind to another time and place. She squeezed them shut with pain and prayed to Frige, wife of Woden, for the strength to survive this.

Hengest

It took several weeks for Hengest and Horsa to make their way back to Jute-land. The cause of much of the delay was Horsa needing time to get to grips with the mast and sail of the *Raven*. He was aware of the general principal but it took a good deal of time to learn how to tack and gybe such a massive vessel. The regular lurching through the swell set Hengest's stomach heaving on the first day out of Frisia that he decided to join Beorn on the *Bloodkeel*, which took a less erratic course.

They stopped off in nearly every port on the way and Horsa had clearly enjoyed showing off to his older brother how well he knew every seedy tavern and muddy trading centre. And while Hengest enjoyed spending time with his brother and seeing some of this world he had never been a part of, he itched to be reunited with his family and grew impatient before Horsa took the hint and pushed on. Finally, they made their way up the narrow river that led from the western coast to Brand's homestead.

The *Bloodkeel* and the *Raven* drifted in on the evening tide through the marshlands, their oars slopping in and out of the water with gentle grace. There was very little snow left now as winter had given way to spring. Renewed energy hummed in the air and the marshes were teeming with life.

The river grew narrower and curved around to the left. It was shallower here and the grinding of the keels on the silt could be felt beneath their feet. They dropped anchor and waded ashore to make camp amongst the reeds. It was not far to Brand's homestead so most of the men were left with the boats whilst Hengest and Horsa set off with a few trusted warriors.

The palisade was visible from a distance and its gate, with its carven protective runes, towered above it. From the gate's crosspiece hung a dark form that twisted and swayed in the breeze. Hengest halted as he spotted it. It resembled a bundle of rags hung up to dry, but as they approached it twisted around and the deathly pale face of a dead man gazed at them, eyes bulging, swollen tongue protruding from black lips pulled taut over a grimace of pain. Hengest's eyes blazed with anguish as he recognised the dead man as Brand. Realisation and horror set in and he let forth a cry, "No!"

The warriors followed him as he ran forward under the creaking figure of death and into the compound of the homestead. It was silent and empty. The forge had been cold for days and no chickens clucked about in the yard; only a few sad-looking feathers drifted about on the wind. Other than the hanged thegn at the gate, there was not a soul in sight.

The door to the hall was not bolted and, as Hengest heaved it open, a vile stench of death rushed out to meet him. The warriors gagged but their leader set his face and stepped in. It was dark. No flames burned in the fire-pit. His foot brushed against something heavy and solid that lay on the floor and he was met with a furious buzzing as a hundred flies hummed angrily at the disturbance.

"Open the doors!" cried Hengest in alarm, "Get some light in here!"

Horsa and the others hurried to open the doors at the other end of the hall and cold daylight illuminated a scene that tore Hengest's heart from his chest. The floor of the hall was littered with bodies. They were all here; ceorls and theows, men, women and children, grotesque and bloated in their decay. Flies swarmed and crawled in and out of their mouths and nostrils. Glazed, dead eyes stared at nothing.

Brand's wife and three children lay heaped in one corner; a mother's arms around her children, shielding them from harm even in death. Hengest stepped between the corpses, his eyes sweeping the floor, searching for his own wife and children, dreading to find them here.

Eventually he stood up and turned to face Horsa.

"They're not here," he said. He was almost relieved by that fact but at the same time his mind reeled at the thought of what other fate they might have suffered. He searched the other rooms in the hall. They had been looted but were free of corpses even though the stench of death drifted in from the main chamber.

He burst out of the hall and into the fresh air, trying to clear the stink from his nostrils. The silence of the yard mocked him. "Halfritha!" he yelled at the top of his lungs. "Aesc! Hronwena!"

There was no sound save for some startled crows that fluttered, cawing and flapping from a nearby tree. He felt as if he were losing his mind. They were gone. Taken. Stolen from him without a trace. Rage overtook him and he roared at the sky, cursing and invoking the wrath of all the gods he could name. He attacked log piles and stacks of tools in a fury of destruction, only to fall to his knees, weeping.

He felt a strong, reassuring hand on his shoulder. It was Horsa, kneeling by him. He turned and fell into his brother's embrace. "Who took them, Horsa? Who took my family?"

"Whoever it was wanted them and them alone," Horsa replied. "They wanted to hurt you. In all probability your wife and children are still alive."

"What makes you so sure?"

"If they wanted to kill them then their bodies would be in there with the rest of them for you to find. And that man hanging at the gate …"

"Brand. One of father's thegns."

"Was that him? I didn't recognise him. He was left as a sign. A sign for you. They are telling you that they have your family and that they have been spared death … for now."

Hengest rose to his feet, his face set with rage. "By the gods I shall take my vengeance on them. I'll tear their lungs from their broken bodies if they harm Halfritha or the children!"

"And I will help you find them," said Horsa. "We will find the ones that did this and spill every last drop of blood from them until they relinquish your family."

Hengest hugged his brother again, allowing himself to feel gratitude for this man who had been gone from his side for far too long. Here was a pillar of strength he had never before counted on and it was at least some comfort to know that he was there now.

The rest of the evening was spent clearing the corpses from the hall. Brand was cut down from the gate and a large pyre was constructed; the bloated carcasses were tossed on top. There was no time for a funeral befitting a man such as Brand and Hengest lamented this. But he would not leave his friend to be found by the nearest neighbours, who may take a month or more to discover his rotten corpse, and so the pyres were lit with the briefest ceremony time would allow. Songs were sung for the souls who were destined for Waelheall and then the warriors left the deserted homestead by the towering light of the funeral pyres.

They rejoined their comrades at the boats where they ate and bedded down for the night. "Tomorrow I shall head out for the islands," said Horsa. "I know many people who frequent the ports and towns and more than a few of them owe me favours. If your family have been taken away by sea then somebody I know will have heard something."

"I'm coming with you," said Hengest.

"Absolutely not. Whoever took your family must not know that I am helping you if I am to get any information out of them. I shall go alone so that none shall know me."

"And what shall I be doing?" asked Hengest. "Sitting on my arse keeping this fire going?" He felt helpless and lost. At least Horsa had the sea on his side. He had nothing; no friends or allies he could call on for favours.

"You must keep a low profile," Horsa said. "At least for the time being. Once I have found a lead, I shall alert you and we can move on these bastards together. Beorn will come with me and act as our contact. I shall send him back to you with any news. For the time being, you shall be in command of both the *Bloodkeel* and the *Raven*."

"Very well," grumbled Hengest. "I shall scour the coastline while you are gone and see if I can find out anything. They may have been taken over land."

"Is there anyone you know who might bear you ill intent?"

"None that I can think of. Father perhaps, but I doubt he would kidnap his own grandchildren just to spite the son he already banished." He thought hard for a moment. "Garulf," he said at last.

"The Jutish traitor?" asked Horsa. "Isn't he dead?"

"He has family. Sons in Frisia, perhaps. People who would bear me ill will for the death of their lord."

"But you didn't kill Garulf."

"No, but I ensured the victory of the Danes over the Jutes; our own countrymen. And I took command of Hnaef's men upon his death, the very men who killed his father. What better reason could somebody have to harm my family?"

Horsa nodded solemnly. "Most likely it is our own countrymen then. They may want a ransom from you, or they may be bait for a trap. Either way, you must keep your name hidden whilst you are in these lands. If word got around that you have returned before I am able to find out who they are, then all our plans could be undone."

Halfritha

The crossing from Jute-land to the islands in the east had been a terrifying one for Halfritha and her children. The waves rode high and the ship rose and dipped alarmingly. They had spent the journey wedged down in the hull of the boat, huddled together as the craft hurled them from side to side and the icy salt spray soaked through the cloak Halga had given them. They were fed, but rations were meagre and the salty taste of dried fish and stale bread was hard for them to swallow day after day. Halfritha thanked the gods that none of them suffered from the awful seasickness that her husband did.

They hugged the coastline like a child not wanting to venture too far from its mother's hearth, putting in at various bays and inlets along the way. Each time the tents would go up, fires would be lit and men would scour the surrounding countryside for food and fresh water. Once the drinking was underway and the light of the fires spread beneath the glow of the stars, Halga would come and take Halfritha to his tent, leaving the children alone in the darkness.

She could not remember how many times she had let him take her; how many times she had let him spread her out on the furs and felt his hard, rough hands run along the contours of her body, and smelt his rancid breath on her naked flesh. But her mind was put at ease by the knowledge that whilst Halga had his way with her, his attentions were diverted from her young daughter.

But now their lives had taken another change and Halfritha would be forced to protect Aesc and

Hronwena in other ways. The time that Halfritha had dreaded had finally arrived.

Halga was leaving them.

Their eventual destination was a small island. Halfritha knew not where for her knowledge of lands beyond the coastline of Jute-land was poor. A settlement of sorts had been constructed on the island, but few people lived there. Several huts stood on the headland surrounding a square area of turf upon which a scaffold had been built. Below them was a bay where a few jetties hung above the water, green with slime and half rotten. The raiding vessel dropped anchor in the shallows and the crew waded ashore, bringing their prisoners with them.

A company of men was waiting on the shore to receive them. One of them, a short, tubby man with a receding clump of matted black hair approached Halga with open arms as one greeting an old acquaintance.

"How went the trip, Halga?" the fat man asked.

"As well as hoped for, Theomund."

"Any losses?"

Halga snorted. "My men can handle farmers and theows."

"Prisoners give you any trouble?" Theomund asked, eyeing Halfritha and the children.

"None."

"My, my, the girls are fine specimens. They'll catch a good price come market day."

"The word is to keep them until my employer arrives."

"No trouble. There won't be another market for a good few weeks yet. Most of the traders and merchants are still land-locked. I must say, Halga, you surprised me with a trip so early in the season."

"If the price is right I'll sail my crew through the Mistlands and back."

"Am I to understand that you are to grace us with another visit this season?"

"My employer wants us to return for market day to act as guards should there be any trouble. But in the meantime I shall run another slaving trip. North probably."

"We rarely have trouble here," said Theomund in a concerned voice. "Ealdorman Aescgar and his wolves are too occupied chasing you and your kind about than interfering in slave markets. But that may change should you spend too much time with us."

"That's a risk you'll have to take," said Halga, with a flare of irritation at the mention of Ealdorman Aescgar. "Besides, these prisoners have powerful family members who will be looking for them. If my employer pays me to be here, then here is where I'll be."

Halfritha had no idea who Halga's employer might be but the situation was clear. Halga was a regular slaver and this Theomund was his buyer; his middleman. There was no sign of silver changing hands this day and it seemed apparent that Halga had been paid in advance to capture her and her children.

Halga led his men back to his boat and Theomund's guards came to take the prisoners. Halfritha watched Halga leave with mixed feelings. This man had ravaged her again and again on the trip over here but he had been protection of a sort. Now he had handed her over to another man and the immediate future was much less certain.

"Come on, pretty," said Theomund, grabbing hold of her and pulling her away. "Don't be setting your heart on him. There's plenty more men to satisfy you here." His men sniggered at this.

Hronwena and Aesc struggled as they were manhandled away. Halfritha's heart sank but not for herself. Without Halga to protect her daughter, what lay in store for her children now?

Aelfstan

There were many islands clustered in the sea between the lands of the Jutes, the Danes and the Geats. Those islands had once been inhabited by the Heruli tribe – a fierce seafaring people – until the Dane tribes forced them south. Some were inhabited but most were not, deemed too barren and bleak for the ealdormen and kings of the surrounding lands to bother claiming, and so the islands had fallen to the worst elements of society.

Raiders, slavers and outcasts had made their bases on these islands, protected on all sides by the sea and beyond the reach of whatever tribes had spurned them. They recognised no authority other than their own and the only laws they followed were those set down by their corrupt chieftains who lived like petty ealdormen, growing rich on the profits of slavery and piracy.

In the bay of one of these islands a boat rode at anchor. It was a large forty-oared vessel and its prow was decorated with the carven head of a ferocious drake. It was called the *Fafnir* after the famous fire-drake Sigemund had slain and was instantly recognisable to anyone who was unfortunate to see its grinning head emerging from the mist.

The captain of the *Fafnir* was Halga Eadwulfson.

Halga and his men sat drinking in a local tavern; a large wooden building with an earthen floor into which a fire pit had been dug. The room was smoky and seethed with people. Geats, Danes, Jutes and even a few Northmen all spoke a confusing babble of languages. Some were bartering for goods and others were paying bribes to agents of the local governor. Skins and furs decorated the place and flaxen-haired serving girls stumbled about distributing mead and ale, dodging the groping hands of the men as they passed. The place stank of wood smoke, stale mead and urine.

Halga oversaw his men from his seat at the head of the building, absently stroking the bared breasts of a trembling slave girl who sat in his lap. His face was usually ruddy, but tonight it was all the more so on account of the drink and warmth of the seedy tavern.

A commotion broke out among his men and one of them drew a saex upon a stranger who appeared to have beaten him one too many times at a dice game. The stranger, a youthful man with dark hair, drew a similar weapon and prepared to defend himself.

"I'll carve your stinking heart out, you cheating whore's whelp!" spat Halga's man, as he made to attack.

"Cease!" bellowed Halga, and the man halted his advance instantly. No man disobeyed Halga Eadwulfson.

"This man is a cheat!" protested the raider. He had curling black hair and a thick bushy beard that was separated on one side by a nasty scar that ran the length of his cheek. "Nobody can win seven times in a row without some trickery!"

"Then kill him outside," Halga replied. "If any blood is spilled in here I have to pay the owner a fine."

"Why pay?" asked Daegal, his first mate, drunkenly sitting up from the fur on which he was sprawled. "Spill the owner's blood too if he complains." He looked around for the owner, but the proprietor was wisely keeping himself out of sight.

"Because he is the governor's man," Halga said bitterly. "And we are running out of safe ports. Wet your blade outside, I say!" as he turned back to nuzzling the slave girl's breasts.

Two of the dice players made to haul the stranger away but the youth struggled free and called out to Halga, "My lord! I am no cheat! I used the same dice as my opponents. I am just more skilled in the throwing of them."

Halga irritably drew his face away from the girl to look at the man. "I have no interest in dice games, boy. If my men take issue with you then that is between you and them. Remove him from here!"

"A challenge then!" cried out the young man. At this the room fell silent. The stranger was making a meal out of a petty matter no doubt to give himself a fighting chance. But the promise of a contest excited them. "I challenge this man who accuses me of cheating! He cannot deny me the chance to prove my honour!"

"What's your name, boy?" asked Halga, eying him.

"Aelfstan," replied the youth.

"Just Aelfstan? Have you no father?"

"None that I choose to remember, much less name. I grew up with my mother on the western side of the island."

"A local. You look like you have experience of the sea."

"I have travelled, yes," replied the youth. "With merchants, mostly, but it was a raider that brought me home."

"Well, Aelfstan. I suppose you know what a challenge in these parts means? If you kill one of my men, even if it is over a matter of honour, then you are honour-bound to take his place at my oars. If you can defeat him that is."

There was laughter at this and the black-bearded man with the scar grinned at Aelfstan.

"I am aware of the custom, my lord."

Halga smiled and tossed the slave girl from him as he stood up. "Then a challenge it is."

There was a cheer from his men. Such entertainment was rare and always appreciated. The entire tavern spilled out into the muddy yard and formed a loose circle.

Aelfstan was pushed and shoved into the centre where his grim-faced opponent was standing, already accepting a shield from a friend and testing the weight of a single-handed war axe. A similar weapon was thrust into Aelfstan's hand and a round shield with a red bird painted on it was handed to him.

"Do you object to axe and shield combat?" asked Halga.

"Not at all," replied the youth, trying to look more confident than he felt. The axe was slippery in his wet grasp and the shield felt enormously heavy. In more noble surroundings, a man was allowed three shields, and upon the destruction of the third he would be forced to fight without one. It seemed like shields were in short supply on this island.

The crowd watched, eager for blood. No betting was taking place; that was unusual but probably indicated how little faith they had in the insolent local boy defeating Halga's hardened raider.

Halga stood to one side. He gave the order to fight with a drop of his hand and the black-bearded man swung at Aelfstan without hesitation. The axe's edge slithered off the boss of Aelfstan's upraised shield and he slashed out in a counterattack but was blocked by his opponent's own shield.

Cheered on by his shipmates, blackbeard swung again, slamming his weapon hard against Aelfstan's defence again and again, cracking the wood and tearing out great chunks of the shield. Knowing that it would not withstand much more, Aelfstan made a daring push forward and slammed its iron rim into his opponent's jaw.

The crowd winced as their comrade staggered backwards, stunned, blood pouring from behind his teeth where he had bitten through his tongue. Now he was enraged.

A man in the crowd called for bets and Aelfstan smiled. He had impressed them and his odds had suddenly increased, at least in their eyes. He let his opponent come to him this time, ducking and sidestepping his swings, tiring him out.

He caught a blow on his shield and it cracked along the grain, breaking away and cutting his hand in the process. He shook his arm free of the straps and cast the broken shield aside. His opponent came at him again and Aelfstan stuck his boot out, tripping him. As the man fell forward, Aelfstan whirled around and connected his axe blade with the back of black-beard's head. It was a fatal blow. The axe bit deep, crunching through skull and sinking into the brain.

Blackbeard sank to his knees and Aelfstan wrenched the weapon free, tearing out a chunk of grey matter with it. The dead man slumped forward, face down in the mud.

A few local spectators applauded but quickly subsided when they saw that none of Halga's men were saying anything. Aelfstan had not expected wild cheers of praise. He knew that he had killed one of their comrades and, honourably or not, that was rarely received well. He turned to face them defiantly.

"Who now calls me a cheat?" he said.

The men continued to stare at him. They had misjudged him. The boy could fight and fight well. Now the newcomer was left to wonder if they would stick to their piratical code or let their ill feelings get the better of them and tear him to pieces. Their captain eventually spoke.

"You have killed a member of my crew," he said. "Now you must either pay us his weregild or, if you are unable to, you must take his place at my oar bench."

"I have no money," Aelfstan replied. "And I am a good seaman, so it looks like I'll be joining you."

The crew grumbled.

"We leave tonight on the ebb tide," Halga said. "Be at the wharves where the *Fafnir* is anchored. If you try to run, you will never leave this island alive."

"I'll be there," Aelfstan replied. "I will pay your man's weregild with my sweat and my steel. You will come to remember this day as a blessing."

"Unlikely," said Halga as he turned to leave. "The man you killed was my nephew."

Halga Eadwulfson was not a man to break the laws of piracy even when a family member had been killed and so, by the brutal law of the sea, the young stranger joined the crew of one of the most feared raiding vessels in the northern world.

Since his arrival in the islands, Horsa had been on the scent of information concerning his brother's kidnapped family like a wolfhound. He had frequented nearly every filthy tavern and muddy shoreside village, every seedy haunt of the most fearsome types known to prowl the islands. He had met with every old shipmate and called in every favour owed him in return for information. He had quaffed mead with murderers and oath-breakers, played dice with slavers and mercenaries, and roared with laughter at the obscene jokes of the worst piratical scum in his pursuit of a lead.

Eventually a scrap of information was tossed his way; a small scrap, but of such valuable importance. In hushed tones in a smoky corner of a dilapidated tavern a man had mentioned to him that the fearsome captain Halga of the *Fafnir* was in the business of gathering slaves that were to be auctioned off sometime later in the season. It was rumoured that he and his crew had been paid a large sum of money to kidnap a noble Jutish family. Hardly the usual activity for lowlife slavers who, for the most part, stuck to raiding out of the way villages and poorly defended settlements.

This was all Horsa needed to know. He had not crossed paths with Halga Eadwulfson himself, but he knew many men who had. His ruthlessness was unparalleled and his cunning unmatched. Winning a place on his crew would be difficult and keeping his identity secret in a world where his name was not wholly unknown, would be even trickier.

The next few days were nothing but hard work for Aelfstan. The crew still bore a grudge for his slaying of one of their number and they worked him like a dog for it. Forced to do the most menial and dirty tasks, Aelfstan took it without complaint. They were a rougher lot than his own crew back aboard the *Bloodkeel*. Viciousness and cruelty seemed to be innate in them and in-fighting was common. Only Halga's word had any effect on them and he ruled with an iron fist. Punishments were severe and twice Aelfstan witnessed the captain beat a man to the deck with a heavy length of wood and continue beating him until his bloodied body was no longer twitching. Salt water would then be thrown on the senseless man and he would arise groggily and continue with his work as if nothing had happened.

Aelfstan wondered if any of the men harboured resentment of their chief, or if any of them secretly considered taking his place as captain as he himself had done aboard the *Bloodkeel*. Certainly nobody mentioned it, so he wondered if this type of yielding crew was not more dangerous to a captain than one that openly voiced its opinions, for how could a captain know who to trust if all were silent and obedient?

It seemed a hazardous crew to be a part of, but he was at last aboard the *Fafnir*, and that was good enough for him. It would only be a matter of time before one of his new shipmates would let slip a scrap of information concerning his brother's kidnapped family.

On the fourth day a trading vessel was spotted off the tip of Jute-land. It rode low in the waist, laden with its heavy cargo of glassware, amber and wool. The *Fafnir* pursued it for a day and a half around the headland like a wolf stalking a stray sheep. The trader was sluggish and its captain was too proud or too foolhardy to cast his wares over the side to lighten the load. It probably wouldn't have made a difference, for Halga's ship was tightly disciplined and outfitted for speed, but it would have postponed the inevitable death that trod its foamy wake.

As they closed on the trader, Halga and his first mate Daegal handed out blades to the crew. They were simple, cheap affairs, heavy and poorly oiled, but they would do the job. Some of the crew pulled out helmets and simple garments of boiled leather from the wooden chests that served as the oar benches. Several of the men armed themselves with grappling hooks and formed a line on the side facing the trader. Aelfstan was well used to such activities from all his years aboard the *Bloodkeel*, but he did his best to appear new to it.

"Ever killed a man before?" Daegal asked him, handing him a sword that was flecked with rust.

"Only once," Aelfstan lied, for in truth he had killed too many to number. "A man who tried to steal my purse in Reddasporth."

"Well, let's see how you do today," the first mate replied with a grin. "These are traders, not warriors, but don't be fooled. Some of them will be good fighters. Careful you don't let one of them knock you overboard or you'll be left behind."

Aelfstan appreciated the first mate's words of advice for it was the first half-friendly thing anybody had said to him in days. Normally the crew took delight in ill-advising him when it came to his tasks and then roaring with laughter when he failed at them. But this was battle and attitudes changed when death was near.

"When we board them," Daegal continued, "you stay put and make sure that none of the bastards cut the grappling lines. Leave the hard fighting to us but keep them off the *Fafnir*."

Aelfstan nodded, a little irked at being given such a dull job when he knew that he could best a good deal of his new comrades in a fight. But appearances had to be upheld.

The *Fafnir* crept alongside the trader, knot by knot, edging ever closer. The men with the grappling hooks stood by, ready for Halga's signal. A spear sung through the air and thudded into the bilge of the *Fafnir* followed by a garbled insult from one of the traders.

"Feisty lot, aren't they?" commented Daegal, before three of the crew returned the gesture by hurling their own spears at the trader. Two of them found marks, piercing a couple of men who screamed and fell back behind the bulwarks.

"Grab them!" shouted Halga. The grappling hooks were sent out across the gap of water, their rusty barbs embedding into the dark wood of the trader. The crew heaved on the ropes and drew the gap closer. When the distance was small enough, there was a great rush as the crew of the *Fafnir* stormed the trader.

Their prey was ready for them and brandished small shields and spears as the hardened warriors fell upon them, stabbing and hacking with their blades. Aelfstan took his position at the bow and watched the slaughter with a lustful interest. The straining grappling lines creaked as the two vessels tried to drift apart. Sure enough, one of the traders weaselled his way through the heaving throng and raised a short-handled axe to one of the ropes.

The axe stroke never fell. Aelfstan smashed the pommel of his sword into the man's face and heard the bone and teeth crunch as the man fell down to the red deck, screaming. One of his mates stepped up and stabbed at Aelfstan with a blade. Aelfstan parried the stroke and fought back, but over the man's shoulder he could see a similar situation further down at the stern of the boat.

One of the *Fafnir's* crew – a youth called Asse – was standing with one foot on either side of the gap, trying desperately to get aboard the trader and join the fight. A big man with an axe was preventing him and between his legs, Aelfstan could see a second trader, sawing through one of the grappling ropes with a saex.

The rope snapped and the stern of the *Fafnir* began to drift away from the trader. Asse found his legs moving further apart, and the gap below reached up to swallow him. Soon he would be off balance and would plunge into the sea.

Aelfstan heaved his opponent aside and ran the length of the boat, hopping over oar benches and crossing over to the trader at the last moment. The big man with the axe raised his weapon to hew through Asse's leg but Aelfstan got there first, barrelling into the man and sinking his sword in between his ribs. Turning quickly, he reached out a hand to the panicked Asse and hauled him aboard the trader.

"My thanks, Aelfstan," said Asse, rubbing his stretched and aching groin. "I thought I was about to lose a leg there, and I nearly lost more."

It was the first time any of the *Fafnir's* crew had called Aelfstan by name rather than just "boy" or one of the more inventive names they had concocted for him. He could see the gratitude in Asse's eyes. They were of a similar age and had rarely spoken but he had saved Asse's life and that was the kind of deed that even raiders honoured.

The fight was all but over and Halga's men finished off the traders with swift efficiency. They were keen to begin checking the cargo of the trader. Soon they were transferring the sacks of wool and chests of amber to the *Fafnir* amidst laughter and cheerful song.

Once the trader was empty and riding high in the water next to the *Fafnir*, a fire was lit in its belly and the grappling hooks were reeled in. As they rowed away they watched the smouldering flames catch at the mast and torn sail, licking along the bulwarks as they ate through the hull. Soon there would be no sign of the ship other than smoke and a few pieces of charred driftwood.

Aelfstan saw something small and black sitting atop the mast of the burning vessel. It ruffled its feathers with its beak and he recognised it as a raven.

They were far from land. The sight of the black bird of death was surreal, but none of the other crewmembers seemed to see it and Aelfstan wondered if it was visible to his eyes only. It cawed loudly and took off in a flurry of feathers before vanishing into the grey sky.

The trading vessel began to sink, and by the time it was on the horizon, there was little left of it other than a pillar of black smoke.

Hengest

The *Bloodkeel* and the *Raven* rode at anchor, gently dipping up and down upon the evening tide. The Danes and the raiders sat in separate camps on the shore, their fires burning bright in the fading light.

They would not share hearths, these proud Danes and landless pirates. They came from different ends of society. Hengest's men were the sons of noblemen, born with swords in their hands and trained to use them from an early age. Horsa's men were banished, rootless drifters, exiled by the very types that sat just across the sand from them in their polished iron helms and costly hauberks.

The raiders poured scorn on the Danes for their loftiness and the Danes in turn, turned their noses up at the tattered and mismatched clothes of the raiders and the ancient hand axes and swords they carried. These were two groups of warriors that had never had to share a beach.

Hengest barely registered the tension between the men under his command. Neither food nor drink could sate him and he kicked at tufts of long grass irritably. Over the past few weeks he had dragged this mismatched crew along the coast seeking answers where there were none. None had heard anything of Garulf's family. Nobody could even tell him if the Jute had any sons that might wish to avenge him. It was as if the last remnants of Ealdorman Guthulf's descendants had been wiped away at Finnesburg.

Where was Horsa? Why had he not returned or sent word? For all Hengest knew his family was already dead. If they had been split up then it would be near impossible to recover all three of them. Every day that went by was a day Halfritha and the children drifted further from him.

"I've reached a decision," he said to the men that night. They looked up from their evening meal at him. "Upon the dawn tide we set out for the islands. There are enough men here to scour each island until my family is found."

"We do not depart without the captain," said an Angle who Hengest recognised as Aelfhere, one of his brother's most loyal companions.

There were many murmurs of agreement from the rest of the *Bloodkeel's* crew.

"And if my brother should not return?" Hengest asked. "How long are you prepared to wait? Anything is better than just sitting here."

They made no answer and most returned their attentions to their meals. Hengest realised that he was forgetting himself. These weren't his men. He was the leader of a handful of Danes who would be no match for his brother's men should any unrest break out between the two groups. He stared away from them at the black line of the horizon, feeling tears of frustrating sting his eyes. Ordlaf and Guthlaf appeared at his side.

"You know that such action is folly, my lord," said Ordlaf. "If we begin tearing up the islands looking for your family now, then whoever has them will be alerted and will be forced to get rid of them quickly. We must wait for your brother's word."

Hengest turned to him and spoke in a hushed tone so that the rest of the men would not hear the anguish that made his voice tremble. "But my family's life hangs in the balance, Ordlaf," he said. "I cannot just sit around here waiting; it's killing me. And where is this Beorn fellow? He was supposed to report back from time to time. It's been weeks and still no word. Suppose my brother is dead. What then? Am I forced to remain here whilst my wife and children are kept prisoners or sold as slaves or worse?"

"Wait but a little longer," Guthlaf advised. "The raiders' trust in your brother is unwavering. They are certain that he will return, and when he does, we shall set out as you said and tear those islands apart to find your family."

Hengest nodded and clutched the old warrior's shoulder for support. Out in the darkness of the night, the waves gently lapped the shore bringing no news from other lands but their own soft and mocking chuckle.

Aelfstan

They headed back to land and spirits were high. The crew sang as they rowed, elated by their rich haul. Aelfstan had feared some kind of punishment from Halga or Daegal for his failure to protect all of the grappling lines, but word had got around of how he had saved Asse's life and killed two of the traders, so nobody said a word to him. That was good. He had climbed a few rungs of the slippery ladder of respect and the crew now looked on him a little better. He even dared to think that they respected him as an equal. He smiled as he heaved on his oar. It had been a good day.

They put in at a small, deserted inlet on the northern tip of Jute-land and made camp. It had been their first landfall since they had set out from the islands four days ago and, after eating nothing but salted fish and stale bread, they were all glad of the comforting warmth of a fire and the succulent taste of roasting meat. A barrel of mead was opened and they all drank and ate well while the stars gazed down from their inky seclusion.

The stolen amber was divided up amongst the crew and each got a share depending on how many men they had killed. Aelfstan was pleased to receive his own quota for the two men he had slain and he gazed upon the hardened lumps of resin that seemed to glow by the light of the fire like frozen honey. The sacks of wool were to be sold for silver at the next port they reached and the profits would again be divided up with Halga naturally taking the lion's share.

Aelfstan, his head buzzing with the drink, looked around at the dark dunes that rose up from the beach, vast and seemingly desolate, undisturbed by the roaring and laughing of the encamped raiders. Something moved out in the night and he squinted into it.

Two figures were approaching; a man and a woman. The man was tall and wore a loose-fitting garment of leather. He bore a sword at his belt and walked with the swagger of a man who had been at sea for many years. The woman was a slender thing, with dark hair that whipped about her on the wind as they made their way across the sands towards the campfire.

"Captain," spoke Aelfstan. "Strangers approach."

"They are not strangers, boy," said Halga, heaving himself upright and dusting the sand off his breeches. "This is my good friend Beorhtwulf, who agreed to meet me here tonight. *Hwæt*, Beorhtwulf!" he called out to the man who approached.

The two men embraced and by the light of the fire, Aelfstan could better see the two strangers.

Beorhtwulf was of a similar age to Halga and just as large, although he dressed in a considerably less conspicuous fashion than the dandified captain. His beard and hair was the colour of dirty straw and he wore it long in braids. But it was the woman who accompanied him that caught Aelfstan's eye.

She was young, but no child. Her hair was dark and her eyes were bright and keen, surrounded by smudges of charcoal. Her slender body was concealed in a swathe of black wool. No gold or other ornamentation decorated her and she would have seemed the plainest of women if it were not for her eyes. They showed a depth that seemed to echo ages far greater than the twenty or so winters her body had seen, and she cast them about the men seated before her like a hawk scanning the fields for food. There was something predatory about her and Aelfstan had difficulty taking his eyes off her, yet he felt a mild terror as hers met his, as if she could see things within a man that only he knew.

"Stay away from that one," warned a voice in his ear. It was Asse.

"Who is she?" Aelfstan asked, finally managing to tear his eyes away from that terrible gaze.

"She's Ealhwaru, Beorhtwulf's girl. A Saxon slave he picked up when she was no more than a child. He's practically raised her and, although she is still his slave, he treats her as if she were his daughter and lover combined."

Aelfstan wrinkled his nose at this dubious mix of roles. The woman sat down by the fire and men offered her food and drink. She refused the mead but accepted a shank of goat that the men were passing about, which she nibbled on delicately. Behind her Halga was showing off their latest haul to Beorhtwulf.

"We took this from a bloated slug of a trader earlier today," he said. "It's not the best of hauls but it will suffice for now until our real payday arrives. But what of you since we last met? Last I heard you were fighting off Ealdorman Aescgar's wolves in the Eastern Sea."

"I was," Beorhtwulf replied. "The bastard is finally dead, rot his soul. But this winter I received word that my brother is slain."

"I am sorry," Halga replied. "Ingvar was a good man. One of the best raider captains I ever knew."

Aelfstan's ears pricked up at this. *Ingvar?*

"His death was a blow to me," admitted Beorhtwulf. "But when I learned that it was his own first mate who had killed him, I decided to leave the life of raiding for a while until I hunt down his spineless worm of a murderer."

"His first mate?" inquired Halga. "What treachery is this?"

"A man called Horsa, son of the Jutish Ealdorman Wictgils. He killed my brother in cold blood and took command of his vessel. The rest of the crew were clearly just as spineless for they still follow this worm among sea-wolves. But when I find him, I shall carve such bloody vengeance on his screaming body that he will wish he had never heard of the sons of Wolof!"

Aelfstan involuntarily looked away, casting his face in shadow, his heart hammering in his chest. *Ingvar's brother!* Some member of the *Bloodkeel's* crew must have been talking about the events in Dane-land during the winter and for that they could not be blamed. He had taken Ingvar's life in a fair fight and had vowed none to secrecy about it. But surely, this man would not recognise him. He thanked the gods that they had given him the sense to fabricate a name before joining the crew of the *Fafnir*. And after all, with a new name, how could Beorhtwulf suspect him? None here knew his true identity.

He hoped that it would stay that way.

The night wore on and there was music of sorts. One of the men pounded on a simple skin drum and the other piped away on a reed pipe. Beorhtwulf sat by Halga and seemed to enjoy himself as much as any man.

"Why do you not dance for us, Ealhwaru, my dear?" he said after a while.

At first, the Saxon theow refused but after much persuasion from the crew and the gentle firmness in Beorhtwulf's voice, she at last stood up, dusted herself off and moved into the centre of the circle, her frame outlined by the crackling fire. A faster rhythm was picked up by the drummer and the piper whistled a merry tune that rose and fell erratically. And then Ealhwaru began to dance.

Aelfstan had never seen anything like it. He had always enjoyed the dances of wenches in taverns and his father's hall but this was something else. The Saxon woman ducked and weaved to the primitive music, her contorting body its perfect match. It was primal, bestial even. She began to sweat and the glow of the fire off her shining limbs put Aelfstan in mind of the rippling scales of a snake.

The tempo increased and the men began to cheer as Ealhwaru spun and spun, her eyes half closed as if she were in a trance, her wild hair flailing about. She edged closer to Aelfstan and as he watched, he felt as if she was dancing for him and him alone.

He was aware of the eyes of the crew upon him and that made him feel uncomfortable. Being the centre of attention was the last thing he wanted with Beorhtwulf sitting a short distance away. But the gyrating, curling form of Ealhwaru entranced him and he was unable to look anywhere but at the glistening ivory skin and jet-black hair as she spun, drifting closer and closer so that he could almost smell the woman's scent.

She stopped spinning but continued to dance and weave, her eyes fixed on his, her face close. And in those eyes he saw his own reflection, pale-faced and awe-struck. But there was something else too; a shadow, a dark blot that squatted behind him, its claws resting on his shoulder. It frightened him and he wished that the woman would move away.

Then the music stopped and Ealhwaru flopped down on the sand, exhausted. The men went wild with applause and began chanting for a second dance. Aelfstan got up and walked away from the campfire, not wishing to stay for a second round against those dark, all-knowing eyes.

He stared out to sea and breathed deeply. Behind him the drumming and piping began once more and the crew began to cheer as Ealhwaru danced for them again. To his left, over by the beached *Fafnir*, Aelfstan heard voices. It was Halga and Beorhtwulf conversing in low tones. He had not noticed them slip away.

Not wishing to be seen, Aelfstan crept towards the hull of the *Fafnir* and squatted down in its shadow, listening to the voices coming from the other side.

"You're welcome to join us," Halga was telling Beorhtwulf. "I could use an extra pair of hands."

"Another slaving expedition?" Beorhtwulf asked. "Didn't you just come back from one?"

"That was just a small bit of business for a little extra silver. It was a favour really. One Jutish bitch and her two babes. Hardly the big money like a voyage north would bring in."

Aelfstan breathed hard. There was no doubt now that it had been Halga's crew who had abducted Halfritha and the children and it was clear that it had been a special job for somebody. But who? He would have to worm more information from the crew, but to do it without drawing suspicion upon himself was going to be tricky.

"Besides," Halga continued, "I can get a better price for the wool we took in the north. We'll pick up some slaves there and head back to the islands for market day. What do you say?"

Market day.

Finally Aelfstan had some news to send back to his brother. It was almost certain that his wife and children were alive and awaiting sale, most probably in the same location that Halga intended to drop off his next shipment of slaves. All he had to do was wait out the voyage and get word to Hengest before they made their move.

But that would take some time. If Halga intended to set sail for the north, then it would be difficult to pass on what he had learned to Beorn who was lurking somewhere in these parts, keeping an eye on the *Fafnir's* movements.

The conversation continued between Halga and Beorhtwulf and it was agreed that the Angle would join the expedition along with his Saxon woman. This was bad news to Aelfstan's ears as he wanted to put as much distance as possible between himself and the brother of the late Ingvar.

But go on he must, for the sake of his niece and nephew; the children he had never met. And for the sake of Hengest.

Halfritha

The baking sun beat down on the slave huts making the stink of rotting fish that rose from the piles of nets all the more potent. Halfritha's fingers bled as she worked, untangling the mounds of ropes and nets, breathing through her mouth to block out the stench.

This was the work the slaves were set to on the island; a way of earning their keep. They were all awaiting sale, all one hundred and fifty odd of them, culled from every coastline of the northern world; dragged from their homes, their families murdered, awaiting the dreaded market day where their fates would be decided by the haggling of merchants and the jingling of silver as it passed through greedy hands.

Halfritha nearly gagged every time she took a breath for the stink only increased her nausea. She felt ill most mornings now and had not bled this month, cementing her deepest, most horrifying fears.

She was with child.

Nobody had noticed yet but it was only a matter of time before her belly would begin to swell with new life inside it. It was Halga's, that was certain, for Hengest had been gone too long for it to be his.

Halga's child.

The thought made her sick. He had taken her many times on the journey across from Jute-land and the thought of the seed of that brute quickening deep within her womb caused a shiver to run through her. But she could not bring herself to blame the child for its father's evil. A child was a child and deserved all the love its mother could give it.

But how could she bring the poor, fatherless creature into a world where she herself was a slave?

What future lay ahead of it other than poverty and hardship? The situation was bad enough for her existing children without condemning another life to slavery without it ever tasting free air.

Her children were coping well enough. Aesc was as fierce as ever, refusing to do the work set him until the guards' beatings and Halfritha's desperate pleading convinced him to play the part of a slave, if only for a little while. The boy had grown up in a wealthy household with theows of his own to order about. Bowing his head to others came hard to him, but he managed, even if Halfritha knew that it was for her sake only.

Hronwena on the other hand had grown distant. They had always been close but since their capture Hronwena had developed a coldness which she cast on her mother like frost. Some days she would not talk to anybody at all and worked alongside her mother in sullen silence. It was not hard to see why she had changed. The previous weeks had been a brutal introduction to adulthood for her. Night after night she had seen Halga take her mother away to his tent. She was no longer the rosy-cheeked child with quick laughter and her mother's smile.

Halfritha had always returned when Halga finished with her to find her daughter sleeping, disturbed by bad dreams. She prayed to the gods that her daughter's young mind retained its innocence and did not guess what went on in that tent, but she feared that her daughter was not as naive as all that. It was not too hard to imagine that her coldness was borne of a disgust at her mother for sleeping with the enemy. If only she could make her understand that it was done out of love for her. But Halfritha did not know how to begin to broach the subject with her.

There was a woman on the island who ran a brothel for Theomund's men. Her name was Leola. Her girls – the prettiest of the slaves hand-picked by Theomund – lived apart from the main camp where they were kept clean and perfumed for the men's enjoyment. Halfritha had seen them on occasion and had thanked the gods that Theomund had not picked her or Hronwena for this little harem. Perhaps this was due to the orders of Halga's mysterious employer but whatever the reason, she much preferred to pick apart fishing nets than spend night after night warming the beds of their captors.

Surely those girls were no strangers to the problem of pregnancy? She had heard of certain herbs that could bring about the birth of a child before it had fully formed inside a woman's belly. The child died, of course, but before the gods had breathed the spirit of life into it and made it whole.

The brothel was part of the settlement near the wharves on the other side of the island. As the slaves were hardly allowed to wander about freely on the island, getting to the brothel was something of a problem. Every five days or so, a couple of the guards would take a small group of slaves to collect food from the wharves to carry back to the camp. It was well known that the guards often liked to enjoy a few drinks in the tavern whilst the slaves loaded up the food. It was presumably a dull life to be guarding a slave camp away from the ale and women that their comrades had the privilege of.

Halfritha managed to convince one of the regular slaves to swap places with her for the way was long and the baskets of salted pork and grain were heavy. When the guards came to round up the usual group of five, Halfritha squeezed her way to the front and got herself picked for the trip. Sure enough, once they had reached the settlement, the slaves were left to load up the baskets from the granary while their guards headed towards the tavern on the wharves. Security was rather lax on the island for no slave could leave without a boat.

"Where's the brothel?" Halfritha asked her neighbour, an elderly, odorous man who had spent many years on the island, for no visiting merchant wanted to buy him. He regarded her curiously.

"What on earth do you want to know that for, girl?"

"Just tell me," Halfritha said irritably, for her window of opportunity was tight.

"Other side of that warehouse," the man said, nodding to a large, warped old building where a couple of men were loitering about outside, shirking their work.

Halfritha took a quick glance about to make sure nobody was watching them. She could feel the shocked eyes of the other slaves on her back as she covered her hair with her tattered shawl and scurried across the mud towards the warehouse. If she was caught leaving the group she would be flogged. She had seen it done to several wretched souls who had attempted theft or insubordination during her stay on the island and it was incentive enough for them all to toe the line.

The men hanging about the entrance to the warehouse called at her as she passed, barking some jest in their guttural Danish tongue and laughing, but they did not molest or challenge her and she offered a silent prayer to Frige for it.

Behind the old warehouse, as the old man had said, stood the brothel. It was an unassuming sort of place and, looking at it from across the street, Halfritha had not known what she should have expected. It was little more than a hut with a low, dark doorway covered by a hide.

As she entered, the stink of sweat and unwashed male bodies hit her, mingled with the sickly-sweet perfumes the women splashed on themselves to cover their own odours. A couple of them were lounging about by the hearth. They were scrawny things wearing extremely short tunics and faces painted with ash and pig's blood. They looked at her muddy clothes and plain face with scorn. Several chambers led away from the central hearth, screened by wickerwork and tattered curtains. At least one of them was occupied for Halfritha could hear the bestial grunting of a man and the soft moaning of the object of his efforts.

A curtain was drawn aside and a middle-aged woman emerged. Her face was painted in a similar fashion to the two girls but she wore a long dress. Her bearing marked her out as a woman who commanded the respect of the other girls. This had to be Leola.

"Who are you?" she asked, an eyebrow raised. "Theomund send you? I already told him I've no more room and, no offence dearie, but you're a bit older than the types these men usually want."

"No, madam, I …" stumbled Halfritha, "I wish to speak with you about something urgent. And private," she added, glancing at the two girls who watched her.

"Very well," said Leola with a sigh. "Come into the back room. But I warn you, if you're a thief, I'm armed and skilled at using a blade."

Halfritha ignored this and followed the woman behind the curtain into the room that served as Leola's private office. It was dim but she could make out the shapes of many strange artefacts hanging from the beams. As well as combs, brushes and other items of beautification, there were many bunches of dried herbs and clay jars along with the twisted, petrified forms of various animals; lizards, snakes, fish, bats and other creatures that she could not identify. Medicines, probably, and she felt a touch of gladness knowing that she had come to the right place.

"Well then?" prompted Leola. "I'm a busy woman."

"My name is Halfritha. I'm one of the slaves from the other side of the island. I want to ask you a favour."

Leola's eyes watched her keenly, like an old cat.

"I think I might be … with child," continued Halfritha, unconsciously cradling her belly.

Leola's eyebrows lifted just a little. "And what exactly do you want from me?"

"I'm told that women in your profession know of certain herbs that can make the baby go away."

Leola sighed. "Look my dear, I feel for you, but really, it's not my business if one of the bastards here knocked you up. It certainly wouldn't be the first time it's happened on this island. But having a baby isn't all that bad. It'll be taken away from you and raised somewhere else. You won't have to look after it all on your own; the gods know that this isn't the place for it. It won't be your responsibility. All you have to do is bring it into the world and others will take care of everything else."

"But I don't want to bring it into the world!" cried Halfritha in frantic annoyance. Why couldn't this old woman see? "I want it gone! To never have existed!"

"I want lots of things, child," replied Leola coldly, "but I don't expect to receive them. Go away and have your baby. There's nothing I can do for you."

"But there must be! What's all this stuff around here?" she indicated the hanging bundles of herbs and dried animals. "If not for saving women from the horrors of bringing children into the world, where they will be raised as slaves, as whores?"

That last remark stirred something in Leola and for a moment she looked angry. "Look, girl, we're all slaves here. It's a rotten lot in life I know, and if one of Theomund's men wants to have his way with you lot over at the camp instead of paying for it here then that's his privilege. Every month I have to give some of my girls potions that destroy the lives these scum plant inside them, and it nearly kills them too. I've lost several girls that way and it's not something I enjoy doing, but I do it anyway because I'm a slave just like you. The only difference is that years ago I learned to accept my lot in life so tried to make the best of it. That's why I run a brothel on this god-forsaken island instead of just working in one. It's what sets me apart from all the other hopeless women I see passing through my doors; poor little wretches that don't even know what they are.

"I watch them come and go. The ones that stay are the smart ones who, like me, accept their wyrd. The others, well they're the ones that get flogged, murdered, cast into the sea or need me to patch them up because

254

they refused to do what a man commands of them. These girls here don't get a say in life but they have to keep working, and if they get pregnant, well the baby has to come out because no man wants to fuck a swollen sow of a girl. You don't have such worries, so I'm telling you to keep your damned baby and be grateful that a good grain of life has come out of this damned island. Leave me my small amounts of herbs for the women who don't have it so lucky."

This speech would have knocked most women aback and made them feel guilty for whining on so, but Leola had not counted on the desperation in Halfritha's heart and the love she still kept for her husband. She would not have this child that was not Hengest's! And if Leola could be angry, then so could she. "I won't have this child!" she shouted. "I won't! What kind of a mother would I be to it if I let it become a part of this world where only coldness and brutality await it? To become a whore in this wretched hovel if it's a girl or work its fingers to the bone under the lash if it's a boy! I will not do it! I'd rather die!"

This last remark was not quite true for if she were to die then who would look out for Aesc and Hronwena? But she was not finished with this woman yet. "You sit here on your perch and tell me that I'm lucky not to be a whore like you and your girls, well what about my child? Will it be lucky too? And it wasn't some man on this island who fathered it. It was a pirate captain called Halga, a wicked evil man if ever there was one."

Leola had been starring coolly at Halfritha up to this point. But her last remark had made her sit up. She gazed into Halfritha's weeping eyes and a touch of sympathy crossed her aged features. There was something else there too, a dark remembrance. "Sit down, child," she said, indicating a stool. Her voice was softer now, lacking all of the hostility it had shown a moment ago.

Halfritha obeyed and wiped her eyes on the hem of her shawl.

"You should have told me," said Leola.

Halfritha sniffed. "What difference does it make to you who the father is?"

"Because I just might be prepared to help you if it means preventing the spread of that evil bastard's seed."

Halfritha looked up at the woman in surprise.

"Halga was the one who brought me to this island twenty years ago. I was due to be married when he and his raiders took me from my village. He killed my husband-to-be along with my whole family. Like you I became his whore on the journey across. My first child was his. A boy. Where he is now, the gods alone know. I gave birth to him in this very hut. A different woman was in charge back then and she helped me through it. Then he was taken from my arms and sold off to some merchant who would raise him as a theow in a foreign land. Never saw him again and I never will."

"Are you glad that he was born?" asked Halfritha.

Leola looked at her with an expression she could not read. She reached behind her and fished up a pouch of some sort of herb. "This is rue," she said, tossing it onto the table. "Mix it into hot water and drink all of it in one go. It will bring about the bleeding required to flush out the child. I should tell you that it is risky but you are not too far along that it is not worth trying. If you run into any problems, or it hurts too badly, send for me immediately."

256

"I can't thank you enough," said Halfritha. "And I'm sorry if I spoke too harshly a moment ago."

Leola waved aside this apology.

"I don't have much to pay you with …"

"I don't require payment. We are all sisters in suffering on this island."

Halfritha stood up to leave. The old woman had gone very silent. She thanked her again, but Leola seemed not to hear. She turned and slipped out through the curtain, leaving the old woman alone with her ghosts.

Aelfstan

The voyage north was rough. Great waves knocked the *Fafnir* about from side to side and the crew heaved on their oars with every fibre of their beings. Salt spray washed over the bulwarks and the crew were constantly soaked, sore and grumbling. Food was short and the dull taste of dried fish and hard bread did nothing to raise their spirits.

It grew colder and the wind was bitter. The crew dug out their furs but, with the constant waves soaking them every time the ship crested a swell, the garments were too damp and cold to provide much comfort. Eventually, after what seemed an eternity on the turbulent sea, they sighted land.

Aelfstan had never been this far north so the bulging, wet rocks that glistened in the sun were a new sight to him. Sand dunes and fens dominated the coastline of the lands he was used to but here everything was rock and moss, as if the teeth and bones of the giant Ymir – whom the gods had slain to form the world – were more prominent up here in the lands of the Northmen. There was even a little snow left over on some of the higher boulders. It lay in streaks in the shaded places like sleep in the eyes of the land after its winter slumber. Tall pine forests rose behind the shoreline and were dark green against the greys and blues of the sea and sky. Colonies of seals barked curiously at the *Fafnir* as its crew rowed her along the coastline looking for the inlet that Halga knew from previous visits.

They passed close to a village tucked away in a corner of the fjord. Wooden houses with thatched roofs were layered up the side of the hill behind the wharves and their inhabitants jumped up and down on the shoreline in alarm at the sight of the raider. Some held shields aloft and hammered weapons on them menacingly in an effort to drive away the doom that the dragon-prow heralded. But the settlement was not Halga's target and the Fafnir drifted by, its crew laughing at the panicked villagers, as they sought their intended spot further along the coast.

It was after midday by the time they found it; a pretty and secluded inlet shaded by pines and firs. They dragged the *Fafnir* into the shallows and then set about making camp. Halga sent men off in search of food. They were in luck, for a little way down the shore a whale had beached itself and died, leaving its dark, rich meat for the taking.

It had only been there a couple of days or so, but already several locals from nearby settlements were carving off thick strips of blubber and meat to take back to their families. Halga's men were initially met with curses and insults from the locals, but the sight of their spears and their large number was enough to frighten them off.

They took shifts in cutting through the blubber to reach the juicy red meat beneath, which was brought back to their camp and cooked, while Daegal took a select few of the crew to the village they had passed to get a good price for the wool.

Beorhtwulf put Ealhwaru to work with the men and she did not complain. During the voyage she and Beorhtwulf had shared a fur on the deck at night and several times Aelfstan had been kept awake by their lovemaking. Seeing her standing knee-deep in whale blubber, her arms red to the elbows while Beorhtwulf lounged about with Halga back at camp, Aelfstan couldn't help himself from asking her; "Are you Beorhtwulf's lover or his slave?"

She looked at him with those cruel, keen eyes and replied, "I was his slave once. When I was a little girl he took me from my village after my parents had been butchered by Angle swords. I have travelled with him since, crossing the seas and the forests and the marshes of Middangeard."

"Why do you not flee him? Are you still his slave?"

"We are all slaves to something." As she said this she looked deeply into his eyes and he recognised the same look she had given him the night she and Beorhtwulf had joined them; the look of somebody seeing a shadow over somebody else's shoulder.

"You love him," he said.

"Yes, I love him. Besides, what need have I of freedom? I have never known hunger, or thirst or need of any kind whilst I have been in his company."

"Are you not worried that he will tire of you? Men often discard slaves they no longer require with a quick blade if they find no buyer for them."

She smiled at this and wiped a fleck of blood from her delicate chin with her shoulder. "He needs me just as I need him. Therefore he will not tire of me. He requires my thoughts and my dreams."

"What need has he of somebody else's dreams?" asked Aelfstan, dumping a huge chunk of flesh onto the bundle of fir branches that had been lashed together to form a crude bearer. "Has he none of his own?"

"My connection to the Old Ones," said Ealhwaru. "The ancient spirits of the earth and sea that were old when Woden and his kin came."

Aelfstan halted as he felt a shadow fall across his soul. "What do you know of the Old Ones?" he asked, the chilling memory of the cave of Gefion coming back to him.

"All women are connected to the Old Ones," she replied. "But only some are aware of this connection. The three sisters who weave men's fate into their great tapestry are the kindred of the ancient spirits who ruled before Esegeard came into being. Women who share a bond to the Wyrd Sisters often display gifts like foresight and the ability to see that which others do not. My mother was such a woman. She was highly respected in the villages of my homeland. Men and women went to her for it was said that she could see their fates and could speak with the gods themselves."

It suddenly made sense to Aelfstan. Ealhwaru's mother had been a seeress, one of those dark-shrouded women who dabble in mysticism and runespells. A wicce or a haeg; depending on one's dialect.

"I inherited my mother's gift," she went on, "and I have seen that which follows you."

"What follows me?" he asked.

"I saw it on the first night, when Beorhtwulf and I joined your crew in Jute-land. A great black raven, sitting on your shoulder."

"A raven?"

"Woden's messenger," she continued. "It watches you, protects you. But for what reason I cannot tell."

Aelfstan remembered the raven he had seen atop the mast of the burning trader, and before that at Finnesburg. Both times his life had been saved. Was Woden safeguarding him? *What for?*

And then he remembered.

Screaming. Burning. A blazing hall, and a dynasty ended. A sunken idol and a goddess destroyed. The crackling of the flames as Ealdorman Herogar and his people perished; murdered, *sacrificed* by Horsa, son of Wictgils, who had taken their lives in Woden's name. The words he had shouted into the thunder-wracked sky returned to him like an echo in a dark, dripping cavern. The gods had been listening! They had accepted his sacrifice. And they were protecting him.

He surged with a fiery exuberance brought on by this sudden understanding. The gods were protecting him! Memories of recent events were revealed in a wholly new light to him. The turbulent crossing from Angle-land to Frisia to rescue his brother. He could have been sunk. The battle in Finnesburg where his attacker had been warded off by a raven. He could have been killed. And again during the fight aboard the trader. Luck had been with him again.

Luck?

Wyrd.

How many times should he have been killed but hadn't been? Was he immortal? Would Woden keep him safe, guard him as a warrior of the gods? He felt elated by these findings. Surely he could not fail in his quest now. He would find Hengest's family and not a blade nor a spear could harm him.

He was gods-chosen!

"You look pleased with yourself," Ealhwaru said, eyeing him suspiciously.

"I am," he replied. "For I am Woden's man!"

"A blessing and a curse."

"What do you mean by that?"

"Those chosen by the gods often find it a heavy burden to bear. No matter how much they seem to help us, there is always a price to pay and often it is dearer than we would like. Woden is known to tire of his chosen ones and abandon them when they least expect it. The old tales are full of such instances. And there is something else that follows you that might take the raven's place should it fly from your shoulder."

"You speak in riddles, woman."

"Wyrd is always a riddle," she retorted. "A riddle for us to solve. It is not runes cut in birch or stone. It is open to interpretation. I tell you, there is a second presence that follows you; one far older than the Allfather and his ravens."

"Something to do with the Old Ones?" he asked, feeling suddenly cold.

"Yes. Something female."

"Female?"

"The Old Ones were a matriarchy. They were concerned with fertility, nature and foresight. The perfect flipside to Woden's warrior-cult. I would have to cast the runes to know for certain, but I suspect a woman will be your downfall."

A woman? The idea was laughable and yet it made Aelfstan angry. "You hold the Old Ones in very high regard for a wicce," he said. "I thought you were supposed to be on the side of the Ese."

Ealhwaru turned angry at this and snapped, "It is not for me to pick sides. Things are as they are and I just speak what I see." She walked away leaving Aelfstan to carry back their load of meat.

Later that evening, a visitor approached the camp. He was an elderly man whose red hair and beard were streaked with grey and, although he was a Northman, he spoke the dialect of the southern lands well.

"Clear off, old man," snapped Daegal, who had recently returned from the village and was in a bad mood for they had not managed to get as high a price for the wool as they had hoped. "You'll get no table scraps from us."

The man seemed affronted at this and continued walking towards them. "I have come to trade, not to beg," he said, as he threw down a bundle of wolf pelts upon the wet sand.

Something about the man seemed familiar to Aelfstan, but he could not quite put his finger upon it. Then he recognised the white bearskin the stranger wore as a cloak.

Ketil!

The bearskin was even more filthy and tattered than he remembered it being as a child. A surge of memories flooded his mind. This was the salty old dog who had put the idea of running away to sea in his young head all those years ago. He had aged considerably during the last twelve years. His eyes were lined at the corners and the ragged flesh that surrounded his missing ear was snow white where it had been purplish before.

And then Aelfstan began to panic. Would Ketil recognise him? *Impossible.* He had been no more than a boy the last time they had met, and the years had been tough enough on the both of them to fudge the old raider's memories.

Several of the men came forward to take a look at the wolf skins.

"Hunted them myself up in the northern lands," Ketil told them. "I was planning to sell them on in the village but then I saw your encampment and I know how much sailors appreciate good quality furs."

He was laying it on thick, and it seemed to be working, for silver and amber was produced from many purses and soon several of the crew were sitting comfortably with new furs around their shoulders.

"Will you sit with us and eat a while?" Halga asked Ketil, honouring a common courtesy between men who had just completed a business transaction.

Aelfstan prayed that the old man would decline and be off on his way but he was disappointed. Ketil found a comfortable spot by the fire and basked in its warmth as a mead skin was handed to him.

"Where are you lads off to next then?" Ketil asked the men.

There were murmurs of trading, recruiting and other legitimate activities but no mention of the real purpose of their expedition north.

Ketil smiled. "I remember my voyaging days well but they are all behind me now. I used to travel from Dane-land to the land of the Saxons and beyond to Frisia. Now I'm just a simple trader making my living along the coasts of my homeland. But oh, to feel the sway of a ship's deck beneath my feet again! To smell the salt of the ocean and set eyes on foreign lands once more …"

Aelfstan wished that he had met Ketil under different circumstances for he really wanted to shake the old man's hand and reintroduce himself. He had fond memories of listening to the old raider's tales on the wharves of his father's settlement. All the places he had spoken of and the people who lived in them all sounded so exotic and far away to him then.

But Horsa's naivety had been replaced by worldliness. He had seen much of the world now, and it was a cold and dark place full of violence and evil of which he was now a part. It wreaked damage on them all. He looked up at the man who had been a mentor to him, the man who had seemed so strong and powerful to his child's eyes. Now he was a seller of pelts in his old age. Did time treat everybody so cruelly?

He noticed that Ketil was looking right back at him.

"Don't I know you from somewhere?" the old Northman asked him, a puzzled frown on his face.

Aelfstan's heart hammered in his chest. "No, I don't think so," he replied.

"I'm sure we met a long time ago," Ketil persisted. "Weren't you the son of some ealdorman down south?"

Aelfstan was acutely aware of Beorhtwulf sitting nearby, chewing on a strip of whale meat. *Vengeful Beorhtwulf. Blood seeking Beorhtwulf, hungry for the butchery of his brother's killer.* Aelfstan groaned inwardly. What cruel mockery were the gods enjoying at his expense now? What sort of protection was this? To throw this old man and his keen memory against him now when they had been doing such a good job of keeping him alive?

"I'm the son of no ealdorman," said Aelfstan firmly. "You are mistaken."

But Ketil was not listening to him and was busy scratching his head. "What was the name of that ealdorman in Jute-land?" he mumbled to himself, racking his brains for the faces and names of the past. "Wictgils!" he exclaimed at last. "That's him! Ealdorman Wictgils! You're little Horsa, the ealdorman's youngest son."

Beorhtwulf's eyes darted up from his meal to fix on Aelfstan. Aelfstan desperately tried to avoid his gaze, wishing that Thunor would send down a thunderbolt to silence the old fool. But he was not finished.

"I remember you sitting at my feet down on the wharves, listening to my tales," Ketil rambled on. "Such a keen lad. Well, I am glad that you took up the life of a seaman. Roving the whale-road, answerable to no one. It's the closest us mortal men can get to being gods."

"You are mistaken," Aelfstan repeated, grinding his teeth together for he was aware that several other members of the crew were now looking at him with interest. Next to Beorhtwulf, Ealhwaru watched him, a half smile on her lips.

"Truly you are mistaken, old man," said Halga. "We picked this youth up not one month ago in the islands. He's a wandering vagabond, certainly no ealdorman's son that I can see."

Ketil stared at Aelfstan. "Oh, perhaps you're right," he said. "My memory isn't what it used to be. I've spent so many years travelling, I often get places and people confused. My apologies, young man."

Aelfstan nodded and continued eating his meal. The talk turned to other things and eventually Ketil stood and told them all that he had to be getting home.

Darkness had begun to approach and the crew of the *Fafnir* carried on drinking and eating into the night; enjoying the brief moment of warmth and comfort that was sure to end with the coming of the dawn, when Halga would kick them into action and they would leave the small inlet and continue with their journey.

Aelfstan was hugely relieved that old Ketil had left them and his cover was still intact. Perhaps it had just been a small jest of the gods for they had brought him through it unscathed. But it had been a frightening experience. Every so often he could feel Beorhtwulf's eyes upon him, paying him close attention as if the raider was waiting for him to let something slip, confirming what the old man had said.

He did not sleep easy that night.

Hengest

"I'd be tempted to leave the silly bastards to their fate," said Ordlaf. "Serves the scum right."

"It is tempting," admitted Hengest, "but I need to prevent my brother's men from deserting me and going on the warpath. They'll tear this coast apart and bring all the men Ealdorman Healfdane can levy down on us."

"An example needs to be made of them," said Guthlaf, "but I don't see how you can stop them from doing what they want. We Danes are too few to keep your brother's rabble in check."

Hengest tossed the twig he was idly toying with into the flames in frustration. Horsa's men were so like their captain it was uncanny; no thought of consequences or the inconvenience of others. Although food was running short, Hengest had expressly forbidden them from pillaging the neighbouring lands but, as usual, the raiders had reminded him that they owed no fealty to him and they would do just as they pleased.

Now three of them were in the hands of Ealdorman Healfdane – the ruler of these parts – for stealing some pigs from a local farm. They would no doubt be executed but Healfdane had probably heard of the warband encamped on his shores and that made hostages valuable; at least until he could call his thegns to him and marshal enough men to fight Hengest.

"I knew this Healfdane of old," Hengest said. "He came to my father's hall when I was but a stripling. Perhaps I can persuade him to let the men go."

"Why would he give up his most valuable game pieces?" Ordlaf asked. "Those prisoners are all that keep your brother's men from burning his thatch over his head. And they are champing at the bit to do just that, hostages or no."

"And another thing," said Guthlaf, "surely this Healfdane has heard of your banishment. If he is an ally to your father, he may not be disposed to bargain with you."

"That is a chance I will have to take," said Hengest. "News can travel slowly and it has not yet been a year since I left Jute-land to join Hnaef. Luck may be with us. You shall both come with me and I shall take one of the raiders too to ensure my brother's men do not think I am attempting any treachery."

"This is highly dangerous," said Guthlaf. "Why do you risk so much for three thieving scoundrels?"

"Because this is a chance to bring my brother's men into the fold and I will not let it slip by me."

Aelfhere was the one chosen to accompany Hengest and the two Danes to Ealdorman Healfdane's settlement. The rest of the raiders seemed uninterested in whatever Hengest was trying to prove and probably thought he'd end up with his head on Healfdane's gables, but Aelfhere was willing enough to come along.

With no horses it took the best part of a day to reach the settlement. They were picked up by a company of scouts and escorted the last few miles to a walled enclosure that contained the ealdorman's hall and other buildings. They were disarmed at the gate and their reception was a hostile one. Warriors stood by with their swords half drawn, ready for treachery.

At the doors to the hall they were told that only one of them may enter to speak with the ealdorman. Hengest bade his three companions to stay put.

"This is ridiculous," said Ordlaf. "You can't go in there alone. It would be madness!"

"I have no choice," Hengest replied. "If they wanted to kill us they could have done so as soon as we gave up our swords at the gate."

"Even so," said Guthlaf, "you don't know what's awaiting you in that hall. Maybe this ealdorman wants to get his hands on a fourth and more valuable hostage."

Hengest did not answer. His nerves were taut and he had a sick feeling in his gut. He wanted to get this over with as soon as possible so he strode in through the doors, leaving his friends and Aelfhere waiting in the chamber behind him.

The hall was dark and smoky and the ealdorman sat alone at his table while the hearth burned low, the evening meal finished and the theows and thegns departed. Two guards with spears stood at the wall behind him.

"It is a strange leader of raiders," Healfdane began, "who camps his men on my shores without permission, steals from my people, and then strides up to my own doors with a paltry three-man escort."

"I am no raider," said Hengest. "You may not remember me, but I met you when I was little more than a boy. You came to the hall of my father, your friend, Ealdorman Wictgils. I hope that you still honour that friendship."

"Ealdorman Wictgils's son?" said Healfdane, his eyebrows raised. "Yes, you have the look of him. But I heard rumour that his son had been exiled."

"That was my brother, Horsa," said Hengest, thinking quickly. Perhaps Healfdane had heard of Horsa's desertion or maybe his own exile, but he did not seem to have a full grasp of the facts and Hengest hoped that he could bluff his way through this. "I have come to apologise, my lord," he went on. "The three men who stole from you were under my command and disobeyed my orders."

"This all seems very strange," said Healfdane. "Why should you, an aetheling, be at the head of such a mixed band of cutthroats? Two of them are Angles and the other a Geat of all things. What happened to the Jutish thegns your father commands?"

"In truth they are mercenaries," said Hengest. "My father has sent me to sea to learn how to command men. He employed this band of villains as his own thegns would follow me too readily. He wanted me to be forced to instil discipline in men who did not fear him. I am ashamed to admit that it is harder than it looks."

At this Healfdane's face creased into a smile for the first time. "That sounds like old Wictgils! Always one to make things difficult, even for his own kin!"

"I will not give up on men under my command, even though they deserve to be left to your justice," said Hengest. "I hope that you can see this and will consider the payment of a gild in exchange for their freedom so that I may punish them in my own manner."

Healfdane frowned. "If you were not the son of a man I used to know better in happier times, I would refuse," he said. "But in this case, a gild would suffice I suppose, on the condition that you leave my shores on the dawn tide. I cannot have a warband encamped on my doorstep. Where in all the blazes were you taking them anyway?"

"We had hoped to join up with Ealdorman Aescgar's fleet," said Hengest. "Some hard fighting against the raiders would knock some sense into my men but we are having some trouble locating him. He barely camps long enough to be found before moving on."

"He's driven the raiders as far as Geatland, or so I've heard," replied Healfdane. "I caught wind of some large battle on the open sea, but no indication of who won. You might not find any raiders left to fight. Or Ealdorman Aescgar's corpse in the water."

Food and drink were brought for Hengest and his three companions who were allowed into the hall at last, and discussion turned to the gild that was to be paid for the theft of the pigs. They slept the night there by the hearth, and on the following morning, were presented with the three thieves who had been kept in a stockade since their capture. They were grubby, irritable and beaten black and blue. Swollen eyes and broken lips were evidence of how unwelcome foreign thieves were in these lands.

They were grateful to Hengest for securing their release as they set out for the coast on horses loaned from Healfdane's stables. A company of guards escorted them and would take the horses and the gild back to their ealdorman.

The raiders were astounded to see Hengest return with their lost companions and gave a cheer when they dismounted and rejoined their crew. Hengest hoped that the cheer was directed at him and, although none of the raiders openly praised him, he knew that he had at last won them over and drawn the two bands of men a little closer.

Aelfstan

The settlement that Halga had chosen to raid for slaves was situated at the northern end of the fjord. It was a small village of thirty to forty huts and a meagre hall that faced a collection of wharves where fishing boats bobbed about gently. Backed by tall pines and hidden behind the jagged curve of the fjord, the villagers probably considered themselves safe from the eyes of raiders. But Halga knew this fjord well and this was not his first raiding expedition in the lands of the Northmen.

Although Aelfstan had spent a large part of his life as a raider, he had never been comfortable with taking slaves. He had been part of two slaving runs onboard the *Bloodkeel* and they had been ugly, sordid affairs that left him feeling like the lowest type of scum. Taking somebody's livestock and possessions was one thing for those could be replaced if the unfortunate villager was willing to work hard enough. But taking somebody as a slave was the same as taking their life. Once somebody purchased them, their years as a theow would be short and hard.

It took a special type of raider to deal in slavery, Aelfstan had decided, and he was not that kind of person. But he was not about to express his moral stance on the matter to his new comrades when he was so close to learning the whereabouts of his brother's family.

The *Fafnir* anchored behind the spit of land that concealed the village, and twenty of its crew waded ashore. The rest remained aboard the ship with orders to row around the headland and block the village from the other side while Halga led the attack through the

273

trees. This would prevent any of the valuable villagers from escaping in their small fishing boats.

Beorhtwulf accompanied the group of fighters, as did Ealhwaru, much to Aelfstan's surprise. He had heard of female warriors before but until now he had never set eyes on one. He did not doubt that the dark, mysterious woman could be as cunning with a blade as she was with her tongue.

The forest grew thick down to the water's edge and muffled the sound of Halga's men as they swept through it, ascending the hill, swords and spears in hand. The scent of wood smoke and drying fish penetrated the gloom of the forest where spotted mushrooms grew in abundance and rotting pine needles were soft underfoot.

They could hear voices. Nearby, a stream wound its way down into the fjord and several women were squatting by its edge, scrubbing cooking pots with sand. They laughed and sang, oblivious to the sharp blades and hungry eyes that watched them from the darkness of the trees.

Halga's men attacked without warning, grasping the element of surprise before it passed them by. The women looked up in terror as the twenty raiders charged from the trees, brandishing their weapons and creating as much noise as possible to terrify their prey. They knocked the women to the ground with the hilts and flats of their swords and produced thick ropes to bind their hands. One of the women escaped and ran screaming through the trees towards the village.

"Stop her!" Halga cried. "She'll alert the whole settlement!"

Without thinking, Aelfstan set off at a sprint in pursuit of the woman. The slope was steep down to the village and already he could see the cluster of buildings from which wisps of smoke curled up peacefully into the morning sky. Several of the men looked up as the screaming woman came down towards them, shrieking and waving her arms about.

Then they saw Aelfstan, but it was too late to save the woman. Catching her by her braided hair, Aelfstan drove his sword into her back, its red tip bursting through her chest. He ripped the blade upwards and pulled it free, letting the dead woman sink to the ground.

Looking up, he saw the outraged villagemen as they ran towards him, holding axes, tools and clubs. He could see the hatred in their eyes. It gave him a sense of power, a dirty, soiled sense of power and he smiled. He was, after all, Woden's man now. What were mere men to him?

The angry faces of the villagers turned to expressions of surprise and horror as the rest of Halga's men emerged from the trees, their screams filling the air. Aelfstan yelled a war-cry from the bottom of his lungs and charged, running ahead of his comrades. They swept through the village, killing the men who were foolish enough to stand against them, cutting them down where they stood, for such men who resisted made poor slaves.

Women and children screamed in terror. Some fled to their homes and bolted their doors. These were futile actions as the raiders booted down the flimsy doors and set fire to the thatch, dragging the howling wretches out into the mud. Some made a hurried retreat down to the wharves where the boats were waiting, but the great carven grimace of the *Fafnir* was already making its way around the headland and drifting into sight, its grinning

275

face mocking their attempts as its crew rowed it closer to shore.

Aelfstan felt lightheaded as the screaming of the butchered villagers filled his ears and the stench of blood and opened bowels pervaded his nostrils. It was intoxicating. The gods were with him! He waded through the would-be warriors of the village, cutting open arteries and slashing through guts like a farmer harvesting corn.

One of the men managed to skewer a hunting spear into his shoulder but Aelfstan did not register the pain, only the pathetic attempt of one man to stop him. With one swift stroke, he hacked through the ash shaft and split the man who wielded it from shoulder to breastbone.

He felt the impressed gazes of Asse, Daegal and the rest of the crew on him. Here was a real warrior! Who would have thought it of the young dice player they had picked up in the islands? His words to Halga that day were ringing true; he was a fine replacement for the man he had killed.

The resistance in the village was ended now. The bodies of those who had bravely defended their homes and families littered the muddy ground. Those who were to be sold as slaves were rounded up and restrained whilst those who were too sick or old were quickly dispatched by Halga and his men. Houses were raided and stores looted. Mead was being drunk by the victorious raiders and the prettiest of the women screamed as they were ravished.

Aelfstan entered one of the huts and was attacked by a fisherman wielding a long knife. He drew his blade across the man's belly, spilling his intestines out onto the floor. The man sank to his knees and Aelfstan found himself looking at a young mother and her child who cowered behind a table strewn with the makings of a meal.

He looked down at the guts and spreading pool of blood at his feet. The man had been protecting his family, that was all. The eyes of his family looked up at him in pure terror and, as the haze of slaughter cleared a little from his eyes, he pitied them.

The door slammed open and another man entered. Aelfstan whirled about to face Beorhtwulf.

"You seem quite the warrior," said the Angle. "Aelfstan, isn't it? You are very handy with a blade for a travelling vagabond. One would almost think you had been born an aetheling."

Aelfstan stared at him. He saw the same mocking cruelty in his eyes that had been so evident in his brother, Ingvar. He was sure that Beorhtwulf suspected him after Ketil's words the night before. This was the one man who could stand in his way, the one man who could foil his mission and doom Hengest's family to their fate.

He screamed, letting all of his hatred and frustration surge through him as he charged at Beorhtwulf. Their swords clanged together and the terrified mother and child took the opportunity to flee the hut. Steel slithered against steel and Aelfstan swung high, knocking the helm from Beorhtwulf's head and gashing the side of his face open.

The Angle staggered backwards and Aelfstan ducked as a defensive swipe whistled over his head. He cut his opponent's feet from under him and Beorhtwulf fell heavily with a cry of pain. One of his feet was severed and the other one cut to the bone. Blood pumped freely onto the floor of the hut. Aelfstan stood over the fallen brother of his former captain, his bloody sword tip pointed at the man's throat.

"Who … who are you?" managed Beorhtwulf through his agonising pain.

"Don't you know?" Aelfstan asked him, grinning savagely, knowing that he could reveal his true identity and it would not matter now. "I am Horsa, son of Wictgils."

Beorhtwulf stared at him, the pain in his face replaced by a burning hatred.

"I killed your brother," Aelfstan continued. "I severed his ugly head and took his ship. And do you know what I did with his body? I pissed on it and left it for the wolves." This was a lie, but the anger at this man who had so nearly thwarted his plans was so great that he wanted to hurt him beyond the pains of defeat and death.

Beorhtwulf howled with rage and agony. His sword lay a few feet away where it had slid out of his grasp when he had fallen. It was beyond his reach.

"And now, Beorhtwulf, son of Wolof," continued Aelfstan, "I'm going to kill you." He raised his blade and saw the fear in his enemy's eyes before he brought it down hard, tip first.

It sank almost noiselessly into Beorhtwulf, slithering through flesh and puncturing the chest cavity.

Aelfstan briefly registered a shadow in the doorway before the screaming started. It was Ealhwaru. She gazed upon the bleeding corpse of her lover and master and cried out in rage before flinging herself at Aelfstan. He tried to wrench his sword free but was unable to as the screaming hellcat of a woman was upon him, scratching at his eyes and clawing at his face.

He grunted with pain as her nails raked his cheeks. Grabbing her around the torso, he flung her away from him. Like an animal, she landed on all fours and was then upon him again, drawing a saex from her belt.

This time he was ready for her and he grasped the wrist that held the knife and was surprised by her strength. She pushed him against one of the walls of the hut and he kicked out backwards, propelling them both towards the table. Ealhwaru's back arched as he bent her backwards onto the flat wooden surface. She gripped his middle with her thighs the way a lover might amidst the throes of passion and he pressed down on her, slamming her clenched fist against the table again and again. The saex fell free and skittered across the wood. Now he had her!

He planted his forearm on Ealhwaru's neck and leaned down, choking her. She gripped him harder, her crushing thighs drawing him closer. She looked so fierce and defiant with her black hair plastered across her sweating face; a warrior-woman that would surely make Woden's shield maidens proud; and Aelfstan felt desire rise up in his loins.

He wanted her. He had wanted her since the day he had first seen her. And now he would take her.

He tore her dress to expose her round, perfect breasts and then he leaned forward and kissed her hard on the mouth. She bit him and he cried out in pain. If he had had a hand free he would have struck her.

But then she relaxed a little. He felt her rigid muscles soften under his arms and he let her draw him closer. They kissed, no biting this time. Aelfstan smiled. Was he successfully taming this wild Saxon woman? He released his grip on her wrists and her slender arms wound their way around him. He hastened to unbuckle his belt and loosen his breeches. Lowering them down to his knees, he worked his hands beneath her skirt and grasped her firm buttocks before thrusting into her. He kissed her neck and breasts, moving backwards and forwards, working himself towards climax.

He was vaguely aware that only one of her hands was caressing his neck now and did not heed the other one until it was almost too late. She had reached across the table to where the saex lay and had grasped its bone handle. With a swift motion, she drove it towards his neck but he caught her wrist as before, slamming her arm down hard on the table.

Bitch! He began thrusting harder, feeling the ecstasy rising up within him; nearly out now. She screamed her hatred of him as he rammed her again and again, and then the release came, shivering through his body.

He felt himself weakening. The energy and rage that had fuelled his slaughter that day was abating. Woden's battle-spirit was leaving his mortal body and Ealhwaru's words to him the other night stirred in his mind; 'something else might take the raven's place should it fly from your shoulder'.

He pulled the saex from her grasp and as she tried to rise, sensing his weakening strength, he drove the blade hard into her chest. She screamed and writhed beneath the pressing weight of his body and he dragged the blade up, cutting through her guts. She coughed blood and struggled a little more before eventually lying still.

Aelfstan felt her abdominal muscles loosen and he pulled himself free of her. She lay motionless on the table, blood seeping from the ugly slice in her body, her senseless eyes staring up at the shadows between the beams and the thatch. She had been so beautiful in life and now she was mutilated, violated. Dead.

He felt sick, every ounce of his lust and thirst for death and slaughter had deserted him now, leaving him cold and disgusted with himself. What had he become? He quickly pulled up his breeches and buckled them before stepping outside into the sunshine.

The slaughter and enslavement of the villagers was complete. Buildings burned while the raiders dragged loot about, drinking the mead and raping the women. Daegal saw Aelfstan leave the hut and walked over to him. "Enjoying yourself?" he asked.

"What?" replied Aelfstan, in a daze.

"This must be your first raid, although you bear yourself as if it were your tenth."

"Oh, yes. It is." Aelfstan lied.

"Have you seen Beorhtwulf and his lady? I'm sure they were with us when we attacked, but the captain can't find them."

"In there," Aelfstan jerked his thumb towards the hut he had just left.

Daegal peered into the gloom and emerged, his face white as snow.

"Gods!" he exclaimed. "What happened?"

"Some bastard villager managed to kill Beorhtwulf," Aelfstan replied. "He also killed Ealhwaru and was raping her corpse when I came in and gutted him."

"That's a bad turn of luck for a man if ever I saw it," Daegal said, spitting to keep the ill fortune from rubbing off on him. "Beorhtwulf was a seasoned warrior. How could a simple fisherman have killed him?"

"As you say," said Aelfstan. "Bad luck. Perhaps he offended the wrong god."

Halga's satisfaction at raiding the village was dampened somewhat by the death of his friend. The fishing boats that were tied up at the wharves were sunk to make room for the vast keel of the *Fafnir* to be brought in and the slaves and booty were loaded aboard.

At their backs the village burned and a pyre was constructed to send Beorhtwulf to Waelheall. The body of Ealhwaru was placed next to her master so that she might continue to serve him beyond life, although some commented that Woden might claim her as one of his shield maidens, so impressive she had been in battle. Aelfstan cared little. They were both dead and his position amongst the crew was all the safer for it.

The pyre burned away on the shoreline as they rowed away, the slaves whimpering down in the hull between the rows of oars. The fjord receded and soon they were out on the Western Sea, with the white caps breaking around them and the crew pushing them homewards.

Halfritha

The bleeding began sometime in the night. Halfritha was not aware of it until she rolled over and felt the coldness of the wet sheets. There was a deep, throbbing pain in her abdomen and by the dim moonlight shining in through the slats in the roof she could see that her sheets were dark. She tried to sit up but the pain was too great and she fell back with a cry.

Hronwena, who slept nearby, stirred and sat up. She took one look at her mother's condition and let out an ear-splitting scream.

The slave camp was soon in a flurry of excitement. Several women ran outside and cried out that Halfritha was dying. This aroused some of the men in their own hut and they came out to see what all the fuss was about. Aesc, hearing his mother's name being shouted by the wailing women, came dashing out and across the muddy yard, but was restrained as he tried to force his way into the hut.

"What's all this noise?" shouted a guard who came over with his whip in his hand. "Get back into your huts or I'll have the hides off each and every one of you!"

"It's Halfritha!" cried one of the women, brave enough to face the guard. "Something's wrong, she's bleeding to death!"

"No!" cried Aesc, and he redoubled his efforts to break through the barricade of women.

"There'll be some bleeding alright if this is some sort of trick," said the guard, as he waded his way through the terrified women. They let him pass, and he entered the hut, stooping below the low beam. His face turned to one of uncomprehending horror as he gazed upon the blood-soaked sheets. It only took him a moment to gather his senses and stumble backwards out of the hut.

"Mother, don't die!" wept Hronwena. "Don't leave us all alone!"

Halfritha drew her close. "Listen to me, Hronwena," she said. "I want you to go to the other side of the island and find Leola. Bring her back here as fast as you can."

"But the guards …"

"They'll have to let you go, she's the only one who can help. Ask for directions to the brothel. But you must hurry!"

Hronwena wiped the tears from her eyes and nodded. The women stood back to let her pass as she fled from the hut into the darkness.

"Why didn't you tell us you were with child?" one of the women asked Halfritha.

Halfritha tried to answer but could not.

"She didn't know," said an elderly woman who knelt down by her side. "I've seen many young girls not even know it. Hush, child. Don't speak. You need to save your strength. Your daughter will be back with that woman soon." She turned to the others. "Well, don't just stand there gawping, ladies, fetch clean rags, sheets, anything. We must try to halt the bleeding as best we can."

With all the bustle in the search for clean linen, and the guards distracted by Hronwena's pleas to let her pass, Aesc was able to work his way into the hut.

"Out of here, boy, this is no place for you," snapped the old woman.

Aesc ignored her and approached his mother. "Why are you bleeding?" he asked, his eyes red with tears.

"Come here, my son," Halfritha said, grasping his hand. "Your sister has gone to fetch help. I'll be alright, you'll see. But when she returns, I want you to step outside and let the women do their work. Can you be brave for me?"

He nodded and wiped the tears from his eyes.

It seemed to take an age before Hronwena returned with old Leola in tow. "Hold it, whore," said one of the guards at the doorway as he put a restraining hand on her arm.

"I'd remove that if I were you," Leola told him, a small knife appearing in her hand as if by magic. "Unless you want to explain to Theomund what happened to your manhood."

The hand was removed and she was allowed to enter.

"Right, put on water to boil, somebody," she said, immediately taking charge. "I'm glad to see that you girls had the sense enough to plug the bleeding until I got here. Good. Now get these children out of here."

"We're staying," said Hronwena.

"No," said Aesc, and he took his sister by the hand. "Let's leave them to it, please, Hronwena."

Hronwena looked from her little brother to Halfritha.

"Go, child," she told her daughter. "Look after your brother for me."

Hronwena let Aesc lead her outside.

The next couple of hours were a blur for Halfritha: she remembered little. Dawn light was peeping in behind the hide covering of the door by the time Leola carried away the bloodied sheets and began to scrub her hands in the rest of the hot water.

Aesc and Hronwena were called in and they flung themselves around their mother's neck.

"Do not trouble her too much," said Leola, drying her hands on a cloth. "The bleeding has stopped, but she needs rest more than anything."

"My children ..." Halfritha mumbled, grasping them to her with weak strength.

"We thought you were going to die," said Aesc in an accusing voice.

"I'm sorry," Halfritha replied. "I'm so sorry. But I will remain by your sides as long as there is breath left in my body."

"Alright, everyone back to their beds," shouted the guard outside. "Get that boy out of there and back to his own hut. Gods, what a night!"

Aesc didn't want to leave, but Halfritha persuaded him, and reluctantly he left Hronwena and his mother alone as the women began filling up the hut once more, eager for their beds after the lengthy interruption of their sleep.

"Mother, what was it?" Hronwena asked, as she snuggled down next to her. "Why did you nearly die?"

Halfritha sighed and decided that it was time for Hronwena to know the truth, for a misunderstood fragment of the truth was worse than no truth at all. "What I am about to tell you now, Hronwena, is to stay between us. Aesc must never know."

Hronwena nodded, her eyes wide in the darkness.

"It was a baby."

Hronwena stared at her mother, uncomprehending. "A baby?"

"It was growing inside me, just as you and Aesc did once, but … it died. Leola helped me get rid of it."

Hronwena was silent for a long time. "If it had lived," she said slowly, "would it have been Father's, like Aesc and I are?"

"No, Hronwena. It would not have been your father's."

"Halga."

The awful word confirmed an understanding that Halfritha would have thought beyond her young daughter. But Hronwena was a clever girl and had somehow associated the night's events with all those times Halga had taken her mother away, only to return her when dawn was turning the sky pale just as it was now. That unspoken horror that had caused such a rift between them over the past few weeks had finally worked itself out in Hronwena's mind, and for that Halfritha was sorry.

"You have to understand, Hronwena," she said, "that what I did, I did for your protection. I let Halga take me away so that he would not take you in my place. I couldn't let him take you, you understand. I just couldn't."

Hronwena said nothing. Halfritha knew that they should have had this conversation weeks ago. Then, her daughter turned and buried her face in her chest and began to weep.

"I'm sorry, mother," she cried. "I'm so sorry."

Aelfstan

The crossing was easier on the way back and no storms assailed the *Fafnir*. They made the tip of Jute-land in good time and headed eastwards towards the islands.

Aelfstan grew restless as they neared the straits that connected the two seas, for he knew that time was running out for his brother's family and he would be forced to make his move. If only he knew which island the market was to be held on, he could warn Hengest in advance.

With fresh slaves in the hull that required constant guarding, market day was on everybody else's mind too and talk turned to it that night when they made camp.

"What is our next heading once we have sold this lot, captain?" Asse asked, chewing on a mouthful of dried fish.

Halga sniffed. "We shall be spending a few days on the island," he said. "Our employer wishes us to stand guard whilst the market is taking place."

"Forty men to guard a market?" asked another member of the crew.

"They are frightened that the relatives of that Jutish family we captured during the winter will try to cause a disturbance," said Halga. "We only need to be a presence on the island."

"I don't know why we didn't just ransom them if their family is so important," said Asse.

"Hold your tongue," said Daegal. "It's the captain's business what we do with our slaves. You'll get your cut and that should be enough for you."

"What Jutish family is this?" Aelfstan asked.

"Oh, that was before you joined us," Halga replied. "A private job that earned us a little extra pay."

"What market are we taking them to? Anywhere I know?"

"There is a small island off the shore of western Dane-land. Markets are regularly held there in the summer months."

"Is this the sort of thing fitting for men such as us?" another of the crew asked Halga, his drink getting the better of him. "We all respect your wish to help out a friend, but are we raiders or hired skull-crackers?"

Several of the other crewmembers voiced their agreement. They were not happy with the arrangement and saw it as beneath them.

"Silence!" roared Halga. "We are being paid more than enough for our time, and it is I who am captain here, remember that!"

The crew piped down and scowled into the flames, eating the rest of their meal solemnly.

There was little more discussion that night and, as sleep eventually took hold of them, they bedded down on the sand. Aelfstan had grown to like Asse and he felt that if was going to get any more information from the crew, then it would be from him.

"Any idea who told the captain to grab that Jutish family?" he asked him, as he rolled up his blanket beneath his head as a pillow.

"Some friend of the captain's back in Dane-land," said Asse. "He arranged it without discussing it. It didn't sit well with us as he wouldn't let us take any other slaves from the settlement or much loot for that matter. It was hardly worth the effort. Halga can do his friends' favours if he wants, but we want decent pay. And now he wants us to hang around the slave market like levied farmhands."

"Who is this friend of his?"

Asse shrugged and placed his hands behind his head as he got comfortable on the sand. "Somebody he knew from way back before he took to the life of raiding. He never discusses his past but I heard it from the others that he's of noble stock. The Hocings, no less. A distant cousin of King Hnaef, perhaps. Anyway, the raider's life seemed to suit him better than following the banner of the West-Danes. Although he is not unwelcome in Dane-land, so it can't have been the result of a quarrel. Halga spends his winters there, holed up in some safe haven."

Aelfstan said nothing. *The Hocings.* That was interesting.

The moon was high when Horsa rose from his fur. The fires had died low and the rest of the crew were slumbering, their humped forms like small hills in the moonlight. The only sound, apart from the occasional snore, was of the waves calmly lapping the beach.

He had been pretending to sleep until he was sure that none of the others were still talking, for he could not afford to be seen leaving the camp. He rose silently and began weaving his way through the motionless forms of his comrades. As soon as he reached a safe distance, he risked a glance over his shoulder to make sure that nobody was following him before breaking into a run.

The tall grass of the island whipped at his legs as he ran; a dark shadow in a landscape of silver. No trees grew on this island and he felt alarmingly exposed out under the dark, cloudless sky with its brilliant moon.

He did not stop running until he had reached the other side of the island. Panting for air and his back sticky with sweat, he rested his hands on his knees and breathed deeply.

Down on the beach stood the dark figure of a man, waiting patiently. Next to him, grounded on the sand, was a small, one-man boat fashioned from hides stretched over a wicker frame.

Horsa smiled and approached the man. "You don't know how good it is to see you, Beorn," he said, embracing his oldest friend. "Sorry to keep you waiting, I got away as quickly as I could."

Beorn beamed a silvery smile at his captain. "I thought I had lost you," he said. "When the *Fafnir* headed north, I was unable to follow. But fortune smiled and I sighted it off the headland this afternoon."

"Sorry," said Horsa. "Had I known that we were heading to the Northlands, I would have warned you but there was no time. This Halga likes to keep things to himself until the last minute."

"It's a good thing he is confident enough to camp in plain sight, or I might not have found the right island after darkness fell."

"His confidence will be his undoing. I have seen his type before and they rarely die straw deaths. How is my brother?"

"He is well but impatient. The men have taken to him a little now. Any news with you?"

Horsa's heart ached at the mention of his crew. He longed to be treading the familiar planks of the *Bloodkeel* and laugh with its crew once more. But an end to it all was finally in sight.

"Tomorrow we leave for a small island off the coast of West Dane-land," he told Beorn. "Do you think you can follow us?"

Beorn nodded.

"There is to be a slave auction in a day or so and Halga's men are to play guard duty. My brother's family are sure to be there along with whoever ordered their kidnapping. Tell Hengest to be there in the market place with a small group of men and to have the *Bloodkeel* and the *Raven* hidden nearby with our men ready to storm the island at my signal."

"What will you be doing?"

"I'll think of something. The wind is due to change aboard the *Fafnir*, and when it does, I shall be helping it along with all the puff in my lungs."

Beorn smiled. "Good luck then, captain."

Horsa helped Beorn launch his tiny craft into the water and watched as his loyal friend paddled away into the darkness, back to Hengest with the news.

Horsa turned and headed back across the island towards camp where he prayed that his absence had not been noticed.

PART VI

(Æsc) "Æsc byþ oferheah, eldum dyre.
Stiþ on staþule, stede rihte hylt,
ðeah him feohtan on firas monige."

(Ash) "The ash is exceedingly high and precious to
men. With its sturdy trunk it offers a stubborn
resistance, though attacked by many a man."

Hengest

The bay was crowded with boats by the time Guthlaf and Ordlaf rowed the small craft up to the wharves. Hengest stood in the prow and frowned at the lack of moorings. Several other vessels that could not find a spot were beached on the wet sand with clusters of grim-looking men hanging about them, conversing in low tones. The huts that made up the settlement rose up behind the bay and already people thronged about them.

It was market day.

After beaching their craft, Hengest and his two companions made their way up the hill towards the cluster of decaying huts. Hengest wore a long, grey cloak that concealed his mail and an eye patch that covered his left eye. He couldn't afford to be recognised by whoever had taken his family until he was ready to make his move. Beneath the cloak he felt the reassuring weight of *Hildeleoma* hanging from his belt and he was looking forward to the time when he could draw its shimmering blade and exact his vengeance.

The *Fafnir* and its crew were nowhere in sight and Hengest guessed that they must be anchored in some bay on the other side of the island. The overseers of the market wouldn't want to frighten the potential customers away by having a great longship in the harbour with its forty armed men milling about the wharves. But Hengest was confident that Horsa was putting whatever plans he had into action and would be ready to fight by his side once his enemy had been identified.

As they passed the first of the shacks, Hengest saw a blacksmith at work in a makeshift forge. The fire blazed and roared as the bellows fed it air and on the wall behind hung iron torques in a variety of sizes. These would be fastened around the necks of new theows, marking them out as the lowest members of society. For an extra fee, the blacksmith would engrave the runes of their master, so if any escaped it would be known to whom they belonged.

Hengest gritted his teeth at the thought of his wife and children wearing somebody's name around their necks. He pushed it from his mind. He was here to save them from that fate and could not afford to get distracted now.

The huts opened onto a wide space where a raised stage of rotten planking stood. A mass of people thronged about it watching the sale of two young girls, probably sisters, dragged from their homes after their parents had been butchered. They stared at the wooden floor, their faces blank of all emotion while a fat man haggled with members of the crowd who called out offers of silver.

The girls were not much older than Hronwena, and again, Hengest clenched his teeth as the fat man called out obscene remarks regarding their virtues to the murmured interest of the crowd.

He scanned the onlookers for anyone he might recognise, anyone eying him suspiciously, but there was no one. The two girls were sold and ushered off the stage where their new master was waiting for them. Hengest watched them disappear as a new slave, this time a young man, was dragged onto the scaffolding and the bidding began once more.

Slave by slave came to the stage and each was sold. Men haggled and silver passed from purse to hand much in the same way as at a cattle market. Hengest began to grow anxious. His wife and children were nowhere to be seen.

Halfritha

The guards had begun to take slaves away, one by one, down to the marketplace. It was unclear how many of them were to be sold that day. Perhaps all of them. Halfritha's heart was filled with dread at the thought of being separated from Hronwena and Aesc. There was no guarantee that the same buyer would purchase all three of them.

The talk of the slave market had been circulating the camp for days now and all were on edge. Halfritha's strength had returned, bit by bit over the days. The other women had looked after her and nursed her back to health but now it felt like it had all been for nothing. What good was her strength if she was not around to look after her children?

A group of guards approached the women where they worked at the fishing nets and began scanning faces, looking for certain specimens of quality to be sold.

"Keep your head down," Halfritha said to Hronwena. "Don't give them any excuse to take you."

But it was too late. One of the guards was already walking over to them. "These two," he said, pointing at Halfritha and Hronwena.

Halfritha looked around frantically. Where was Aesc? The men had been herded up for inspection but she saw no sign of her son among them. She felt the rough hands of one of the guards land on her shoulders and she struggled. She had to find Aesc!

"Bring her along," said the first guard. "Don't let her give you any trouble."

"No!" screamed Halfritha. "Not without my son! Not without my boy!"

The guard did as he had been ordered and Halfritha barely felt the heavy blow across her cheek. Hronwena began to weep.

"Not so hard on the face, damn you!" snapped the other guard. "They don't sell as well if they're all bruised up. Come on, we're wasting time."

Halfritha and Hronwena were dragged to a cart and pushed inside with a dozen other slaves before they set off towards the other side of the island.

The marketplace was a terrifying scene. The crowd bayed like hungry dogs and shouted out prices as Theomund stomped up and down on the rotten scaffolding – a man in his element – calling out to the crowd and accepting bids with a greedy grin.

As Halfritha and Hronwena were hauled down from the cart and pushed up onto the stage, an adult male was being led away by his new master, off to get his collar fixed at the blacksmith's.

"And what have we here?" asked Theomund jovially, as Halfritha and Hronwena were pushed forward. "A mother and her daughter, what a precious sight! They can both be yours at a discount. Who'll start me?"

Halfritha held Hronwena close as they were led out across the boards where the baying crowds howled their fate at them.

Hengest

Hengest's breath caught in his throat as he saw his wife and daughter. He fought to restrain himself as they were manhandled onto the stage. *But where was Aesc?* His heart burned as he saw Halfritha and Hronwena alive and well but his son was nowhere to be seen.

"Seven silver pieces, can't say fairer than that!" bellowed the auctioneer. "Who'll start the bidding at seven silver pieces? These young ladies have many years of work left in them and they're pretty too if you fancy them for your bedchamber!"

He placed his hand on Hronwena's shoulder and the young girl took the opportunity to sink her teeth into the soft, fat flesh. He howled with pain and there was a burst of laughter from the crowd. The enraged man struck Hronwena savagely across the face.

Hengest could bear no more. "Seven silver pieces!" he called out. He would buy his wife and daughter back if necessary before collecting the heads of every slaver here in compensation.

"I have seven silver bits," said the fat man, his throbbing hand forgotten. "Who'll advance it to ten?"

"Ten here!" called out another man on the other side of the marketplace.

"Twenty!" shouted Hengest, and there was a stunned murmuring from the crowd. He didn't care. He wasn't going to let anybody else bid for his wife and daughter as if they were cattle.

The auctioneer's eyes twinkled at the high price, eager to seal the deal before the buyer had a chance to change his mind. "Done sir!" he bellowed, and gestured for his men to take the two slaves down behind the scaffolding where their new master could collect them and pay their price.

Hengest made his way around the back, pushing through the crowds. Guthlaf and Ordlaf followed him close, their hands on their sword hilts beneath their cloaks. Behind the stage a table had been set up with a set of scales for the weighing out of silver.

"You must either be very wealthy or have very particular tastes, friend," said the auctioneer as Hengest approached. "Not that these girls aren't worth the price, of course!"

"I am just a man who is willing to pay for what he wants," Hengest replied, as he counted out the correct pieces of silver and handed them to the man at the scales.

He became aware of the presence of several heavy-set men at his back. He could not tell if they were armed but got the uncomfortable feeling that they were being surrounded. "Well?" he asked the auctioneer, as he dropped the last silver ingot onto the table. "Where are my theows?"

The auctioneer flashed a nasty grin at him. "Seize him!" he said, and the men at Hengest's back moved suddenly.

Guthlaf and Ordlaf drew their swords and spun to face the half dozen men who had produced weapons and were pressing against them. They were hopelessly outnumbered. Hengest did not move. He merely stared into the fat man's eyes.

"Now then, Hengest Wictgilsson," said the auctioneer, still grinning, spitting out his name as if it were sour mead. "If you would be so kind as to go with these men quietly. I don't want any blood spilled in my marketplace. There is someone who wants to give you a warm welcome."

"When I've dealt with him, I'll come back and kill you," Hengest told him. "That I promise."

One of the men extended a hand and Hengest unbuckled *Hildeleoma* and handed it to him. It was met with a low whistle of awe as the guard took the magnificent blade.

"Father!"

Hengest looked up. It was Hronwena. Two guards restrained her as she struggled to break free and run to him. Halfritha was next to her, already held in a tight grip by the men. Tears at the sight of him streamed down her face.

"I'll come for you both!" Hengest called out to them, but already he was being pulled away by the guards. "I'll come back, I promise!"

"Take those women back around," said the auctioneer, as Hengest and his companions were led away. He jingled the silver ingots Hengest had paid him in his hand playfully. "I rarely have the chance to sell the same slaves twice!"

Aelfstan

The crew of the *Fafnir* were not in the highest of spirits that morning. They had waited for several days on the barren side of the island and they were restless and irritable. Finally, with market day upon them, Halga had given the order to head around to the bay where they were to stop any boats from leaving once the market had started. They grumbled as they rowed, none of them daring to raise their voices above much more than a whisper, less Halga or Daegal hear them.

The prospect of butchering mere brawlers held little interest for them. Even if trouble broke out, such lowlifes were unlikely to carry much silver or offer much in the way of a fight. It was demeaning for the toughest bunch of raiders on the known seas to be bought as guards for a slave camp. Aelfstan smiled. He could almost taste the discontent at the oar benches and the air crackled around his ears like a brewing thunderstorm.

And now it was time for the first stroke of lightning.

As the ship began to round the headland, he leaped up from his bench and called down to his comrades. "Halt what you are doing!"

Thirty-nine faces turned to stare at him in astonishment.

"Leave the oars where they are!"

Halga strode the length of the boat towards him, his face flushed with rage. "Have you lost your mind, boy? I give the orders on this ship!"

"How much are you being paid to play guard duty?" Horsa demanded of him.

"That is not your concern! I pick the jobs for this crew and ensure that all get a fair share. Of course, if you would rather opt out, then you are free to leave at any time!" He pointed a thick finger at the rolling waves whilst his other hand rested upon the handle of his saex.

Horsa looked to the crew again. They seemed unsure as to whether their comrade was insane or stupidly brave. "Whatever you are being paid for this petty, humiliating job, I promise to double it if you follow me instead," he said to them.

"What, by Thunor's cock, are you playing at?" bellowed Halga. "If you want to be captain, then have the guts to challenge me for the position instead of trying to buy my crew's loyalty. And how would a penniless vagabond pay double what I have been offered, eh? Tell me that Aelfstan!"

"My name is not Aelfstan! I am Horsa, son of Wictgils!"

There was an awed silence as this revelation sank in. Even Halga was taken aback. There was whispering and murmuring throughout the crew. His name was well known and there were stories about him. *Horsa? The fearless first mate of the Bloodkeel? The exiled son of an ealdorman who had raided a troll's lair and took part in the slaughter at Finnesburg?*

"Then it was you who killed Beorhtwulf," said Daegal, his eyes like daggers. "I knew there was something odd about that day."

"Aye, I killed him and his Saxon bitch just as I killed his brother, Ingvar, who had been my captain for too many years."

"You shall pay for your treachery with your blood and your screams," said Halga through gritted teeth.

304

Horsa ignored him. His position was precarious. If he had misjudged the crew then the rest of his time on Middengeard would be short and painful. But if he had guessed them right …

"On that island is the family of my brother, Hengest," he said. "They are the noble Jutish family you captured earlier in the season. I sought a seat on your oar benches to track them down and take vengeance on the man who ordered their capture. I have two vessels of hardened raiders headed towards this island to reinforce me. Together, my brother and I intend to storm this market and take back his family. If you would join us, then I can promise you as much gold as we can loot from these stinking merchants and slavers."

"How do we know that your brother won't seek vengeance against us?" asked Asse.

There was a chorus of agreement and Horsa smiled. He had caught their interest, made them consider their options. That they had not torn him limb from limb yet meant that Halga was as good as finished.

"My brother only seeks revenge on the one who employed you," he told them. "He has no interest in raiders who follow their captain's orders. If you would help him then I promise you that he will be generous, and those of you who wish can remain as part of this crew under my command. You have my word on this."

"I'll be dead before you command this ship," roared Halga, drawing his saex. "This is mutiny!" He turned to the crew. "When I am finished with Horsa, any man who stands with him will regret the day he was born!"

Daegal stood at his captain's side, but the rest of the crew no longer cared for the threats of their captain and first mate. They looked to Horsa, their minds made up. In their hands they held oars, clubs and knives. They were no longer Halga's crew. All the threats, the beatings, the mutilations and the humiliations burned in their memories as they advanced on their captain.

"Your command is over, Halga," said Horsa. "The *Fafnir* belongs to me now."

Something snapped in Halga's mind. Perhaps it was the anger at losing his ship to the arrogant youth who had killed his nephew and his best friend. Or perhaps he was merely running on stark terror now; a cornered rat that will bite the foot that tries to stamp on it. He leaped, saex slashing through the air.

Horsa was ready for him. Gripping his wrist, he tossed the bigger man to the deck and drew his own blade.

A knife fight is an ugly thing. Unlike swords or axes, it is not easy to strike a mortal blow. Most people who die in knife fights do so through loss of blood and exhaustion, punctured by many wounds. The scars on many a raider's arms and torso are a testament to that fact.

Halga rolled and came up at lightning speed, cutting low. Horsa leapt back, warding off the blow with his arm. The blade sliced through his flesh, opening it nearly to the bone. Gritting his teeth against the sharp pain, he lunged at the man and the two fighters were locked in a deadly grasp, both unable to wield their weapons properly. Horsa brought his knee into Halga's abdomen with brutal force, knocking the wind from him. As he bent double, Horsa switched the grip on his blade and brought it point down into Halga's exposed neck.

The blade sank in easily and Halga gasped. His own knife clattered to the deck and he stumbled forward, clutching behind him for the source of the needle-like pain that was just out of his reach. Horsa wrenched the blade free and tripped the man so that he went down heavily on his knees.

Standing behind him, Horsa reached around and drew his already bloodied blade across Halga's throat, severing through tendons and windpipe. Halga gurgled in an agonised quest for air, blood soaking into the front of his tunic. He coughed and tumbled forward, face down upon the deck. So died the scourge of the seas, in a pool of spreading blood in the bilge of his own ship.

Daegal, loyal to his captain to the end, made for Horsa, his sword drawn; but the crew were ready for him, clawing at him with hungry hands. He screamed as he was dragged down between the benches, the blows of clubs, oars and fists rained down upon him until his body twitched no more. The crew stripped the corpse of any valuables and tossed it over the side, shortly followed by Halga's.

"Let the fish dine on them," said Horsa.

And so Horsa earned the captainship of a vessel through single combat for the second time in his life. He tore off a strip of cloth from the hem of his tunic and tied it tightly around his wounded arm. The crew stared at him, wide-eyed. Their killing of their first mate had aroused the battle-lust in them and they were eager for orders.

"What now, captain?" asked Asse.

"Put in at the nearest inlet," replied Horsa. "We'll advance on my brother's enemies over land. They won't know what hit them. Oh, and you are first mate now, Asse."

The young man beamed at him and immediately began giving orders to drop oars and make for land. Horsa smiled and took a position at the bow of the ship.

It was time to re-join Hengest.

Hengest

Hengest, Guthlaf and Ordlaf were led across the island to a festering old shack that stood upon a headland. A thin wisp of smoke wound out of the hole in the rotting thatch and several guards lounged about the place. They were conversing in Danish and stood up as the prisoners approached. The door to the hut was opened and Hengest and his companions were pushed inside.

It was dark and smoky. More guards were sitting by the fire and all about the place was the stench of damp and decaying straw. A shadowed form sat on a chair on the other side of the hut. The dim light prevented Hengest from seeing who it was, but by the dress she wore, he knew it was a woman.

"The mighty Jute comes to claim his family at last," she said in a thin, cold voice. "Just as he dampened the light of my life, so I have damped the light of his."

Hengest knew the voice. It was not one he had ever counted on hearing again. "Hildeburh!" he gasped.

She rose and approached the fire. Her face was gaunt, racked by the grief she had been unable to shake during the months since the massacre at Finnesburg. Black circles ringed her eyes but they still blazed with the light of hatred for him.

"It was you who kidnapped my family?" asked Hengest.

"You killed my husband," she replied. "You destroyed my home and sent my youngest boy and I off to Dane-land with my brother's men, to a hearth long since foreign to me. I wept bitter tears in my brother's old home, a prisoner of the man who now rules the West Danes; a man I do not know. My son was less fortunate. Frealaf did not survive the winter, removed from the only home he ever knew, broken by the loss of his father and brother. I have no sons now. I know it was you who slew Frithuwulf. You took everything from me. So yes, I wanted you to feel that pain."

"Frithuwulf's death was no fault of mine!" protested Hengest. "And I let you and your son live when many a man would have put you both to the sword."

"Do not lie to me, Jute!" she screamed. "It was your sword that cut Frithuwulf down! It was your feet that trampled him to death, smashing his beautiful body into a bloody ruin. And yet my husband gave you your life and offered you a home and service in his warband. But you threw this in his face, calling your brother to Finnesburg and wreaking a bloody slaughter on my people."

"Your husband's offer to me was an offer of imprisonment in exchange for the lives of my men who had done no wrong. He had no right to insult me like that!"

"Frithuwulf was just a boy," said Hildeburh. "He was just my beautiful baby boy. He was innocent!"

"So are my family!" snapped Hengest. "And your son knew what he was doing. He chose to defy your husband's orders and stand against your brother. He chose his death."

Hildeburh's eyes narrowed. "Don't ever speak of him! Your family are nothing to him. Their sacrifice is necessary to make you feel the agony of losing the thing you love best in life! You shall die today with the knowledge that your family are theows and have lifetimes of hardship and degradation ahead of them!"

Hengest snorted. "Did you really think that I would come here with only two thegns? I suspected that some treachery lay at the heart of all this. There was too much planning, too much purpose behind it all. I knew that it was not just the work of simple slavers. I have two ships on their way with fifty men between them. You'll never leave this island alive."

The threat did not have the desired effect on Hildeburh for she smiled at him, a cold, unfeeling smile. "I expected that you would enlist the help of that brutish brother of yours and his gang of villains again. And that is why I took the precaution of employing the most feared raiders in these islands to join me here today."

Almost as if on cue, there was a commotion outside. Shouts and the sound of clashing steel rang out. The guards in the hut leaped up and stormed out, drawing their blades.

Hengest, Guthlaf and Ordlaf saw their opportunity and seized it. As one of the men rushed past, Ordlaf grabbed his sword arm and wrenched it around, twisting the joint until an audible 'crack' was heard. The man screamed and dropped his sword which Guthlaf plucked up and thrust into the belly of another man. Hengest meanwhile, slammed his fist into a guard's jaw, knocking him to the ground. There was a brief struggle for the man's saex which Hengest won and slashed the man's throat with one clean sweep before turning upon Hildeburh, grim intent in his eyes.

She showed no sign of fear and merely retreated into the shadows of the hut. Hengest stepped towards her and then thought better of it. She could wait. He turned and followed Guthlaf and Ordlaf out of the hut.

Outside they found a massacre in full swing. Around forty men had charged the hut and were making quick work of Hildeburh's hired Danes. It was the crew of the *Fafnir* but there was no sign of Halga Eadwulfson. Instead they were led by a stocky man with dark hair who swung a blade with a savagery equal to that of any of them.

"Horsa!" bellowed Hengest.

The younger brother grinned back at him. Soon Hengest had *Hildeleoma* back in his hand and was thoroughly enjoying the crunching of the blade through mail, wood, flesh and bone; every cut a stroke of vengeance. But the irony of the situation was not lost on him. These very men who fought at his side had been the ones who had torn his family from their home and had butchered Brand.

The bitter memories of the ruined farm and the bloated, stinking corpses came back to him, but he pushed them away. Wherever the loyalties of these men had lain in the past, they served his purpose now.

It was short work and soon all the mercenaries lay about dead, their blood feeding the damp earth.

"As well timed as ever," Hengest said, embracing his brother. "Where are the rest of your men?"

"Storming the harbour if they know what's good for them," Horsa replied. "I saw the *Bloodkeel* and the *Raven* rounding the headland before we attacked. Nobody will be leaving the island now. Have you rescued your family?"

"No. They were waiting for me and took us here before I could get them away. I saw Halfritha and Hronwena down at the auction but where Aesc is, Woden only knows."

"We'll find him," said Horsa reassuringly. "We'll tear that place apart, but we'll find him."

"Fine. First I have one more thing to take care of here." He strode over to the hut and booted open the door.

They stood in the doorway, letting their eyes grow accustomed to the light. Something moved fast, a blurring sliver of light in the darkness. Hengest lashed out with *Hildeleoma* and the saex wielded by Hildeburh spun out of her grip and clattered down by the hearth. Hengest grabbed her by the wrists and forced her down to her knees. The light fell on her hateful face and she looked up at him with the scorn of the defeated on her fine features.

"Her?" remarked Horsa in astonishment. "Finn's queen?"

Hengest nodded. "After we left Finnesburg she returned to Dane-land where she remained for a while. But her hatred for me burned too bright. She blamed me for her son's death and she could never let it lie. After fleeing her brother's successor, she set about exacting her vengeance."

"She hired Halga's men to kidnap Halfritha and the children."

"Yes."

"It wasn't difficult for her to arrange. Halga is a Dane and kin to the Hocings. This I learned from his crew. He has a safe haven in West Dane-land. Probably knew Hnaef when they were youngsters."

"She knew that I would come looking for them," said Hengest, "and that I would probably recruit your help. That's why she had Halga's men here today with the aim of destroying us. But she didn't count on my brother being the most cunning little bastard on the Eastern and Western Seas! Now she has no more cards left to play."

313

"You should have killed her back in Finnesburg," said Horsa.

"Yes," he agreed. "Now, leave me, Horsa. I want to do this alone."

"Brother, there's nothing I haven't seen, believe me."

"Please, Horsa. I don't want you to see me do this."

Horsa nodded and left the hut. He closed the door softly behind him.

After a while, Hengest emerged from the hut. All eyes were on him. His forearms were red to the elbows and his face showed the expression of a man who has just performed an unpleasant but necessary job.

"She didn't even scream," he said. "It was almost like she wanted me to end it." He was shaking. He had killed men before but never a woman and never in such a manner.

"Don't dwell on it," said Horsa. "For better or for worse, we've all done terrible things. There are no perfect men standing here today."

They found the marketplace in a state of chaos. The *Bloodkeel* and the *Raven* had drifted into the bay and the sight of the longships with their rows of oars manned by warriors had thrown everybody into a panic. By the time the crews had descended upon the wet sand, Theomund had ordered his guards to form a measly shield wall in the face of the attackers.

The customers ran in every direction, not knowing where to go. Those who had already bought slaves wanted to get into their boats and row away with all haste. but that was impossible with the raiders standing between them and the wharves. Most of them simply gave up and looked for a place to hide, hoping that whatever the raiders were after it would not involve them.

Beorn led the men up the beach and ordered the seizure of all theows. The guards were cut down in seconds, simply overwhelmed by the sheer number of the raiders. Newly purchased theows were wrestled from the hands of their owners and those who sought to hold onto their property were slain out of hand.

Theomund looked around at the chaos in horror. He turned and tried to make his way down from the scaffolding but froze as he saw the crew of the *Fafnir* heading towards him from the opposite direction. He saw Hengest at their head and his face paled.

"My wife and daughter, scum!" bellowed Hengest, striding up on to the stage. "Where arc they?"

Theomund stammered and shook so much that Hengest grabbed him by his tunic and pulled his fat face close, the tip of *Hildeleoma* pressing painfully into his windpipe. "Th … they have been s … s … sold!" he babbled.

"To who?"

"To a wealthy merchant! He took them away to the eastern side of the island!"

"Why?"

"His boat is m … moored there. He d … doesn't like the crowds of the wharves."

"And my son?"

"Wh … what?"

Hengest flung the wretched creature to the wood, and with one swift stroke of *Hildeleoma*, sent his ugly head rolling across the planks.

"Find Aesc!" Hengest shouted to Horsa. "I'm going after the merchant!" and he was off, racing through the marketplace towards the sandy bay on the eastern side of the island.

Horsa

Guthlaf and Ordlaf set off after Hengest whilst Horsa joined Beorn and helped with the rounding up of the theows. There was a large number of them; men, women and children both young and old. Horsa searched the miserable and frightened faces but he didn't even know what his nephew looked like.

"Is this all of them?" he asked Beorn.

"We emptied the huts and took every slave from their owners," the Angle replied. "But some may have already departed before we landed."

Horsa spotted a young boy who looked to be of Aesc's age. "What's your name, boy?" he asked.

"Scyld, lord," replied the lad.

Horsa cursed. This was the only likely lad within sight. "Have you seen one the same age as you? Dark hair, healthy-looking, by the name of Aesc?"

The boy shook his head and backed away, his lip quivering at the sight of Horsa's bloodied sword.

"Think carefully!"

"There was one," said an elderly man nearby. "A real fighter he was too. Didn't take to being sold at all well."

"Where is he?" demanded Horsa.

"Sold!" the man replied. "To a group of seafaring men. Maybe they wanted him as a new deckhand. They headed off in a small keel just before you lot landed. Might catch them if you hurry."

But Horsa was already off at a run, shouting orders to his men to alert the *Bloodkeel* and make her ready to put out immediately.

Hengest

Sweat poured down Hengest's back as he ran. The salty smell of the sea and the cool breeze refreshed him as he jumped down onto the beach. In the distance a small boat lay on the sand and a group of people approached it. One of them wore a long cloak of blue and looked to be a merchant.

Hengest's heart surged with joy as he saw the two women that were being manhandled behind him. *Halfritha and Hronwena!* He set off across the sand at a sprint and, as he approached, two of the men turned to face him, their saexes drawn.

"Father!" shouted Hronwena for the second time that day. It was sweet music in Hengest's ears and he was determined that his wife and daughter would not slip from his sight again.

Guthlaf and Ordlaf came up beside him, puffing and gasping for air. One of the merchant's men thrust with his saex. Hengest stepped to the side and sliced through the man's arm with Hildeleoma, before bringing his blade down on his head, splitting it open.

The other man tried to attack Hengest but found himself intercepted by Ordlaf who slammed the pommel of his sword into his face. The man fell down heavily and Ordlaf finished him with a downwards stab.

The merchant watched the fight with wide eyes and grabbed Hronwena as his last man fell, holding a knife to her throat as Hengest advanced on him. "Take another step, stranger and I'll gut this girl."

Hengest fumbled for his pouch and tossed it at the man's feet. It opened and the glint of silver ingots spilled out. "You can take all of that in exchange for the two women," he said, "and you can leave with no loss other than the two servants of yours that lie dead here."

He was throwing his money at a complete stranger when he could easily kill him but Hengest no longer cared. He was sick of killing and only wanted his family back.

The merchant seemed to consider this. His eyes flicked from the two dead men to the pouch of silver. "Take them," he said, sheathing his blade and pushing Hronwena towards Hengest. He reached down and scooped up the pouch before hastily turning back to the boat.

"Father!" cried Hronwena, flinging herself into Hengest's arms. "I knew you would come!"

He clutched her close, hugging her so tightly as if he was terrified of letting her go again. "Daughter," he said. "I would go to the Mistlands and back for you!"

Halfritha hugged her husband and kissed him passionately on the lips. "I had given up hope," she admitted, her eyes brimming with tears. "Forgive me. But Hronwena never gave up on you. And Aesc ..." she trailed off.

"Horsa is looking for him," Hengest told her, kissing her forehead reassuringly. "He's tearing the marketplace apart. We'll find him. And then we'll leave this island for good."

"Halga," she said, looking up at her husband. "The raider who took us. He is on the island ..."

"Dead," Hengest replied. "Horsa killed him. I am only grieved that I was not able to do the job myself."

Halfritha relaxed and hugged him closer.

They saw Horsa running across the sand towards them along with several of his men.

"Aesc has been taken off the island!" he shouted to Hengest. "A small group of seafarers have him. Look!" he pointed out to sea and sure enough, a small craft could be seen rowing out towards the horizon.

Halfritha began to sob. The nightmare was not over. Spurred into action, Hengest dashed over to where the merchant was pushing his vessel out into the shallows. Swords drawn, Hengest, and his companions splashed into the surf and seized the vessel.

Cursing, the unfortunate merchant was tossed into the shallows and the craft set out with Guthlaf and Ordlaf taking great digs at the waves with Horsa at the rudder and Hengest at the prow, his hands gripping the top strake so that the knuckles showed white.

Aesc

Aesc crouched at the stern of the small boat and looked around miserably. The iron collar that had recently been fitted around his neck lay heavy and cold against his skin, and his face was marked by a large purplish bruise from where his new owner had hit him as he had resisted being carried onboard.

He had no idea where he was being taken or what the future held for him, but he was fairly confident that he would never see his mother or sister again. This made him want to weep, but he forced the tears back, determined not to show weakness in front of his enemies. His father had taught him that much.

There were ten men in the boat and the oars rose and dipped with regular precision, powering the craft out to sea. The island and its marketplace were fast shrinking behind them. As one of the men looked behind at it, he called to his mates in alarm. "Someone's following us!"

Aesc stood up and looked at the small boat way behind them, its oars digging at the water furiously. At its stern stood a man with long, light hair and Aesc let out a whoop of joy. "It's my father!" he shouted. "Come to rescue me! You'll all suffer for this now!"

"Whelp!" roared his master and he cuffed Aesc soundly, knocking him into the hull. "Row harder! We can outrun these water rats!"

The men hauled on the oars harder and the boat sped through the water.

There was a sudden cry of alarm from the prow and men leapt up in a panic, pointing ahead. There, emerging from behind the spit of land came a longship, its forty oars ploughing the water and its dragon head leering at them as it came about to block their path. Aesc's heart sank as he recognised it as the *Fafnir*.

"Hard to steorbord!" shouted the captain and the ship drifted slowly about.

"We can't pass them, captain!" said one of the men. "Not forty oars!"

The captain spun around to look at the small craft that was pursuing them. It was close now. "Let them come alongside," he said. "Prepare to repel them when they do."

There was a great scurrying of activity aboard the small boat as the men rummaged about for shields, swords and axes.

Aesc looked back and saw his father and his men ship oars and drift alongside. One of the crew made to hurl a throwing axe at the approaching boat and Aesc rose quickly to his feet, flinging himself at the man. They crashed down into the hull and rolled about before Aesc found himself being hauled roughly to his feet and grasped in a headlock that cut off his air supply.

He reached down and seized the saex from his master's belt and drove it hard into the man's thigh, twisting it; another thing his father had taught him. The man howled and flung the boy from him, bringing his sword up in an overhand swing.

The blow never fell. In the intervening moments, Hengest and his men had swarmed the boat, leaping into it with swords swinging. Seeing Aesc at the mercy of a man wielding a blade, Hengest had rushed the length of the boat and swung his blade down, cleaving the man's shoulder down to the breast.

As the man toppled into the bloody hull with a splash, Hengest dropped his sword and scooped up

Aesc in a mighty bear hug. "My boy!" he cried. "My boy!"

"Father!" said Aesc, his voice a hoarse whisper, choked with the long held back tears that he now allowed to flow freely.

The hull of the boat was awash with red slaughter. Not a single member of its crew was left alive. Hengest took his son over to meet his men. "Aesc," he said, these are my loyal thegns Guthlaf and Ordlaf whom you have already met. And this, is your uncle Horsa."

The man called Horsa ruffled his hair. "Glad to meet you at last, nephew," he said.

"Is it over?" Aesc asked his father.

"It's over," replied Hengest. He fingered the collar around Aesc's neck which bore the name of a dead man etched in runes. "The first thing we do when we get back to that island is get that damned thing off."

As the *Fafnir* cruised closer its crew cheered, pounding the air with weapons and fists.

Aesc shrank back, not understanding. His father noticed and said; "Relax son. Halga is dead and these men helped us storm the island. They saved my life."

"They're good lads," said Horsa, "I thought we might keep them unless you have any objections."

Hengest frowned. "I don't think my wife and children will take to them after what they've been through but the head has been cut off the serpent, so to speak. And what is really left? A group of seafarers who make their way in the world just as we do. I suppose we might find a use for them."

A father and son had been reunited; an event that all the powers of wyrd had seemingly tried to prevent. But even the gods themselves could not keep that kind of love at bay. Above them the grey sky was clearing

323

and, in the distance, rays of sunlight tickled the water like spears of hope thrown down from Esegeard.

Hengest

In the lands of the Angles it was high summer. Cattle grazed in the meadows and theows worked the fields. Within the home of Beorn the Bald, the hearth fire crackled. Horsa and Beorn laughed and drank to old adventures whilst Hronwena and Aesc played with Beorn's great old hound down on the furs. Hengest lay with Halfritha in his arms, watching all the people he loved share the same room. It felt like his life was complete.

Almost.

Deep down he was uneasy. The future was far from certain. Beorn had offered them his home indefinitely but they could not stay here. Not after what had happened to Brand. They had defeated one enemy but had probably made many more in the doing of it. They could not stay here forever.

The *Fafnir*, the *Bloodkeel* and the *Raven* rode at anchor on the coast, watched over by the hundred odd men he and his brother now commanded. They were rich too, with gold and silver enough to last a lifetime.

"What troubles you, husband?" Halfritha asked him, sensing his worried mind.

"Our wyrd, love, just our wyrd."

"I've always found that it is best not to worry too much about what those mad wenches weave into our tapestries," said Beorn. "All we need do is ride the waves and pay the proper respects to the gods and all will be well."

Hengest smiled. Spoken like a true raider. No care for tomorrow as long as today was good. No wonder he and Horsa got along so well.

325

"I say we head out for one final raid this season," said Horsa, throwing the rest of his mead down his throat. "We have three ships under our command, enough to rival even the fleet of Ealdorman Aescgar were he still alive. The entire northern world will be at our mercy!"

"Don't you ever think that you are destined for something better than the life of a common raider?" Hengest asked his brother.

"Aha!" said Horsa with a chuckle. "Here speaks my noble older brother. He's the son of an ealdorman, you know!"

"I'm serious, Horsa," said Hengest. "As you say, we command one of the most powerful fleets in the northern world. Do you not think it would benefit us greater to look beyond the borders of Dane-land and Jute-land?"

"What's so bad about the life of a raider?" demanded Horsa. "There's loot and battle to be had. And women, of course, oh the women!" He suddenly noticed Halfritha glaring at him and he grinned at her sheepishly.

"I remember you saying that you wanted to see the world, Horsa," Hengest said. "You said you wanted to make something of yourself."

"Aye, and I did. I'm the most well-known raider in these parts. Have you heard that they tell tales about how I raided a trolls' nest?"

"Our names could be bigger."

"Ah, you've spent too much time in the company of kings," Horsa told him. "All that pomp and power has gone to your head."

"What if I have?" Hengest asked. "I've seen how kings live. They build mighty halls that make the dwellings of ealdormen look like fisherman's huts. You talk of battle and wealth and women but what good are those things if you do not have a home to return to, a place to enjoy your wealth when winter descends?"

"You've a point there," admitted Horsa. "Winter is no fun out in the wilderness, I can tell you that."

"We have no home, brother. Beorn is kind but these lands are not welcoming to us. Jute-land, Frisia, Dane-land; none of these places are safe havens anymore. No matter how much wealth we amass and no matter how many men we command, we are still exiles, just as our father made us."

They were silent for a time. The mention of their father cast a shadow over their happiness. Even though they were far from his reach, their lives were still subject to the old drunk's whim.

"Where would you want to go?" asked Horsa.

"I don't know," replied Hengest. "Maybe south to Frankia. Or perhaps the Burgundian lands. There's a whole world out there that knows nothing of us. We could start anew, build new lives where none are our masters."

"There's always Britta," said Beorn.

"That island at the end of the Western Sea?" asked Horsa. "Isn't that Roman lands?"

"No, they abandoned it when Alaric and the West-Geats sacked Rome," said Beorn. "Nobody rules it now apart from petty kings and chieftains. And they spend most of the time fighting each other. Many of my own countrymen have gone there already. They say it's good, farmable land. And there has been a Saxon presence on its south-east coast since the last days of Roman rule. They recruited Saxons in their armies, you see. When the Romans left, the Saxons stayed. It's easy pickings, I tell you."

"And what of the Britons?" asked Hengest.

"Fragmented and leaderless," replied Beorn. "Christians mostly."

"Christians?" remarked Horsa. They had all heard of the followers of the Christ-messiah but none of them had met one before. Few such people ventured as far north. There were rumours that Christians were weaklings and cowards, forbidden by their single god to take up arms in vengeance. Instead they were expected to pray and turn the other cheek should anyone slight them. "They don't sound like much of a challenge."

"As I said," said Beorn. "Easy pickings."

Horsa looked at Hengest and Hengest looked back at Horsa. A silent moment passed between them.

Halfritha squeezed Hengest's hand. "Are you seriously considering going?" she asked him.

"I might consider heading a reconnaissance voyage," he replied. "Just to spy out the land. Who knows? It might be just the place for us to build a new home."

"But it's so far."

"It will only be for a while. You and the children shall remain here and if I decide that it is safe and prosperous enough, then I shall send for you. It may be the beginning of a grand new adventure for all of us."

"I've only just got you back, husband. I thought you were lost for good. We all did."

"It is for you and the children that I'm considering this, Halfritha," Hengest said. "You deserve something better. I shall find land for us and build us a home where we can grow old and live out the rest of our lives in peace and safety."

"It's a long way," said Horsa, chewing on his lip. "And rough waters too. Few vessels can make such a trip. The *Raven*, perhaps."

"Is there anything that can be done to the other two to make them more seaworthy?" Hengest asked.

"As a matter of fact, I've been playing around with the idea of fitting false keels to them so that they might support masts. It'll take a lot of experimentation, but I think I might be able to get something working before the season is out, if it's this summer you were thinking of going."

"The sooner the better. Horsa, get those boats seaworthy. Beorn, I'm going to need your help in training our men. We need to forge them into a united force unrivalled by any."

"Of course, said Beorn."

Horsa scrambled to his feet. He reached for the mead jug and poured everyone a hornful. "Let us drink then!" he exclaimed. "To Britta, the great whore, and whatever fate she holds for us!"

Horsa

The western sky was clear and full of promise. White gulls wheeled and cawed about the masts of the three ships as if they were waelcyrie escorting their crews to the golden halls of the gods. As the land drifted out of sight behind them, they fell away, one by one, their shrieking voices remaining as tokens of luck. The chant of the rowers throbbed as their oars rose and fell, carrying them out into the blue unknown.

Horsa shouted a command to ship oars and raise sail. The crew scurried about and soon the great black sail was billowing outwards, dragging the *Bloodkeel* on through the waves.

It had taken much of the summer to get the length of the mast and depth of the keel right. He had the *Raven* for a model but the *Bloodkeel* was a much smaller craft and it had been a painstaking process to get the ratio right. But at last, as late summer approached, he had made both the *Bloodkeel* and the *Fafnir* fit for a long sea voyage.

He watched the sail and let the slopping of the waters rushing past the strakes calm his mind. He did not heed the hearty jests and laughter of the crew behind him. His heart and mind were elsewhere.

Perhaps a fresh start in this land of Britta was not such a bad thing after all. There were too many bad memories in the lands behind them, too much blood and guilt. If this new land was all it was cracked up to be, then he swore by Woden, that things would be different from now on. No more mindless slaughter. No more of this Woden's man business. He was nobody's man but his own. If the Allfather wished to keep him safe, then so be it. If he did not, then the gods be damned, he would do his best on his own.

Still he felt the shadow upon his shoulder and the presence behind him that made his spine ripple. Ealhwaru's words haunted him. He had killed a goddess. He had butchered a cult. And deep in his soul, he knew that comeuppance was part of his future.

He looked to the horizon with a heavy heart. Out there lay Britta and beyond that, it was rumoured, lay the edge of the world, spilling into the yawning black nothingness. Gods, was such a place the only land left to him?

Very well. It would have to do.

Hengest

Hengest breathed the salty air deep into his lungs, trying to keep his mind off the swaying deck of the *Raven* that lurched beneath his feet. Travelling across large bodies of water still did not agree with him. Nevertheless, he was captain of a longship with a crew beneath him. A league or so ahead of them was the *Bloodkeel* with Horsa at the prow and behind them was the *Fafnir* under the command of Asse.

Above him, fluttering from the high mast was a pale banner depicting two horses' heads facing away from each other with an intricate tangle of knot work connecting the two. It had been Halfritha's parting gift to him; a standard for the two brothers to carry into unknown lands so that the gods would see them from their halls in the heavens.

She and Hronwena had been working on it in secret ever since they had arrived in Angle-land that summer and had presented it to him the day they set sail. Although the subject had not been broached, the symbolism in the stitching was clear. Hengest and Horsa; two brothers who often trod different paths but were forever linked by the strands of their wyrd, however tangled they may be.

Before them, the horizon stretched ever onwards into a blue infinity. Somewhere out there was the land of Britta and whatever it held for the men who journeyed towards it in three keels, leaving behind everything they had ever known and loved.

It troubled Hengest to leave his family back in Angle-land and his mind would never be at ease while they were not by his side. But he had left a solid group of warriors behind at Beorn's homestead to protect them this time and besides, as soon as he and Horsa found a safe haven, he would send for them.

If land and plunder were as readily available in Britta as Beorn had said, then he could build a sizable homestead with a hall and stables and maybe even rule his own settlement as an ealdorman, just like his father had done. He smiled. Exile be damned, the Wyrd Sisters had an uncanny way of twisting a man's fate around so that he ended up not too far from where he began in life.

The three ships drifted onwards, their sails full of the eastern wind. The horizon reached out its long blue grasp to claim them as they sailed towards it. One by one, the ships were swallowed by the sky and vanished into legend.

AUTHOR'S NOTE

The Anglo-Saxon migrations to Britain in the fifth century are a muddled and confused affair. The term 'Anglo-Saxon' refers not to just one people but is rather an umbrella term for several Germanic tribes who made the trip to Britain once the Roman legions had departed. The most notable of these were the Jutes (from the Jutland peninsula in modern day Denmark), the Angles (from Angeln in Germany) and the Saxons (from Saxony – also in Germany).

It is not known how extensive these migrations were nor how aggressive as contemporary sources are few. What is apparent however is that during the fifth century, there was a large cultural shift in the east of Britain that saw the culture of the Celtic-speaking, Christianised Britons transform into the pagan, Germanic-speaking culture of the people who would one day be called the English.

Hengest and Horsa are two characters in the midst of this upheaval, accredited with spear-heading the migrations and founding the English kingdom of Kent. They are most likely historical figures and are attested to in three separate sources, beginning with Bede's *Ecclesiastical History of the English People* which was completed sometime in the late eighth century. Their tale was embellished further in *The History of the Britons*, ascribed to the Welsh monk, Nennius. *The Anglo Saxon Chronicle* also mentions them and gives the year for their arrival in Britain as 449.

Nothing is known of Hengest and Horsa's story before their arrival in Britain other than that they were the sons of one Wihtgils who was descended from Woden and that they were exiles. In my attempt to provide a back story for these extraordinary characters, I have turned to other sources for inspiration, notably an Old English poem known as *The Finnesburg Fragment* which tells the story of King Hnaef and his sixty retainers holding a hall against an attacking host. One member of Hnaef's retinue is named as Hengest.

Unfortunately the poem is incomplete so little more is known but the story is told in full in that other great work of Anglo-Saxon literature; *Beowulf*. Here, Hengest's name pops up again and it is revealed that he takes command of Hnaef's retinue upon the king's death. Is this the same Hengest who is mentioned by Bede and Nennius as landing his three boats in Britain? Are the events at Finnesburg the youthful adventures of the man who, with his brother, would one day lay the foundations of the first English kingdom? For the sake of a good story, I choose to believe so.

Beowulf also provided the inspiration for Horsa's adventures. There has long been an argument that the Old English poem concerning a young warrior's fight against a monstrous troll and its water-dwelling mother, is an allegorical tale depicting the overthrow of an older group of fertility gods by a warrior cult that superseded it. Evidence that a fertility goddess (who had a strong connection to water) was being worshiped in the continental homelands of the Anglo-Saxons appeared in the first century work *Germania*.

Written by the Roman Historian Tacitus, *Germania* is an ethnographic account of the Germanic tribes that dwelled on Rome's northern borders. In it, Tacitus tells us of a goddess called Nerthus, who was kept in a sacred grove on an island in the northern sea. Referred to as 'Mother Earth', Nerthus rode a wagon pulled by cows and travelled among the populace who feasted and made merry in her wake. The goddess (possibly represented by a statue) was then cleansed in a sacred lake and her slaves were drowned. The existence of this cult is backed up by archaeological finds of buried ceremonial chariots and several preserved 'bog men' in Denmark who appear to have been ritually sacrificed.

Nerthus appears to be a Latinisation of Njorthr; a god of the sea attested to in later Norse literature. That Nerthus is a male name suggests that we are either dealing with an hermaphroditic deity or a set of twin deities. Perhaps Tacitus only received half of the story and attributed the god's name to the goddess and failed to record her real name at all. Nerthus and his unnamed twin may have been both siblings and lovers. This incestuous arrangement is also seen in Freyr and Freyja (who were the sons of Njorthr according to Snorri Sturluson's *Prose Edda*). Freyr and Freyja are in fact titles meaning 'lord' and 'lady' respectively. Were they really the offspring of Njorthr and his lover as Snorri describes, or were they secondary names for a god of the sea and his partner; mother earth?

Freyr, Freyja, Njorthr and his unnamed twin/lover, were members of the Vanir (Wanes in Old English); a set of deities connected to fertility, prophecy and magic who were often in conflict with the more war-like Aesir (Ese) which included the likes of Odin and Thor. It was the scholar H. M. Chadwick who postulated that the female halves of these pairings were representations of a universal mother goddess worshipped throughout the Germanic world in particular on the island of Zealand in Denmark. Icelandic literature of the 13th century credit the creation of Zealand to a goddess called Gefion, who formed it with her plough by gouging out a piece of Sweden and dumping it into the sea.

Zealand is perhaps the island Tacitus mentions as being the sanctuary of Nerthus. The symbolism of earth and water is hard to ignore and it would be the perfect home for a god and goddess of the sea and the plough. Indeed, Gefion (which appears to mean 'giver') is attested to in the *Beowulf* manuscript with phrases like 'Gefion's bath' meaning the sea. If Freyr and Freyja were just lordly titles for Njorthr and his wife, Gefion may be the previously unnamed partner of Njorthr; the 'lady' to his 'lord'.

The rune poems that accompany each segment of this novel are from a 10th century manuscript from the Cotton library which, unfortunately, was destroyed in a fire in 1731. Luckily, the scholar George Hicks published a facsimile in 1705 and the particular translation I used is from the *Runic and heroic poems of the old Teutonic peoples* (1915, pp. 12-23) by Bruce Dickens.

Hengest and Horsa's adventures continue in *A Warlord's Bargain* and conclude in *A King's Legacy*, both available now. The first few pages of *A Warlord's Bargain* are included here for your enjoyment.

If you liked this book you could do me a huge favour by leaving a review on Amazon or the retailer of your choice. This would be greatly appreciated.

Chris Thorndycroft

A WARLORD'S BARGAIN

CHRIS THORNDYCROFT

*"This year Marcian and Valentinian assumed the empire,
and reigned seven winters. In their days Hengest and Horsa,
invited by Wurtgern, king of the Britons to his assistance, landed
in Britain in a place that is called Ipwinesfleet; first of all to
support the Britons, but they afterwards fought against them. The
king directed them to fight against the Picts; and they did so; and
obtained the victory wheresoever they came"*
- The Anglo Saxon Chronicle

Part I

(Đorn) "Đorn byþ ðearle scearp; ðegna gehwylcum
anfeng ys yfyl, ungemetum reþe
manna gehwelcum, ðe him mid resteð."

(Thorn) "The thorn is exceedingly sharp,
an evil thing for any knight to touch,
uncommonly severe on all who sit among them."

South East Britain, 447 A.D.

Horsa

The white caps heaved and belched spume as the *Bloodkeel* cut through the water. The distant island of Thanet drifted nearer like a grey hump rising from the waves. Horsa the Jute, exiled son of an ealdorman, barked orders and his men heaved on the oars with all the power in their arms. He gripped the bulwarks, his heart pounding to the drumbeat of the coxswain. His nostrils flared, drinking in the salty spray and the cold wind; the thrill of the chase beating its barbaric rhythm deep within him.

The little trader, not more than a league ahead, struggled to outrun its pursuer and make for the island where its crew hoped to skirt the coastline and lose it. The merchant vessel was fast, accustomed to the constant threat of raiders in this stretch of water; being the narrowest trade route between Britta and Gaul. But it could never hope to outrun the tightly disciplined and well experienced raiders that chased it.

Following close behind the *Bloodkeel* was the *Raven*, matching the speed of its companion ship stroke for stroke. At its stern stood Hengest, brother to Horsa, his flaxen hair billowing about in the wind. Horsa grinned. He could almost see the queasy look on his brother's face across the water. Hengest was no seaman and the constant rising and falling of the deck beneath his feet always made him feel sick, despite the sea having largely been their home for the past year.

Thanet drifted closer and Horsa bellowed an order to increase speed. His men were tired, but they could not lose their prey now. Beyond the island lay Horsa's third ship; the *Fafnir*, which he had won after killing its captain. Under the command of his good friend Asse, the *Fafnir's* crew had pledged loyalty to Horsa and his brother in return for pardon in their part in the kidnapping of Hengest's wife and children.

But that was ancient history. The *Fafnir's* crew had proven their worth a dozen times over in the two years of raiding that had followed. Hidden from view, the forty-manned vessel would emerge just as the trader tried to round the tip of the island, blocking its path and forcing it to tack. That would give the *Bloodkeel* and the *Raven* enough time to catch up with it and board it before it passed Thanet.

"Keep her steady!" Horsa shouted to Beorn, his first mate. "Keep on the headland!"

The trader was almost rounding the tip now and Horsa could see the men aboard it, scurrying back and forth, tossing items overboard to lighten the load. It would be no use, no matter how much they were able to increase their speed. The trap was set. There was no escape.

The dragon prow of a ship appeared around the headland. Its carven grimace leered like some nightmarish creature. The merchant vessel quickly tacked, its sail tilted to direct the craft as the new ship soared towards them, threatening to slam into their side.

Too soon! Horsa gritted his teeth. *Blast that Asse!*

But as he watched, he realised that the new ship was not the *Fafnir*. It was some other vessel outfitted for raiding.

"Who, by all the souls in Waelheall...?" he exclaimed.

And then he recognised that carven figurehead. He had encountered it many times since he and his brother had arrived on the shores of Britta. It was the figurehead of their biggest rival.

"Ceolwulf!" spat Horsa as if it were an oath. "What the blazes is he doing here? And where is the *Fafnir*?"

He watched in dismay as his rival drifted into the path of the trader. Cries of alarm floated to him across the water, mingled with the cheers and shouts of the raiders as their vessel crunched into the side of the trader, splintering timbers and shattering the bulwarks. The crew of the raider latched on grappling hooks and stormed the smaller vessel, swinging blades and cutting the traders down with all the savagery pirates were known for.

"Ship oars!" Horsa called to his crew. "Someone's beaten us to it. Beorn! Drift alongside!"

Beorn the Bald, first mate of the *Bloodkeel* - a massive Angle with a single blond plait of hair hanging down from his otherwise bald head - scrambled to his captain's side. "Who is it?" he asked.

"Ceolwulf."

"But what is he doing this far south? His territory is north of Thanet."

"My thoughts exactly," replied Horsa, his voice sour.

The sheer volume of raiders that plagued the south eastern waters of Britta meant that an agreement was necessary regarding territories. Dictated by the various men of power in the coastal towns and ports who creamed the profits from piracy, each raiding crew was assigned its own area. Transgressions always resulted in bloodshed.

"Your brother hails us," said Beorn.

The *Raven* crept close to the *Bloodkeel* and drifted alongside. Hengest called out; "What's going on?"

"Ceolwulf," Horsa shouted back across the small stretch of water between the two vessels.

"Shall we take him?"

Horsa considered this. The *Fafnir* had still not shown itself and that boded ill. Even with one ship down they still commanded nearly sixty men, but Ceolwulf also had a large force. A sea battle now would be bloody and long with much lost on both sides.

Horsa shook his head at his brother. "Too costly. We'll take this up with Eldred when we get back to port. Coxswain, forward! Beorn, bring us alongside the merchant. Pass him close and quick! We'll at least give that bastard a fright."

The two ships ploughed onwards towards the trader where the fight was still underway. As they drifted closer they could see the bilge of the trader awash with blood. Ceolwulf's crew spotted them and let out jeers and provocations.

Horsa's men gripped their oars tightly and glared at them, their hands itching for their swords and axes that would bring death to their rivals. But their captain stood, unwavering, his steely eyes cast upon the helmed head of Ceolwulf who laughed and waved his bloody sword in the air, watching them pass. The fallen trader drifted out of view as the *Bloodkeel* and the *Raven* rounded the furthermost edge of Thanet.

"It churns in my gut to let those bastards get away with plundering our prize," said Beorn, his hand resting upon the head of his large battleaxe.

"You're not alone in that, old friend," Horsa replied. "But it would be too costly to fight them now when we are one ship down. Let us find Asse and then we can plan our vengeance with clear heads."

Beorn grinned at him. "You get more and more like your brother every day. Back home you would have been the first to jump into battle whatever the odds."

Horsa frowned and turned towards the prow.

"Look!" he cried, flinging out a pointed finger. "There's the *Fafnir*!"

In a small inlet lay the third of Hengest and Horsa's raiding vessels. Its sail was down and several of its oars lay floating in the water nearby. There was no activity onboard.

Horsa had the *Bloodkeel* directed alongside it and stepped aboard, carefully treading between the ugly wreckage. The deck was littered with bodies and blood ran freely in the bilge. The *Raven* dropped anchor at the stern of the ship and Hengest joined him.

"I'm going to gut that Ceolwulf from balls to throat," he said.

Horsa didn't reply. He squatted down by the body of Asse and checked his pulse. He was dead. He sighed heavily. Asse had been a good friend to him. All of them had been. He had infiltrated this very crew in order to track down his brother's kidnapped family. They were a rough lot, but he had eventually been accepted by them and had been proud to count himself amongst their number. Now they were all dead.

"Why was he here, Hengest?" Horsa asked. "What business did he have this far south?"

"I don't know," the older brother replied. "Just plain greed, I expect. But by the gods, we shall take this up with Eldred. He can't get away with this."

Horsa nodded. "Take their bodies aboard the *Bloodkeel*," he said to his men. "We'll give them the funerals they deserve when we reach port. Beorn, take ten men and crew the *Fafnir*. We'll head back to Rutupiae and count our losses."

Hengest

The settlements of the south east coast were dominated by the towering walls of the massive shore forts that had been built by the Romans during their final days of control. These rectangular outposts with their rounded towers had been something of a last-ditch attempt to protect the island against the tide of Germanic raiders that had broken upon it when control over Britta been in its death throes.

With the legions now gone, the very people the forts had been built to repulse were free to live within the frowning shadows of their walls, and they did so, mocking the British authorities like errant children might misbehave under the stern eyes of a bedridden parent. Once they had been bitter enemies, but now Briton lived side by side with Saxon, Jute and Angle.

The town of Rutupiae had once been the main port of the province and the gateway to Britta itself. Much of the old settlement had been demolished to build the fortress. The stones of the triumphal arch that had straddled the main road to Londinium and the bricks that had made up the old amphitheatre were now part of the deep walls that overlooked the shabby town.

Rutupiae was now a mixture of styles both Roman and Germanic. The plaster walls and red tiled roofs of the late empire survived beneath a veneer of timber and thatch constructed by the settlers from across the sea. The muddy cobbles of the streets rang with a myriad of tongues and accents. In addition to the Latin of the merchants and clergy, there was the Celtic language of the native Britons and the Germanic flavours of Frisian, Angle, Jutish, Saxon and even Danish, all squabbling for dominance in the crowded marketplaces.

Bread, meats, fruits and fish lined the stalls. Oysters, for which the town was famously credited by the Roman poet Luvenalis, were hauled in everyday and sold by the wagon full. Wine shops, ale houses and brothels were wedged between ramshackle buildings that festered amongst the heaps of refuse and human waste that even the heavy autumn rains could never fully dissipate. Whores sold themselves in broad daylight and crippled beggars lay slumped in the gutters whilst scrawny, feral children played and fought in the streets. Temples and altars reflecting a myriad of gods and religions were scattered throughout the settlement. Most of the British population was Christian and their priests could often be seen standing on street corners, waving their crucifixes about and shouting themselves hoarse, commanding the Germanic portion of the townsfolk to repent their evil pagan ways, and convert to the worship of the Christ-messiah.

The lack of any sort of official governing body in the wake of the Roman withdrawal over twenty years previously only added to the chaos. The old Roman mansio which had been the main administrative building in days gone by had fallen into ruin and was inhabited only by rats and beggars. The military fortifications were abandoned and anything representing law and justice was absent.

That just left Eldred.

Eldred was an Angle whose family had settled in Britta during the early days of the Germanic migrations. A shrewd business man and slippery as an eel, Eldred began by setting up his own silver lending business, progressing to extortion and murder in record time and, before he was forty, he had the entire town in the palm of his hand. There was a similar story in every town in that part of the land. Without any form of law and the remnants of the Romano-British ruling class cowering in their villas further west, it fell to the various criminal gangs to orchestrate order on the east coast.

But Eldred's influence extended beyond the straggling outskirts of Rutupiae. Once he had bullied and extorted the fishing trade into his control, he set his sights upon the various raiders who operated throughout the waters between Britta and Gaul. Building a power base of tough rogues and bloodthirsty profiteers, Eldred had set about organising the pirates and distributing territory to various captains whilst creaming the profits from their activities. The criminal rulers of the other towns looked to Eldred as something of a leader and it was to him that all disputes concerning territory were put.

Eldred operated out of an old bakery in the town. It was a large building that had once provided bread for most of the town's populace. Now it had been converted into something of a tavern with its great stone ovens housing amphorae of Gaulish wine looted from merchant vessels and barrels of mead and ale. A wooden stairway led to an upper floor which was an extension in the Germanic style of timbers and thatch. It was here that Eldred conducted business.

Several faces turned to look at Hengest and Horsa as they stepped into the old bakery. The two Jutes were recognisable to many in the town, Horsa in particular, as he had a reputation for drinking and fighting.

"Business or pleasure, Horsa?" asked a prostitute who had sauntered over to them, her hair bound high up on her head and her tunic parted to reveal her ample breasts. She slid her arm around Horsa's neck and stroked his chestnut, shoulder length hair.

He shoved her away and followed Hengest who was already making for the stairs. Neither of them was in the mood for fun. The woman frowned and muttered some derisive comment before moving on to other potential customers.

A burly man blocked the stairs, his massive arms folded across his chest. This was one of Eldred's cheap security measures. His blond locks had been shaved from his forehead in the Saxon style which made his face seem larger and more intimidating.

"The chief in?" Hengest asked.

"Busy," replied the guard. "Have a few drinks down here, then maybe he'll see you."

"Piss off, Octa," snapped Horsa. "He'll see us now. Unless you'd rather take a wager as to whose saex can gut the other first."

The Saxon's eyes followed Horsa's hand to his belt where the long-bladed knife of the Germanic peoples hung in its seal skin sheath. He stood aside and said nothing.

"Gutless Saxon mercenaries," muttered Horsa under his breath to his brother as they climbed the stairs. "Couldn't keep a pig out of a shit pile."

Eldred was indeed busy when the two brothers entered his office. Hengest recognised the whore who was bent over his desk, her tunic up around her middle and her face looking thoroughly bored by her employer's energetic thrusting.

"Thunor's cock, can't a man be left in peace?" Eldred exclaimed, looking up at the two Jutes who stood on the other side of the desk. "I'm going to hang that Saxon up by his balls!"

Hengest and Horsa waited patiently for him to complete his task. It took about a minute. The prostitute got up and rearranged her tunic. She winked at Horsa before sauntering out of the room. Eldred buckled his breeches and slumped down into his chair before pouring himself a cup of wine. He offered some to his visitors. Hengest shook his head.

"Suit yourself. It's good stuff," said Eldred. "Newly liberated from a trader last week. From Sicily I believe. Wherever the fuck that is."

"And in whose waters was it taken?" asked Hengest. "Or does the treaty no longer apply?"

Eldred glanced at him. "What can I do for you boys?"

"You can start by telling us what in the blazes of Waelheall Ceolwulf and his sea rats were doing in our waters!" said Hengest.

"Ceolwulf?" asked Eldred suspiciously. "His territory is north of Thanet."

"Well perhaps somebody should remind him of that. Or maybe he got lost. Either way he cost us a trader yesterday and butchered an entire crew of ours!"

Eldred sighed and sipped his wine. "What would you have me do? There are too many pirates in these waters. The treaty has done its best to organise things but sometimes lines on a map get blurred in people's heads. Let it go."

"Let it go?" said Horsa. "That's all you have to say on the matter?"

"If I start making threats and putting pressure on Ceolwulf, he might just say that it was you who was in his waters. And then where would we be? Who am I to trust?"

"Ceolwulf is a sneaky bastard," said Horsa. "He knew what he was doing. He slaughtered our men and left one of my ships riding free. I want him dead!"

"Forget it!" replied Eldred. "Ceolwulf brings in too much profit for me to have him killed. Who would take his place? You two?"

"Think we can't handle the extra territory?" asked Hengest.

"As you just said, you are one ship down," Eldred answered with a smile.

Hengest felt his brother stiffen at his side and placed a restraining arm across his chest to prevent him from lunging forward and dragging Eldred across the desk by the throat.

"Listen," Eldred continued, seemingly oblivious to the current threat to his life. "I feel bad. You two have brought me plenty of profit over the past year, so I'll throw something your way. Word has reached me of a trader loaded with grain which is due to put out from Dubris within the week."

"Grain?" asked Hengest. "We're not bakers."

"It is what is hidden within the grain that interests me. Forty of the sacks contain a single bar of gold each. Forty bars of gold, boys. Some British nobleman is fleeing to Gaul and wants to take his wealth with him. That good enough for you?"

"And what will your cut be?" asked Horsa.

"My usual twenty percent. The rest is yours. Now that's a good deal for good friends. Can't say fairer than that."

"And you're sure about this information?"

Eldred frowned. "When have my agents ever failed me?"